Traces

Be Careful What You Wish For

BY JOHNATHAN PHILLIP BLACKWELL

DORRANCE
PUBLISHING CO
EST. 1920
PITTSBURGH, PENNSYLVANIA 15238

The contents of this work, including, but not limited to, the accuracy of events, people, and places depicted; opinions expressed; permission to use previously published materials included; and any advice given or actions advocated are solely the responsibility of the author, who assumes all liability for said work and indemnifies the publisher against any claims stemming from publication of the work.

Dorrance Publishing Co
585 Alpha Drive
Pittsburgh, PA 15238
Visit our website at *www.dorrancebookstore.com*

ISBN: 979-8-89127-963-6
ESIBN: 979-8-89127-461-7

From the Soul of Blackwell's Quill

TRACES

Be Careful What You Wish For

Other Books
from the Soul of Blackwell's Quill
by Johnathan Phillip Blackwell

"Curse thee that hampers the path of my destiny!"

Miller's Mansion

The Dream Lord

East of the Dark Nebula

Essence of the Mind

Wizards and Witches
(Book One)

Whisper
(Book Two)

The Sor Wiz
and the Painted Lady
(Book Three)

Preface
Is it real or an illusion? Can it be both?

What is an illusion? How about something relative to a representation that the brain perceives should be, but truly is not! An example would be the shimmering heat waves on a highway that create optical illusions of water (a mirage) by way of an atmospheric refracted layer of hot air distorting or inverting reflections of distant objects. But illusions can also be something you think you see or hear when your alone in your home because of the brains uncertainty of what it truly is, these are the scary ones! Things such as that of a perceived fleeting shadow of something, or is it someone, crossing the room, or past that doorway over there. But are these illusions truly no more than a perception of the brain? Or is it ......! A gently swaying curtain in a room where there are no open windows for a breeze to cause that curtain to move, and obviously, there is no one else in the room but you! And there! there on the floor, those footprints compressing into the carpet, slowly one step at a time coming towards you without a sound, or anyone visible to make them! Then there is that unrecognizable shadowy motion of something, or is it someone, in that almost dark space of the hallway, or just as you reach the bottom of the basement stairs. And what about those unidentifiable or unjustifiable sounds from uncertain locations within your home? The scratching on a door or window, or 'something' being drug across a wooden or concrete floor somewhere in the house, but there is no one else in the house, but you! Then there's that sudden loud 'bang'!

The slamming of a door, a window or shutter, without any wind or reason for such a thing to happen!? As you sit on your bed, your knees propped up reading a book. Over the top of the book your attention is drawn to the almost inaudible "click" of the doorknob of your bedroom door, slowly turning, then the door quietly opens, but there is no one there to open it. Or maybe its the sudden sound of breaking glasses or dishes in the kitchen; or a hutch falling and breaking for seemingly no reason! An earthquake maybe? You rationalize what could be, to justify your panic and fears, but truly you find no reason for such things! So what was it? Then there's the oddities of books flying across the room in your office, the living room or from a bookshelf, untouched by anyone seen, and you are alone in the house!

Then the lamp stand, or the coffee table, or a chair begins moving from the place it has always been?! The loud horrific scream of a woman in pain or fear. A child crying behind a wall, when there's no one else in the house, and you don't have any children. Then comes the warmth of someone's breath on your neck! Or the soft breathing, or whispers of someone unseen, 'very' close to your shoulder or ear! And what is that fleeting smell now and then? That of a sensuous perfume, or stale flowers, or the smell of a wet dogs hair. As you traverse your abode, you pass through an area that is cool, or much colder than the rest of your home, and there's no reason for it to be that way!

All of these influences and the rapid changes in your 'location of awareness', your thoughts, feelings and emotions, these create sensations of perceived or potential visual responses of a past exposure, and of course the fear that comes with it! That exposure could be from a movie, what someone said in a conversation, or a TV experience. Things you know not to be, yet perceive or believe them to be real. If you allow it, (emotionally, without will) these things can and will create in your brain, the perceptions of fear or even danger! Any of these may be an illusion; but then again, maybe they're not an illusion after all!? Yes, that could be a problem! Because somewhere in your past, you may have had an experience or exposure relative to that very vision or sound afore you. And of it, a fear of, or uncertainty was formed that now creates a caution in your brain. Only the brain creates caution, not the mind!

The 'uncertainty' of that seen or heard by the brain, arouses a segment of the 'mind', the imagination, which will create even 'more' vivid mental images, of possible things or situations you 'could' or may be about to encounter, or be exposed to, that you'd really rather not be!

At any rate, an illusion is 'not' in any form what you think it is! So you ask yourself, where does the perception of that illusion take place and why? It is a 'cognitive fabrication', a mental neurotic misrepresentation, that creates a temporary pretentious psychological psychosis or disorder within the brain, in an attempt to make relative, or sense of what you are looking at, to a past visional exposure of a person, place, thing or event you can relate to, to subdue your fears! Is your perception without bias or prejudice? Is it receptive enough not to rationalize or attempt to justify what you see, because of your beliefs or fears?

Due to the workings of the brain and mind, humans have the ability to create illusions of deceptiveness in a multitude of ways. Sitting on a park bench, watch people; male and females of various ages, each for a full sixty seconds. What do you see, or think you see of them? Because the realm of emotions is so incredibly vast, only a trace of ones persona surfaces at a time, and humans have many, but even those change from second to second!

Locations, (close quarters, open fields or forests) situations,(advantage or disadvantage) and climate, (temperature, or rain) fearful or defensive body language stimulate or subdues their and your intentions, and dictates the illusions they want you to see, or not see of them. Body language includes, positions (still or a pose) or movement (intended or unintended) and the angle of the head, (changes eye language and nonverbal intent), torso (mostly with females and hunters), and extremities that exaggerates other languages. An intended pose, by the placement of arms, hands, and legs, create radical gestures of implications or intentions, reflecting mirids of emotions in constant change within your mind. Yes, that's what I said, "your" mind. But is that what 'they' had in their mind, for you to see? The fine tuning of the intended illusions are in the facial language of the mouth, lips, eyes, and forehead, that creates the invitation or warning. Verbal language creates the finality of the illusion in tone, volume or specific words. Clothing, or lack of it, and types of material, footwear, makeup, hair styles and color, jewelry and tattoos, camouflage or add to the illusion. Then there are thoughts that create desired images within their and your mind that no one else can see. But like the wind, they add to or subtract from the presented illusion.

Lets look at some written or verbal illusions. Why would you put words, phrases, implications or situations on a piece of paper, TV, movie or a book, in many languages, and make it available, or even mandatory for use in different parts of the world? Isn't that what dictionaries, bibles and writers do? Well, sorta.

"Between fantasy and fiction lies the reality of the mind and the truth of us all." Think very carefully about that for a minute.

There are at least two books mentioned that attempt to keep our verbiage and a piece of the past politically correct; the dictionary and the interpretations of the bible; take your choice.

By the multitudes, the words and meanings of these books dictate what you say, how you say it, or how you feel and what you believe about certain things and things you do.

Yet still, they are translated, used out of context, twisted, manipulated and transposed to get across ones meaning of intent, to match a desired intent or situation (another form of illusion). The human race, regardless of country, uses the contents of these two books to hide in, or behind, or to facilitate the creation of our illusional intent. Are these books not supposedly the authoritarians in their fields? There are eighteen different bibles that I know of for sure, and probably more. I had all eighteen of them in one place at one time in a library. A visitor to my library studied the covers of the bibles for about ten minutes then asked, "which one is the right one, or the correct one?" The answer to that comes down to what you were taught, what your religious preference is now, or what you believe, really believe and fear. That could get quit complicated, and sometimes scary!

And then there are several kinds and types of dictionaries. So, which of these are you supposed to use or believe; and what do you believe?! There it is again. If what is put in these books is not true or real, then who or what are you to believe? And why should you believe any of them, any more than a book of fiction? Is a book of fiction no more than a conglomerate of what's in the dictionaries? However, if the word you say (or create) is not in the dictionary, does that make it not right or unreal? What happened to originality? Where and from whom did the words and meanings in these books come from? And what makes them more legitimate than what you're reading at the moment? And who's to say they are? And who gave them that right? Most people think its easier to go along with the system than to attempt to create one of your own? What is an implication? An assumed implied suggestive or inferred phrase, motion or gesture. Yet in another system, that word implies guilt.

What does it mean to 'conjure up' something? Stay with me. To bring from its core, an entity, possibly a living one, onto your plane or dimension. Where do fables, myths or just unexplainable beliefs come from? (misconceptions and fears about something that is often implied or believed to be true, when in fact it is not!) To explain that one would take a book bigger than any dictionary, and most of us wouldn't believe that one either.

So, what has any of this got to do with what lies within the pages before you? Everything! Look at the very first two questions at the top of the first page. They are but traces to the insight of what is or is not before you. Maybe!?

Do you believe that traces of things of the past, still do or can exist? And what do you call the traces of beings? Look up the synonyms for "trace". That will give you something to think about! Do you believe in ghosts?! Of course not! But then why not? Descriptions of their 'many' types, pranks and illusional inceptions are in dictionaries across the world, so why do people not believe in them, or so they say? No blasphemy intended, but is the Holy Ghost an illusion or is it real, or both; or metaphorical?

One of my several trusted dictionaries says a "*ghost*" is; **"The visible disembodied soul of a dead person".** Let's see if we can unravel at least part of this can of worms. This might seem complicated, but stay with me.

> **The:** the or that; a thing, or something or someone, or a group of things or someone's?
>
> **Visible:** something you can **see;** "noticeable, obvious to the eye, evident, in sight, big as life;" you get the idea right? You can see it! Or is 'visible' too only a location of awareness or a metaphor? Its part of one of the five senses, so no games there. Well now, if you can see it, it must be real, right? Oops, sorry; I keep forgetting, you don't believe in ghosts! How about different kinds of ghosts; a transmute maybe, yes I know, that one is really complicated? Or a poltergeist? According to hear say, this is a bad one. "A **ghost** that announces its presence with rapping or the creation of chaos and disorder. The supposed manifestation of one or more poltergeists, especially as involving physical objects which move or fly about without warning." They will also rake your flesh and make you bleed! Can a 'supposed' entity of something you don't believe in do that?

Disembodied: something taken out of a body? "not having a material body; disembodied *spirit*: (the vital principle or animating force <u>within living</u> things) any incorporeal supernatural being that can become visible (or audible) to human beings." So how can you see them?

Supernatural being: "an incorporeal being '*believed*' to have powers to affect the course of human events". This one has to be real! Sorta? Maybe not.

Soul: "The *immaterial* 'part of a person'; the *actuating cause* of an individual life, a '<u>*physical*</u>' entity." Immaterial: "ghosts and other <u>*immaterial* entities</u>." How can it be both? This one could be a book unto itself!

Dead: "people, person, animal, or vegetation that are (no longer living or alive); a time when coldness (or some other quality associated with death) is intense; a cadaver."

Person: somebody; being, or entity.

These definitions all came out of a dictionary, so they have to be right, right?! So, these things, these ghosts, according to the dictionary must be out there someplace right? Oh, I see, you still don't believe in ghosts. Ghost's; who would make up such a word, and why? Is that the same as some other made up words; apparition; wraith; **trace**; specter; Wonder how long it took somebody to put them words together?

Now, because you don't believe in ghosts, does that also mean that you don't believe in the dictionary's terminology, definitions, interpretations or explanations of the term 'ghost', or maybe anything else in that book? What do you believe? Why? How is it possible we can read or speak at all without them? Would you not be using something <u>someone else created</u>? Can you write, say or sing a word that someone else hasn't already used in a like manner?

<u>Is it real or an illusion? Can it be both?</u>

If you 'can' see it, in any part; hear it breathing, hear its sound, its voice or the sounds of its motion, does that not mean '<u>something</u>' is there? When it touches you and you can feel it, or see results of its presence, and you can smell it, what does that tell you? Traces of, and *the reach* of the dead do exist, believe me! So, what or who was or is, that thing you and I just saw? A shadow? Of what, or does it make any difference?!

<u>Is it real or an illusion? Can it be both?</u>

Foreword

Charles Ray Aldermon(Charlie), was born and raised on a small farm on the western outskirts of Olathe Kansas. When Charlie was little, James and Lisa Aldermon (his mom and dad) noticed Charlie's choice of toys were woodblocks, Legos and rector sets. Then he started mixing them together to create real looking buildings. In the fourth grade, his math teacher noticed that Charlie, as he was called, drew a lot of two dimensional squares or planes. A bit strange for a child that young. It was like he could see what he wanted to draw, but couldn't express more than its base on paper. One day while the teacher was standing just behind and next to Charlie, watching how meticulous he was with each line, the teacher decided to see if Charlie was wanting to draw a three dimensional unit, and slowly leaned over and extended a line down into the plane from the upper left corner of the plane, creating a dimension within the plane, with Charlie watching intently. Charlie stared at the line and after a minute or so, and with his pencil followed the line the teacher had just drawn. Then Charlie drew another plane halfway down the page. This time the teacher added a vertical line up from each corner of the plane but did not connect the lines. Charlie again followed the lines the teacher had drawn, then to the teachers surprise, took the initiative and connected a line to the tops of each vertical line on his own as the teacher watched. He had it! Now he knew how to draw what he saw in his mind. It truly was what Charlie was trying to do! Soon his drawings became more than complex three dimensional boxes.

The teacher attached another plane to the next box Charlie drew and he became excited. Again he traced the teachers lines in deep thought. The next day, the teacher gave Charlie a geometry book just to see what would come of it. Only a few days later, to the teachers surprise, Charlie's drawings took on some radical and profound features.

At the next parent teacher conference, the teacher excitedly told Charlie's parents about their precocious son's gift, and a gift it was. Then he asked if they could afford a drafting board? Of course the answer was no. These were farmers with barely enough income to make it through the winter. That board comes with a lot of stuff, and all of it was very expensive. That Christmas, the teacher brought Charlie a drafting board, a stand and stool for the board.

There was a T-square, and different kinds of angular and curved plastic pieces, and two very strange looking rulers, he had all of it. This was the true beginning of Charlie's life long career.

In junior high he became fascinated and infatuated with the riddles and magic of the math of geometry and trigonometry. It was about then Charlie began to correlate the numbers of his math, with the numbers in his drawings together in his mind. He used both to create the structural integrity for the buildings in his drawings. In high school, his favorite subject and class was mechanical drawing. On his own, Charlie created not only the exterior designs, but the structural skeletal designs of large and strange looking buildings and their blueprints. In college, he studied and began to understand metallurgy; the tensile strengths of different kinds of iron and steel, and their weights. The weight and strengths of different kinds and mixes of concrete. The effects of gravity stress factors, the erosion factors of rain and rust, and the power of wind sway against the buildings he drew. His professors were more than impressed, and his grades made it obvious. But Charlie was so intent on his studies, he had little or no social life, in or out of school. Girls were no more than friends if that. They seemed more complicated than any of his math problems and took up more time than he was willing to give them. In college, he did a couple courses in drafting, then structural blueprints and majored in the dynamics of structural engineering. These were his favorite subjects, and he had acquired more than a knack for it. He even spent two years in Japan to learn the intricate structural methods they used to build their 9.0 earthquake proof buildings.

Oriental girls seemed to have more than a draw on Charlie. Some were more than attractive, but like the girls back home, they too were just as complicated, and those complications were added to by another language.

After college, Charlie took some specialized high tech courses in engineering. But even with the education and degrees he had, it was more than a struggle to find a job in a small town, and still he was alone. You might say 'he was over qualified' for that neck of the woods. After two years, with a few connections in the national architectural industry, he got a job offer and moved out to California, designing large business buildings, resorts and hotels. Things went well for three or four years, and the pay was good. He saved up a lot of money, but after seven years, the politics more than the earthquakes, started getting on his nerves.

The buildings he designed had no problems withstanding the quakes, but nobody would buy them because of the trust and fear factors of their locations. So he gradually started looking for other options. He even looked at some offers from Canada and Europe. Then an offer came in from New York City with a large corporation; he took it without blinking or thinking!

Again he did alright for a time, but after five or six years in the hub bub of New York City, he was again ready for a change. Too many people, too many cars, too much noise and too many attitudes with entitlement issues in what seems a shrinking, already cramped space. It was also about this time in his life he decided to start looking for a nest, maybe even to start a little family, maybe. But Charlie was a methodical dedicated workaholic. That would mean finding Miss Right, and that was going to be an issue tougher than any of his drawings. So, with the intent of his being, he made a sincere wish from his heart. *"Be careful what you wish for Charlie!"* A wish is only a wish right? A phrase of words coming out of your mouth, mind or brain to the air? Then where does it go? Does a wish mean anything?! You might say the intent alone, even a lingering one, has more than something to do with what happens! And of it's own time, and under some strange circumstances, Charlie's wish was upon him in full! The delusion of grandeur brought about more than the perceptions of reality, passion, material wants, and the potential of true prosperity and contentment. These presented themselves in a strange sequence of events, and included something that was not, but is, and it was close to Charlie's heart!

Charlie was now thirty four years old, stood six foot five, and weighed 235 pounds. He had dark sandy colored wavy hair, and hazel greenish brown colored eyes, and he looked like some kind of movie star. His main drawback was that he was dedicated to his work; he was as said, a workaholic! He was also an opportunist, but tried not to take anything for granted. Because he was so good at his work, someone at the top saw through the veil of his bosses egotistical exaggerations. Then the turmoil of a series of harsh and serious changes began to come into Charlie's life! But it was in fact what he had wished for! Was it real, or was it all an illusion? Or could it be both?

"TRACES"

Chapter 1

It was the morning of August 21, 2011. Through a partially blurred vision, my wristwatch says its six a. m.. I guess that means its time to get my comfy self out of this bed. I had wasted eight hours of doing nothing productive. But it seems to be the function of this thing I am. I used to have an alarm clock, but the first morning it went off, so did I. There wasn't a whole lot left of that thing there on the night stand to tell what it was. I just scraped all the pieces off the nightstand into the trash. Even at this early hour, it's still very warm outside for an autumn morning. Summer is hanging on. The suns glare through the window of my apartment is like a huge spotlight, but that has to be a reflection off of a window from the building across the street, because its on the west side of my apartment. Okay, I'm up! Got places to go, people to talk to; a few I'd rather not, and work that I love to do. But first, there are the adventures of getting to it.

Morning routine; take a leak, hot shower, brush my teeth, mouthwash, deodorant, clean clothes, tie, sports jacket and slacks, comb my mop; uh, I'll worry about the beard tomorrow. Grab my briefcase and I'm out the door like one of those city fellas you see on TV. I'm headed for coffee and my nutritious breakfast; grilled ham and cheese; maybe with an egg today. Charles Ray Aldermon here, but most people I know, just call me Charlie. Nobody special, just a regular guy, doing a nine to five job like most, but only because of the knuckleheads I have to put up with. If I had my druthers, I'd probably never leave the office, cause I love what I do, its kind of an art you might say. I guess for what I do, you could call me an architect.

In front of the elevators, it looks like there's a half price sale on cinnamon sugar donuts or pumpkin pie going on. There's people six deep in a half circle in front of the silver brushed elevator doors. I finally get on a cramped elevator to the ground floor, that leaves my stomach on the fourteenth floor, while I'm down here on the first floor, trying to find my legs. Then I have to pop my ears! Damn that things fast; I think it just falls!

Outside the elevator in the lobby, there's the gauntlet of rotating glass doors. Those things are merciless and will put you right back in the lobby (a couple of times) real quick if your not fully awake. The workforce has already hit the streets, some of them literally, even the sober ones! Hundreds of people going in every direction; jaywalking, or waving down a cab in the middle of the street, or just milling at the corner trying to get across the street. The sidewalks are wide and full of indignant bastards in a hurry to go nowhere. Pushing and shoving like a heard of cattle coming out of a corral. They act like their trying to get to jobs, but they'd really rather be going someplace else. Fortunately for me, the deli is only a half a block down (or is it up) the street. First problem is getting across the street in the middle of downtown New York City. There's traffic lights right? right! So why doesn't anybody stop! I look at the four deep row of cars in three lanes of honking traffic, on a two lane boulevard going north, and the light changes. I'm chicken!

"Go ahead sir; gentleman first, I'll just walk over your body when the driver gets out to make sure you're dead!" I manage to survive the crossing and get in a line I'm hoping leads to breakfast, sorta. After about a ten minute wait, finally I'm next. Get ready Charlie! Then it's my turn. I step up to the deli window, and my brain kicks in, cause things aren't as simple as a coffee and sandwich here. I have to make my selection from five rows of cups, and five rows of sandwiches and condiments. Latte, mocha, espresso, regular coffee, and of course hot creamy chocolate, with, or without marshmallows; then the big decision. Three kinds of sugar; soymilk, cream, milk, or some weird powder creamer that smells and tastes like something a squirrel refused, fresh out of the forest jungles of Grand Central Park. Then comes the sandwiches; grill cheese, ham and cheese, sausage and egg or bacon and egg, or just plain egg salad. Decisions! Pick, pay and get the hell out of the way Charlie, there's a thousand more people waiting in line.

I take my coffee and morning nutrition and stand against the granite wall of the building, because that seems to be the safest place in the city to be for the moment for what I'm doing. Where the hell are all these people going, and where did they come from? There can't be that many jobs or apartments in ten square blocks of this spot.

I'm munching down my ham and cheese in front of a drooling hobo, and carefully sipping my boiling coffee that you can stand up one of those plastic spoons in, if it doesn't melt first! Once I tried to take my coffee back to the office; bad idea! I think all seven million people in this town are looking for someone with a cup of coffee in their hand. They either want what you have, or want to knock it out of your hand because they don't have one.

Oh boy, listen to that; the city music system! It's only eight a. m., but the sirens of the cops, ambulance and the fire department started about four thirty this morning. Must be a lot of people in trouble of one kind or other out there. I've lived in this city going on six years now, and I've been seriously thinking its time for another change in scenery; yeah, Hawaii maybe! Don't believe all the commercials you see of that place. I hear they have problems of their own. Flames coming out of a barrel or a volcano; either way its not good. Here my office job is conveniently located just three blocks up the street on fourth avenue. But even that gets adventurous at times. Its not so bad, except when it snows. Then you get on a snowboard and attach yourself to a snowplow. No, don't try that!

I do the same thing everyday, but I think the tension of the management and this New York attitude is finally getting to me. It's not the job, I love what I do; its just some of the idiots and their entitlements that I have to put up with, including the boss, that's been more than getting on my nerves. I'd love to give him a knuckle sandwich for lunch some day. But us blue-collar workers still need a paycheck to cover the rent, so I calm my animal instincts and put up with his stupidity. The majority of these people don't like their jobs, they complain about being over worked and under paid. That there are too many holidays, so they can't get anything done, but still they complain they need a vacation! Me, I'm starting to acquire an 'I don't give a shit attitude', that's creeping into my work habits and what little there is of my social life. I use to have a girlfriend, wonderful young lady. I'm thinking that was the second year I was here in the city. But that only lasted for awhile.

She got tired of my attitude too, and the fact I was a bit possessive. I don't handle rejection very well, especially when I know it's my fault. Thinking the same thing would happen again, I decided not to go looking anymore. I guess I have a lot of friends at the pub on payday night, but you know how that goes; the money runs out and so do they!

I think I need to go someplace else, someplace out of this city and start all over again, literally! But I can see from the asshole just down the hall in front of my office door, it won't be today. I stroll up to my office and the boss is standing in my doorway.

"Morning boss," I say trying to get by him without letting him rub my ass and still be polite.

"Morning Charles. Got a question I'd like to throw at you," he says, waving a large manila envelope up and down the front of his chest, that has the corporate logo on it, barely covering a loud power tie. I step around my mahogany throne and set my briefcase under it. The boss gets comfy in one of two chairs in front of my desk. I can see the wheels turning, or should I say spinning; but there's no smoke, cause there's nothing in there to burn.

"What's on your mind?" I ask, shuffling some papers and a couple of folders on my desk. This guy doesn't step into anyone's office unless he wants something from you, so I know he's up to no good.

"Corporate office wants to open up a new shop in the next couple of months up north a bit. Seeing's how you know your job pretty well, and are sort of business minded, I put in a good word for you. Besides, it would be nice to have someone in that office we are familiar with. Think you'd be interested?" he asks, with a ho hum attitude. But I know he's not telling the whole story, and has got something up his sleeve. The only person he ever put a good word in for is himself. It's always about him, and he's as straight as a corkscrew. He's probably hoping he'll run out of candidates and they'll offer him the job. The envelope is being brandished for a show of authority; he's on a power trip all the time and no one is better or above him. If he did manage to get me into this new office, he would just use me or whoever goes up there, as leverage on whoever is running the place now. That way he could move in and have an establishment of his own. Then he'll want me to get some dirt on them, whoever that is, and blackmail them right out of there.

Then he'll shine in corporate eyes, get a raise and a promotion right into the corporate office, and I'll be left with the residue of his mistakes and he'll leave his stepping stool high and dry. He should have been a politician. Well, I can play that game as well as he can.

"Well boss, they can't afford me here as a drafter, how are they going to make ends meet if I'm up the ladder a couple of notch's? Hell, I'd need a lavish house, a company car, and a stable financial situation if you know what I mean," I said a bit assertively, with just a hint of sarcasm.

"Besides, you'd need someone there you can keep under your thumb; someone you can manipulate once he's there," I said.

"You'd be running the place in two years and you know it. Might even be a bonus in it for you," he said slyly. Yup, he's up to something, and now I'm for sure he's not telling the whole story.

"Something to think about I guess. I'll let you know in a week or so," I said. Guess he was locked into a time frame, and that wasn't what he wanted to hear. So he quietly got out of his chair and went looking elsewhere for another option in the next office down the hall, Blake Arnold's office. I would have liked to consider the offer, but I hate moving. It costs money to move, then you have to deal with new people, trust factors, getting reestablished, and all that stuff. Besides, I've heard corporate bosses are tougher to get along with than this guy, and they don't really care for people looking for a retirement nest, unless its them. I'm only thirty four, but I'd like to see how it feels to be very comfortable for a change, instead of living in a rats nest from paycheck to paycheck, wondering where my next meal is coming from. I was also thinking about maybe starting a family, maybe. But now that he's mentioned it, I might enjoy living out in the country for a change. But a job like that has a lot of unseen or hidden variables that I'm not sure I want to deal with.

After the boss left, I made my way to the coffee machine and filled my cup from the deli. I never throw those cups away until the end of the day. Blake, the guy in the office next to mine, the one the boss went to after mine, stepped up to get a cup of joe and gave me a strange look.

"Did he make you the same offer?" he asked.

"Yeah, I guess; but I lollygagged around and he seemed to be on a schedule and went to you with his problem," I said.

"Well, I know how dirty he plays, so I gave him a sad story too, and he continued down the hall," Blake said with a snicker. Well, I guess I wasn't the only one that could see through the bosses sheep skin. Then it was back to the part of my inner office I call the glass box.

I'm an architect by trade, designing buildings and an occasional home by request from up top. But here I also deal with structural designers, engineers, and contractors from all over the US. I sat my cup of coffee on a pod that's actually a small spiral planter stand, away from my drawing board. I took off my jacket, rolled up my sleeves to the elbow, loosened my tie and started looking over the set of drawings on the board that looked somewhat familiar. A few years back after I got this job, someone at the corporate level asked my boss to design a special building. They wanted something the wind would just go around from any direction, sorta, but not exactly round, and would pretty much give you a three hundred and sixty degree view of the landscape. My boss didn't have a clue and handed the request down to me. I mulled that over for about a week. Then it hit me, a decagon! A prefab ten sided building with a six pitch roof of insulated metal. They also wanted a wing on each side of the decagon. So much for the wind getting around it. The damn thing was going to be huge, and would look something like the white house. I did a layout then a structural design, then drew up the prints using their dimensions for a building with the wings, that turned out to be big enough for you to put four or five companies in it. Wonder what they wanted with a building that big for? That would be a town in itself, I thought. Anyway, we sent the prints back to the main office in Kingston, but never heard anything more about them. I guess that's either what they wanted, or they were looking at drawings from other architects. The drawing in front of me looks very similar, except it's a lot smaller and its an octagon. It kind of looks like a stop sign from above, but it has the structural dynamics of an aircraft hanger. Maybe it has something to do with the decagon. *And in fact it did!* The request for this building had come from the same place too, but like the first one, without anyone's name on it.

Manipulating my T-square and a thirty-sixty to just past the center of the board, I got the feeling someone's watching me. Very slowly I turned my head, just barely enough to the right to see our public relations officer and lead receptionist Ms. Balintyne in a pose, staring right at me from the middle of the hall outside my glass office.

She's a good looking highspeed piece of equipment, exposing more than is legal on the street, in an hourglass contour. Standing there in a pose that teases your imagination and anatomy, making your mouth water. I'm guessing she's about five years younger than me, but that would be okay I guess.

She's more than quite attractive, but doesn't look like the "mommy" type. Like Blake, she's one of the few people in this place that doesn't have a snotty attitude, she's just persistent and occasionally aggressive. With her, what you see, is what you get, and then some. She's sophisticated and classy, yet just pleasantly herself. I could be wrong, but I think she's looking for a ring on her left hand, or for something else I don't have. I don't ask her out cause I don't think a one night stand would quite cover it, and I don't have anything to offer her except me, and I'm thinking that wouldn't be enough for a woman like that. She's one of those perfectly molded females that you want to slide your arms around and hold very close to you, regardless of the situation or who's in the neighborhood. My God; if that woman ever started anything, I wouldn't be able to refuse her, but then what would I do with her? Besides that!

I put my eyes and brain back to work on my drawing, but that feeling of being watched didn't go away. Now what; or should I say who? I looked in Ms. Balintynes direction, but she's gone; off to entice someone else I guess. Must be one of those feelings that just lingers. Turns out Ms. Balintyne is now standing behind me in the other part of my office, with one of those envelopes similar to the one the boss had this morning. Either I got mail or she's up to something. I step off my stool, grab my coffee and step into the other part of my office. As it is, she's in another enticing pose, then moved close enough to expose the Grand Canyon in all its glory, and was looking expectantly up into my eyes for a few seconds, like she wants to more than tell me something, or ask a question, then ever so quietly says;

"I was forewarned with a phone call from Kingston, this was on its way, and was given instructions of how to receive it, and how to make sure it was personally handed to you, by me; must be important. It got here by courier a few minutes ago," she said softly, just in case someone was listing. Then her mouth and lips made one of those enticing motions either to take a breath, say something, or kiss me. Woah big fella, your thinking with the wrong head again! After she gingerly handed me the envelope, she did one of those saucy turns and slowly swayed away from me.

A few steps away, still in her forward motion, she glanced back over her left shoulder putting all that blond hair into motion to see if I was still looking at the merchandise, and kept walking.

"Chicken; she's too nice for someone like you anyway Charlie" I said to myself. I didn't have the guts to say anything to her but "thanks". She raised her right hand and waved the fingers of her right hand. I took the envelope to my desk and sat down.

Okay, wonder who the hell this is from? I don't even know anybody at the corporate office, no one at all? Maybe shithead did put in a good word for me. (*Remember that wish Charlie?*) *This was going to be more than a surprise, and not just for Charlie!*

Let's see here, it's from the co-owner and VP of the corporation, who I don't know, and it says he's ….oh, oh; he's offering me sort of a promotion. The job of putting together, starting up, and running a new office up state. I'd have a company car, expenses to accommodate a new house, and a paid vacation for the time it took to get settled in. "Holy Shit," fell out of my mouth. I hurriedly put the letter face down on my desk and looked around. No one seems curious, so I put the envelope into my briefcase, and put it back under my desk. This must have been what my boss was inquiring about, but why me? How did I get a personal invite? But he probably sent out several feelers and had yet to make a final choice. Obviously my boss doesn't know anything about this, or he would be sitting on my desk by now. My heart started pounding and my hands began to sweat and shake a bit. "Here's your big chance Charlie, don't blow it," I thought. How the hell could something like this happen to a guy like me? I'm just an architect. And how does this guy even know who I am? *Then vaguely a memory came to his mind. But there were two other parts to that wish!* Apparently, somebody at corporate level, was also onto my boss's bullshit, and had circumvented him, big time. But why me? I'm just a drafter, I'm nobody special. I'm sure there's a lot of big shots in this company he could have picked. Hell, they could have offered it to my boss. He would have jumped at the offer with both feet and hands in the air. This is all more than interesting, I thought. Well, I sure didn't have to think about it anymore, I might just be going to move! Or should I say, "being moved"! Wonder if they'd let me take Ms. Balintyne with me? "Don't push your luck hot shot, she's not your type; besides, she might just say yes, then what would you do?" I said to myself.

Just in case there was a possibility, I sent my reply of acceptance back by courier mail that very morning. Man was I ever nervous. How the hell would I tell my boss about this if I did get the job?

Just as I got through the door of my apartment that evening, my phone rang. "Aldermon," I said.

"Mr. Aldermon; this is Daniel Foster at the main office in Kingston. May I assume you are in your apartment, alone?" he asked.

"Yes sir, I am," I said a bit confused.

"I received your reply to my request. Everything is ready and approved for your startup of the new office in Corinth. Hotel reservations are made, and good until you find a house. Your company vehicle will be at the hotel when you get there. I'll be waiting for your arrival at the new office, and the okay to begin staffing that facility," he said cordially.

"If there's anyone from your present office that you'd prefer at the new office, make it known the next time we talk," he said.

"Question," I said. "How am I supposed to tell my boss about this?" I asked.

"You won't have to. I'm now your boss! He'll be on his way to my office tomorrow morning. Clean out your office while he's here. A moving van will be at your apartment at eleven a.m. tomorrow morning. I'll expect you to call me by noon the day after you get to Corinth. You can call me at this number anytime day or night, if you have any questions at all about anything. I would like this transition to go smoothly for both of us. Any more questions at the moment?" he asked. I said "no sir."

"Then I'll be talking with you when your settled in; good bye Mr. Aldermon," he said and hung up. Holy shit! What the hell have you got yourself into this time Charlie? I almost said out loud. Is my boss ever in for one hell of a shock, not to mention I'm pretty sure he's going to be more than a little pissed at me! I really needed to watch what I was doing with this new job. I didn't want to fall into the same power trip my boss is on. Holy cow! I never dreamt anything like this would ever happen to me, but then I still didn't know the half of it. What I didn't know is, this new place is an empty building with no one in it at the moment, no one! Now, wonder what Ms. Balintynes thoughts might be on moving to this new office? But there had to be a catch. Wonder how long it was going to take before that trap slammed shut?! Was this really happening?

I started packing up some of the little stuff from my kitchen and bathroom and most of my clothes, and put them in my VW, trying to make it a bit easier for the movers. The next morning, without my nutritious deli breakfast, I made a special effort to get to the office very early. I didn't want to have to answer a lot of questions, even I didn't have answers for! I borrowed a few boxes and a cart from the janitors, and had my stuff packed up and was out of there before anyone else even showed up. I was still thinking about asking Ms. Balintyne if she would like to come along, but I didn't think I'd know how to handle the rejection, so I didn't stick around to ask. Still, I was going to miss her. But there might be another way of asking her, I just didn't want to start pulling strings just yet; if I had any to pull. Blake would also be another choice for the new office, along with four other guys that have had more than their share of the bosses abuse and neglect.

The moving guys showed up at my apartment exactly at 11 am sharp, just like Mr. Foster said they would. They seemed in a hurry, but still they were meticulous about what they were doing. I didn't think I had enough stuff in that little apartment to fill the crate on their truck until it was half full and they were still packing boxes of more stuff. My total worldly belongings filled all but the last two feet of the crate. Guess you can accumulate a lot of stuff in six years. The movers already had the address of a storage unit in Corinth. They gave me some paperwork, and they were off. I cleaned up the apartment a bit, then it was my turn to hit the road. On the way out of town, I stopped and got a couple of burgers and a fresh cup of coffee, threw a kiss to New York City, got on highway 87 headed north, and never looked back. Except for the traffic up in Albany, the trip to Corinth was fairly uneventful, but it was still a long drive to start out in the middle of the day. When I got to the hotel I was told to go to, I checked in and the hotel manager himself escorted me to a plush room reserved in my name. This was a really nice place, but hotel rooms make me nervous, their only a temporary stopover to something else. I thought about a shower, then changed my mind; I was hungry! Next stop was dinner at the restaurant downstairs. The staff kept looking at me, then would say something to another staff member. They were acting very strange, but being extremely polite. I didn't think I looked that ragged from the drive, but maybe I did. Maybe I should have freshened up a bit before coming down here.

After a dinner of chicken fried steak, mashed potatoes and gravy, it was straight back up to my room, and a nice hot shower, then off to bed. I was unconscious in a matter of minutes. At some point in my slumber, I had a really bad dream about a horrible looking woman that was shredded into bloody pieces. She kept calling to me;

"Charlie, help me," she said as clear as day. That was one scary looking person, and I was wide awake! I must have really been out of it, cause it was almost five a. m. Time to get myself in gear. This morning was going to be a busy one. Guess if I was going to be some kind of boss, I should at least look the part. Another hot shower, clean shave, fresh pressed clothes, clean socks, shined shoes, then I went downstairs to the restaurant.

From the front desk, I was escorted to a reserved table near a tinted window. I was staring out the window at the cross traffic in the intersection when a gorgeous waitress in a mini uniform stepped up to my table with a pot of coffee, and a lot more to offer. How is it these restaurant's get super models to work for them?

"Good morning Mr. Aldermon," she said softly, as if someone else might hear. Oh my lord! It was difficult to look her in the eye without at least glancing at the rest of the menu! My eyes, brain and a couple other parts of me wanted it all! Breakfast, lunch and dinner! Come on Charlie, calm down. She's just trying to do her job for crying out loud.

"Do I know you," I asked quietly, maybe wishing I did.

"No sir, not yet; but your main office said we should take very special care of you. You must be important for them to do something like that. May I take your order sir," she asked, again in that soft angelic voice that caused a lapse of memory. Then in liquid motion, she rhythmically wiggled into a pose that again enticed another kind of appetite. What's that saying about never looking a gift horse in the mouth? A flush came over me; I had to be blushing. Maybe she wanted to be a little more than friends, and that would have been just fine with me, but there had to be a price, one that wouldn't be on my ticket. More than likely, my macho imagination was somewhere it didn't belong. I was starting to get a little nervous about this elated feeling I was having.

I had a light breakfast and tried to pay my ticket, but that too was on someone else's tab, so I left Ms. Gorgeous a healthy tip; she probably has eleven kids and a jealous animal of a husband to feed.

13

I strolled out to the front desk to see about my company car and got another surprise. I was being watched and tracked wherever I went in the hotel and restaurant. The hotel manager was waiting for me at the front desk.

"Good morning Mr. Aldermon, I hope your lodging is adequate and comfortable. Are you ready for your car sir?" he asked.

"Yes, thank you," I said. This was nothing like the treatment I got in the city. Who did these people think I was? I was being treated like an executive. It felt really good and weird at the same time. The hotel manager made a motion with his hand to a valet that stepped up to us.

"Please bring Mr. Aldermon's company car to the front door," he said politely. Then he handed me an envelope with a key and a note in it. "The front door to your office," it said. The car was a Mercedes sports coupe, with the red corporation seal on the front doors. It wasn't brand new, but pretty close to it. It still had that new car smell. I got on my phone and called the realtor I'd been instructed to call. Basically, I told him what I was looking for, the price range I was pretty much locked into, and approximately where I thought the house should be relative to the office, wherever that was. I asked him to give me a call when he had five locations ready for me to look at.

Turns out he knew more about what I was going to do then I did. While I was on the phone with him, something weird happened. I felt something, a strange feeling came all over me. But then maybe the feeling wasn't coming from him at all. Still, there was a draw of some kind. Who was this guy? Through him, over the phone, something was pulling on my consciousness. I'm thinking maybe this guy is the connection to something else. I gave him my phone number and he said okay. Wow; that feeling just wouldn't go away!

I then headed out to find my new office building. Something that big shouldn't be too hard to find. Still, I had to stop and ask questions; seems everyone knows where it is but me. Turns out the building itself isn't in Corinth, but in a small town nearby called Wilton, close enough I guess.

Then I saw it! Oh my gosh! Now where had I seen this building before? And it did look something like the white house! Sorta; but it wasn't white. It was the same building I designed several years ago, but it looked like someone had upped the scale on it a bit. The property itself was about six acres, with a forest that almost surrounded the north and south ends of the eastern part of the property.

The building was freshly put together, maybe two years old; a prefab building facing west, with a huge parking lot on the west side. There was individual parking and an executive helo pad on the east side of the building. Although I knew this building inside and out intimately, I did a basic facility check. Inside it still had that dusty smell of fresh concrete and mortar. I was thinking 'our' operations would take up at least the entire second floor of the center section. All the architectural, accounting and contract work would be on the second floor. All the administrative stuff like records, mail, employment, visitors and such would be handled on the first floor.

Once inside, it seemed only the center portion of the building was going to be occupied, because only that portion was ready for whoever to move in, right down to the desk supplies, shredders, toilet paper and two functioning coffee machines on each floor. I was sure there would be someone over me, so I started looking for an office with a view. Both wings were absolutely bare inside, with just a tinge of an echo. Now I'm thinking I might have promoted myself right out of my drafting job, into a managerial position. But not being a real sociable type of person, I wasn't sure how that was going to work out. Still, I was willing to make some sacrifices. This was the opportunity I needed to make that start over I had thought about down in the city. I wanted to change my attitude and maybe even learn how to get along with new people, even my new boss, Mr. Foster. But I was more concerned about the corporate office people, than the people here. Then came another of many surprises! It sure didn't take them long to find me! I was standing out in front of the building doing some observations of the parking lot, its lighting, trash containers and stall setups when a UPS courier showed up.

"I have an envelope for a Mr. Aldermon," he said politely, but it sounded more like a question.

"I'm Aldermon," I said, and he handed me the envelope. I took the envelope back into the lobby out of the wind and opened it.

"Dear Mr. Aldermon, as the CEO of this part of our corporation, I have certain expectations of your performance. From what I know of you, I can only assume you received this letter at the new office building, the one you in fact designed. Other than a minor alteration in its scale that was incorporated, it is exactly as you designed it, structurally and otherwise, inside and out.

The entire facility, the building, its property and staff will be under your management and care. I'll expect you to perform, supervise and quality control the proposals, designs, drafts and blueprints coming out of your facility. Acquaint yourself with the appropriate local businesses that may in any way facilitate your operations. Outside of a swimming pool, you will receive funds for any moderations you see fit. As you can see, the wings were not furnished at all. I'm leaving those to your discretion. I'm anxious to put this location into operation, as I already have several contracts for local construction in your area. I'll be waiting on your call for the go ahead to staff your facility and open operations (job sites) in the local community". It was signed by the VP, Mr. Daniel C. Foster, just below the corporate seal.

"Oh my God!" rolled out of my mouth and echoed through the empty first floor. Well, I guess that answered that question, and several others. Now how the hell did I get myself into this one? (*Remember Charlie; you asked for it!*) From a drafter to the CEO of a corporate operation?! "Wow!" I'm just an architect! A nine to five blue collar worker. This is like putting a farm boy in the city and expecting miracles. Oh well, it's just another job. I went back outside and was looking at "my" new building and realized there was no company name on the building. I got to thinking about that for a minute. Then I had an idea. "*FOSTER IND.*" with the corporate logo at the end of it. I was going to need a sign company to take care of that. Guess it was time to start getting serious about this job. "CEO!" Oh my gosh.

I went back to the restaurant for lunch and got escorted to the same table I had that morning. For some reason, the time it took to get from the office to the hotel became bothersome. There had to be someplace closer to get something to eat. Maybe there was someplace in Wilton that was closer? As I waited for my order, I began putting together a list of the names of people I knew that were good at what they did. Not just because they were my friends, and that included Ms. Balintyne as well. She wasn't just a pretty face and whatever, she knew her job well.

She could bump heads with anyone in the tactical political arena, and had a unique structural knowledge of the corporation, not to mention the sociability and communication skills to smooth the rough edges at a steamy board conference table. She also knew how to deal with goons like me with the subtle skillful finesse of a queen.

I just wasn't sure she would accept the job or not? Her job here would require more responsibilities, be considerably larger, and would encompass her communication skills throughout other facilities within the corporation. Blake is as good as I am. If I needed an exec, he could more than fit that position. There were four other drafters; Gibbs, Frank, Tristan and Marrket in the city office that were more than qualified to work here that I also put on the list. It was time for people to see their worth and let them shine. I knew I'd have to hire about fifty or so of the locals to keep peace with the local chamber of commerce, the city or town council and the BBB. A freight elevator also went on my list of wants right off the bat. Don't know why I didn't incorporate that into my drawings. The wings would probably need one or two in each wing as well.

After lunch, back at the office, I was sitting in the parking lot looking back and forth at the north wing, then over at the south wing. Why? What were they for? There had to be a reason or purpose Foster wanted them drawn into the prints. (*And there was, but only with time would Charlie figure this out.*) My eyes swept out across the west side of the property and I got an idea. As we were alongside a major highway, the idea would incorporate two things at the same time. I was thinking about a food franchise that served breakfast, lunch and dinner for dignitaries and employees, just off corporate property within walking distance, so our people wouldn't have to waste so much time driving to lunch or other desired meals. A motel also came to mind too; but according to my calculator, I couldn't see how they could make enough profits to stay alive, even with the highway close by. How about a gas station?! I figured, fully staffed, we'd have about seventy five to a hundred people. That alone would be a decent income for the restaurant. Back inside, I counted required job titles, desks, and parking stalls. So far, so good, but that was only the basics for the center section of the building. Well, let's see what this town has to offer.

Chapter 2

I was just about out the front door of the building when the realtor called. Said he had the five places for me to look at. Again I got that feeling of being drawn to something or was it someone? It was an extremely strong pull, so I'm thinking it was someone! And this guy had to be in someway linked or connected to that someone. It was just past three thirty, so I said okay.

At each of the houses, I tried to gauge the time and distance from the house to the office. Being the CEO, I could now afford a lot better then I'd originally told this guy, but I wasn't going to change my bid, at least not yet. But still another one of those unexpected surprises was to come. The first place we went to was a high maintenance older building, inside and out. It would make a great fixer upper that would probably need to be repiped and rewired just to meet the codes. The next one looked fairly good from the street and was about the same distance from the office, but as soon as I got out of the car, I felt something. Something eerie; some people might call it bad vibes. It was like the house itself said, "not this one!" I just got back in the car and said "lets see the next one." By the time we finally got to the fifth one, I was so tired of looking, I wasn't even sure what I was looking for anymore. But this had to be the place! *All things come in time to those of patients who ask of it; and Charlie had!*

It was a quaint looking oriental house. It looked like a smaller version of one of those temples you see on oriental post cards. I could actually see the office building from the front door. This place felt comfortable, this was a home; *but not mine!* As I got out of the car, I got that same weird feeling I got talking to the realter on the phone, but with an addition. Someone was watching us! *There was a lot more to this house than could be seen.* According to the realter, the house was built in 2002, so it would probably only need a new water heater, and a tune up on the central air system. The price was right at the limit I had given him and just a bit more. But with my new job, I could afford it, and we were only twenty minutes from the office. A lot of TLC had gone into the oriental theme, design and sturdy construction of this place, not to mention a ton of money into the décor, inside and out.

I asked the realtor for the complete stats on the house; the contractors, subs and its residents since it was built. The exterior of the place looked like a picture post card of a plush Chinese or Japanese home, but something about the way the house was situated on the lot seemed out of place! It was a very unique kind of a house, with a lavish exterior that looked really nice even in the snow. I walked around the front yard for a few minutes. It was meticulously cared for Kentucky blue grass. And then came the driveway. There isn't a single crack one. That alone said a lot about its construction and the materials used. The entire time we were in the front yard, there was that constant feeling that someone was watching us from inside the house; maybe the realtor had an assistant, I thought.

The house and landscaping had been artistically and carefully designed, then built by a master craftsman with a purpose in mind. This was more than just a home! It was the elegance of calm and peace. But in a New York country side it looked more than a little out of place! The second story and attic roof is in a pagoda type design with the typical pan tile roof. There was a little pool with a bamboo bush to the right of the front door. There's a large heated koi pool in the shape of the bottom half of a Yin Yang sign, with a double wide sidewalk, and an oriental bridge over the pool to the front door. The front door itself is set back about four feet into a heavy looking, almost full circle of a red and gold structure. Then we went inside.

Just inside the front door is an elaborate mud room, and they had left nothing out. Then came the sliding shoji glass doors into the entrance way; frosted with intricate and elegant gold and green bamboo designs and two storks.

When the realtor opened those glass sliding doors, two things occurred simultaneously. A massive rush of gooseflesh washed over the entire front of my face and body, and I gasped! Oh my God! This was the most magnificently beautiful home I had ever seen in my life! Just inside those doors was a tatami mat in the shape of the back of a queens ratan chair, encircled with a strip of tan carpet, then came a tan marble. This looked like the home of a prince, or some kind of royalty! The bedrooms all had tatami mats, and those that needed space have space. The ones that didn't, were quite cozy and sparsely furnished. Oriental homes don't have that much furniture in them. The bedding, futons, comforters and pillows are kept neatly stacked in a closet. The realtor said it had an attic and basement, but I didn't visit them on this trip.

On the main floor was the kitchen, dining room and a laundry room that doubled as a sewing room. There were also two living rooms, one modern and one oriental. There's one master bedroom and one guestroom, each with their own bath and shower, and a meeting room behind the staircase.

The second floor has four bedrooms, each with their own showered bathrooms. There's also an elaborate office with a library on the second floor at the top of the stairs. Everything in the house seems to be either intricately decorated tile or polished wood. I tried all the faucets, the toilets, the thermostats, all the doors and windows, and every light switch. Whoever decorated this place had a serious OCD problem. Everything in or about the house seems to be symmetrical, exactly where it is supposed to be to the inch, and it all works. It was almost too perfect. Then it hit me, "Feng shui!" This truly was an oriental home, a very expensive one! Feng shui is a kind of Chinese philosophy that has something to do with the flow of energy, water and air, yin and yang. Architects in Hong Kong use it a lot for locating building sites and designing their buildings, inside and out; but this is New York! I should have guessed it by the specifics of the oriental designs of the exterior of the house, and the fact that the placement of the house on the lot was not parallel with the street. Still, here and there was a touch of modern. Inside the house, the walls have no corners of any kind, anywhere; they're all smooth turns or rounded edges to the height of your head, accented with indirect lighting. The floors on the main level of the house are a light tan mix of marble and granite, including the elegantly lavish three level, drop down circular living room floors, with carpeted steps leading to the front of a large rock fireplace.

The rest of the floors are polished wood or tatami mats with wide strips of carpet methodically placed between the tatami and the marble.

There are no doors to open and close, they all slide next to each other, then into a recess in the wall, except for the front door, back door, and the door that goes from the kitchen into the garage. The vaulted ceilings are all open, with beams that look like polished tree logs. Only the kitchen looks a bit out of place. Everything in there is ultra modern and high tech. The bathrooms are diversely marvelous. The toilets are behind curved decorated frosted glass with a crane and gold and green bamboo designs. The showers on the main floor are hid beyond a small maze of floor to ceiling walls.

The walls are made of strategically placed glass blocks, and a high grade of decorated jade green porcelain tile from somewhere across the Pacific. On the main floor there's also a steaming tile bathtub that looks like a miniature swimming pool, but it's more like a hot tub, only hotter; like rare, medium and well done!

I went out the back door to check the gas, electric, and water meters and hookups. I followed the wiring from the house to the power pole that is on the property. I wanted to see if any branches needed to be removed. Goosebumps climbed up the back of my right arm, shoulder and neck. Again I'm having that feeling that someone is watching me, but now the feeling seems strangely different. I think the back yard was designed by the same guy that designed the house. It is more than elaborate and pristine. It includes a partially hidden warm water koi pool in the top half of the Yin-Yang sign, and a ten foot waterfall cascading through a jagged rock wall at the back of a large gazebo. Then I saw something through the thick foliage I thought more than a bit odd!? At that instant, the goosebumps doubled and began crawling tightly over my lower back, right shoulder, and up my neck, into my hair! The feeling of being watched is now intense! The side and back portions of the yard are enclosed with an almost vine covered ten foot spiked chain and pole link fence, with burgundy privacy slats. The support poles of the chain link are three inch galvanize pipes filled with concrete every four feet, considerably more than a bit above code, and the fence is electrified! I didn't ask. Guess that explained the breaker box just inside the back door. That whole fence is definitely not normal for residential codes. Beyond the fence is a thick forest. Maybe there are more than a few bears on the other side of that fence I thought.

To the south, or left of the huge two and a half car garage, is a do it yourself hobby mans dream! It houses a metal, wood and auto shop, complete with drills, saws, lathes, and all the tools to go with it. It looks like something from one of those TV home shows, only better. But why would someone leave all these tools and equipment? Unless they left in a hurry! More than a bit odd I'd say.

The house had obviously been intricately furnished and decorated by pros from across the sea. Someone who intricately knew the cultures and the ways of the people very well. I'm thinking there was a collaborated effort of two cultures on both floors.

The staircase that half spirals to the second floor is a magnificent piece of work. Five foot wide steps with carved and engraved banister rails and poles of thick solid polished ash, highlighted in mahogany stain. There is a thick light tan carpet embedded into each step, and inset gold colored lights on the opposite ends of every other step. That was an odd choice in wood for the staircase, but it was beautiful.

Naturally, all these niceties was going to boost the price of the house a bit, but it is more than worth every penny of it. Hell, it would take more than a lifetime for someone like me just to put all of this stuff together. In my awe, the realtor walked up to me.

"Mr. Foster said you would probably like this one, so he bought it in your name," the realtor said casually looking around.

"Then we didn't really need to look at those other houses?!" I stated a bit taken back.

"No sir, but Mr. Foster wanted to give you some options just in case. As Mr. Foster said, "It's just a house, take it so you can get on with your job,"" the realtor stated passively.

"Just how long have you known Mr. Foster, if I may ask?" I asked quizzically.

"I met him when they broke ground for your office building four years ago," he said assertively. I was starting to get a strange feeling this Mr. Foster knew as much about me as I did about my drawings. Had I been set up? Obviously there's a lot more to this move than is visible.

"Well, I guess I'll just take it and get on with my job then," I said, trying to be jovial.

23

"It's been a pleasure doing business with you Mr. Aldermon. I'll take you back to your car now and you can come back and enjoy your new home," he said, and that's what we did, sorta. But I didn't come right back to the house though, cause I was hungry. The house truly had everything in it you could possibly want, except food! So I went to the restaurant to have dinner and made an attempt to look over the paperwork the realtor had given me. A waitress came to the table with a pot of coffee, and asked if she could take my order. Looking into her eyes, a power surge came over me. The innocent vulnerability, and all that exposed flesh! Should I ask? Would she accept if I did? Then what? What if she said no! Reluctantly I caught myself. For crying out loud Charlie, get a life! Now all of a sudden you want to pickup every girl in town. What the hell is wrong with you?

This must be the feeling all the big shots have when they have too much money, or think they are in some kind of control. Entitlements! But me, I'm just me, and need to get back to work. But what her eyes are insinuating has nothing to do with my job! A guy could become expectant of this kind of treatment after a while. The chicken fried steak sounded good, along with a bowl of potato soup with shredded cheese on top. Then it was back to looking at my paperwork instead of the cleavage and more that was being offered, but not on the menu. Was this the feeling of entitlement that power, money and prestige gives you? Or is it my position that's pushing this powerful sensual urge through my body and mind? Or was it just me wanting to show off my new house? Okay, the bedroom specifically. It seems these people know all about me; who I am, my position, what I do for a living, and they know my boss, Mr. Foster. It seems he's put all of them at my beckon call. Were these girls a test of my willpower? Was he looking for a trust factor? Wonder how much he paid them to do all this? He must be one rich bastard, and I'm probably in for one hell of a shock sooner or later. The paperwork Charlie!

After dinner, I was sitting there with a fresh cup of coffee looking at my paperwork and glancing at the scenery, out the window; thinking about a location for that fast food franchise when my phone rang.

"Aldermon," I said.

"Whatchya doing boss man?" It was Blake.

"How you doing sport?" I replied.

"Hey, some guy up top sent me a letter by courier yesterday. He's saying you can't live without me; what's up with that?" he asked with a chuckle.

"That guy happens to be the corps VP and his name is Foster. He told me to make a list of people I thought would fit in here. I couldn't resist putting the next best architect in the business on it. When you coming up?" I asked.

"Whoa; hang on there boss man, I didn't say anything about going anywhere," he came back.

"Well, I'm actually surprised he gave you a choice. That guy is pretty persistent. You can stay at my place until you get one of your own," I said.

"No need Charlie, he's got me booked in a luxury hotel in Corinth with a company car at my disposal," he said.

"That's the hotel where he's got me staying at the moment. I'm in room 212," I said.

"Charlie, did you by chance put Ms. Balintyne on that list?" he asked slyly.

"As a matter of fact I did, my friend. Along with four other guys that deserve to get out from under shitheads thumb," I said a bit sarcastically.

"You know Charlie, he's already not liking you so much. When he got back from the main office, he was some kinda pissed. He went straight into your empty office and there was a loud crash. I'm thinking he karate chopped your drawing board. Ya sir, I'd say he was more than a little up set, but not so much with you, as himself. You were his ticket to a plush corporation job and he blew it. Serves him right, he's been riding your coat tails for as long as I can remember. Now he's gonna have to work to earn a living," Blake said assertively.

"Foster's got me scheduled up there Monday morning. I'll give you a call when I get to the hotel. See ya boss man," he said and hung up. I switched over to call waiting and melted all over the table.

"Aldermon," I said.

"Hello, Mr. Aldermon," came a sultry seductive whisper.

"This is your new sexatary, and I have a sensual desire to please my new boss," she said, and began laughing out loud.

"Whew! You had me going there for a second. Shelly, I hope moving up here to this new job won't discomfort you in anyway?" I said.

"No; no, not at all. I have an aunt and two cousins that live right there in Corinth," she said when she finally stopped laughing.

"I guess there's four or five others that are packing up as well. What did you do to cause such a commotion Charlie? that guy is really pissed," she said.

"I'll tell you all about it when you get here," I said.

"Okay, see you then; bye," she said and hung up. Well, that takes care of both floors. It was now covered with experienced people. Ms. Balintyne could run the first floor with her expertise, and Blake could run the second floor, and still be my exec. The other four guys would fit right in upstairs as well. Me, I'd just try to look like I knew what the hell I was doing to maintain the whole operation.

The next morning the realtor came by the hotel about seven thirty and had me sign some papers and gave me my copies, along with the final stats I had asked for, and two sets of a lot of keys. I decided to spend one more night at the hotel, and told the manager I'd be checking out the next day. Seemed like I was still at work, but not at the office. Wonder if it's going to be like this all the time? I finished my coffee then went upstairs and took a shower and hit the sack. But I couldn't get to sleep, not for awhile anyway, too much excitement I guess. But even before the sleep came, things started getting a little crazy. I had been in bed about three or four minutes and it came.

"*Charlie* ...," came an angelic soft whisper out of the dark from just to the left side of my bed. I sat up in a start. Who the hell is that?!

"Who's there?" I hurriedly asked. Without a sound, something like a wispy shadow moved between me and the window towards the foot of the bed. I jerked over and turned on the lamp, but there was no one in the room except me! But as soon as I turned that lamp off, the shadow crossed between me and the window again, this time moving towards the head of the bed. I turned on the lamp again, nobody! What the hell is going on?! Maybe the shadow was outside the window. Be real Charlie, you're on the second floor. I turned off the light and rolled over to face away from the window. Only a minute or two later, the bed gently compressed, like someone had just lightly sat down right next to my back, and I heard someone breathing right next to my left shoulder. I shot out of that bed like a rocket and turned on the room light! Nobody! What the hell is going on?! It was about fifteen minutes before I got the nerve to get back in that bed, and I was still leery about what had just happened. What the hell could have caused all that? When I finally did get to sleep, that scary shredded up woman came right up to my face in a nightmare. That was a hell of an alarm clock! Five a.m.. No more sleep; not after a dream like that! I even looked at the bedding to see if there was any blood, but there was none! But whatever it was or is, wasn't finished with me yet.

I went through my morning routine. But even under a hot shower, I suddenly became cold, but didn't relate that to anything but the air conditioner. Then I heard a squeaking on glass. Slowly, I slid open the shower door just a bit and looked around. On the mirror was a heart drawn into the moisture of the shower?! Okay, that's different; I have a secret admirer. One of the waitresses, or a friendly maid maybe. I finished my shower, dried off and gingerly opened the bathroom door. So, where's the lovely that drew the heart? There's no mermaid on my bed, and no one else in the room. Now what the hell was going on? Get yourself ready for work Charlie, this stuff is going to drive you batty if you let it!

I went down to the restaurant and had a light breakfast and a look at all the desserts that were being offered. I was pretty sure they didn't act like this at home. Hell, it looked like I could have my own harem, if I had the nerve to ask. I couldn't stay here any longer. I'd either get in trouble or wind up married.

That morning, I went to the Wilton employment office and talked to the director there about potential job openings and placements. He had one of his people put up four lists of job titles that I was looking for on their board. I was sure there was going to be an influx of people looking for jobs when we finally opened the place up. I'd have Blake and Shelly, (Ms. Balintyne) use the two conference rooms for interviews. Experience, dedication and work ethics were what I was looking for, along with a split mix of genders. We were also going to need a janitorial service for the inside of the building, and a sizeable grounds crew for the outside. I decided to ask around and find out who the best companies were for both of those jobs. After I got to the office that morning, I called the sign company and they said they would send out a rep to do the design. Then it was off to the bank Mr. Foster had set up our accounts in, for payrolls, vehicles, utilities and maintenance. Mr. Foster was sure putting a lot of faith in me. That account amounted to ten million dollars which I kept in confidence. The bank manager treated me like royalty and handled everything himself. It seems the whole town knows about our company and who I am. I didn't want to mar their attitudes or the respect I was being given just to have a good time. Looking over the exteriors and interiors of five or six well kept companies, I went in to see who they employed for their janitorial and exterior maintenance.

I chose two of each. One of each I went to see and signed contracts with, the second one I would keep on file in case I wasn't too thrilled with the first one.

Blake came in a day early. After he got settled in at the hotel, he called and I gave him directions to the office building. I put him to work right off the bat. I gave him a list of things he would be responsible for as my exec, and the assistant CEO, and the authority to accomplish anything else he thought he might need to do. Over the next week, Shelly and the other four guys, Gibbs, Frank, Tristan, and Marrket trickled in. Shelly looked over her area downstairs. I gave her a list of what was to be accomplished there and told her she would be the line boss downstairs, a really big job and responsibility. But I wouldn't have given it to her if I didn't think she couldn't handle it. The other four guys had their drafting jobs and offices on the second floor. I assigned their offices mostly by the type of drawing expertise they had in structure, plumbing and electrical and blueprints. Then told them what was expected of them. They would also help to oversee the new people once the hiring got started. Besides the people I had brought up from the city, I was looking for two more engineers, two contract coordinators, three more drafters, and two secretaries, one for Shelly on the first floor and one for Blake on the second floor. It seemed Mr. Foster was reading my mind. He had also robbed some other facilities of exactly what I was looking for, and they were on their way.

Then I went shopping big time. I ordered four pickups with on site maintenance contracts from a reputable dealer in Corinth. These trucks would be for my contractors and engineers, and would be parked on the east side of the building, along with three company cars. That still left a lot of parking spots open east of both wings. Still hadn't figured out what those wings were for yet, but I was sure it would come to me.

Friday and Saturday we had staff meetings in preparation for the busy coming week. Monday morning we started the interviews as soon as the doors were open, and the applicant's came in droves. Turns out there's a college nearby, but I was trying to stay away from part time employees, unless they were exceptionally knowledgeable in certain tasks. The interviews lasted the whole week, from the time we opened the doors, until closing time.

That Saturday, in the conference room we made our selections. Then we made name and job title tags for the desks, then ordered company name tags and T-shirts with the corps logo through an outfit right here in Wilton.

Sunday morning we started making the confirmation calls. I knew getting started from scratch was going to be a bear, but there was no doubt in my mind we could make it work.

Monday morning we checked the new employees into the lobby, gave them an orientation of the company, the building, fire evacuation procedures and who they reported to. Then came the time cards, their job titles and where they would be working. Then each of the staff members took two employees at a time from the crowd and got them situated at their desks, and briefed them on the basics of their jobs. Most of the people were being assigned to Shelly on the first floor. I assigned Gibbs and Frank down stairs for the time being to help Shelly get her newbies situated and orientated. Blake, Tristan and Marrket would take care of situating the people on the second floor when they got there. The people Mr. Foster commandeered filtered in, in a timely manner that week as well. They too would become part of the corporate staff of this facility. I wanted everything to be ready by the next Friday and we were. Monday morning I called Mr. Foster and told him we were ready for business, and gave him my list of wants. He seemed pleasantly surprised that we were ready so soon. Wednesday morning, a business chopper delivered six tubes of drafts and several tubes of prints for contractors in Corinth, and several for different parts of New York, then the chopper was gone. It never dawned on me to have a reason to know where the choppers came from. We called the contractors to let them know we had their proposals and had started work on them.

Right at noon, a second executive chopper landed on the helo pad. This was the man that had me and the others moved here, my new boss. I met Mr. Foster and two of his assistants just outside the back door. Foster was in his late sixties, about five ten with silver hair and hazel eyes. He had come to take a look at the progress of the new operation. After the introductions, he walked right into the main lobby like he was one of the workers and started looking at what was going on around him. The first floor was kind of busy, but he took it all in stride.

"Wow; impressive! I'm pretty damn sure your previous boss couldn't have accomplished all this in the time you have, if at all. I think I made a good choice and congratulations are in order," he said assertively.

"Thank you sir, but I had a lot of good help in making this happen," I said humbly.

"Well, you were the guiding hand. Make sure your people know I appreciate what they've done for you, and me," he said and went off looking around. I introduced him to Shelly, and let her take him on a tour through the entire first floor. I just followed along with a notepad and took notes. I wanted Shelly and Blake to share the spotlight here, because they were more than a part of what made things come together and happen here. Even for an elderly guy, Foster was more than impressed with Shelly's attitude, personality, and her organizational structure and work methods, and the rest of her of course!

Then we went upstairs. Blake met us at the top of the stairs and I introduced him to Mr. Foster, and let Blake take Foster on a tour of the offices and what they did in each one. Foster looked over some of the contracts, a couple of the designs and several of the blueprints and seemed more than satisfied with our end of the proposals.

"Well Mr. Aldermon," he said coming out of the last office.

"You seem to have everything under control here, so I'll get out of your hair and let you get back to work," he said and headed for his chopper. He said nothing about my boss in the city, or the house he had acquired for me. I can't help but think how prideful I felt of our efforts as that chopper lifted off. With a great staff, I was accomplishing my life's goals in style and it felt great! My wishes were coming true. *Even though part of it was about to become just a bit spooky!*

That night I went home to the house, or my castle as I called it, to see how that was going to work out. It was massively huge compared to the studio apartment I had in the city. Damn, just walking around in this house by myself, I couldn't help think this is more than a lot of space for one person. Hell, this is a lot of space for five people! I wound up going to the restaurant at the hotel for dinner anyway, because with everything else that was going on, I had neglected to go shopping for myself.

Chapter 3

I gave Blake and Shelly directions on how to get to my place, and told them not to be strangers, not that they'd ever show up; they had their own lives to live. Even though I was their boss, I wanted to maintain a cordial friendship with them.

On the way back from dinner, I stopped at the supermarket in Wilton and got the survival essentials; enough TV dinners for breakfast and dinner to last the rest of the week! Then it was off to my new house again.

As I pulled up in front of the house to turn into the driveway, I couldn't help notice the glow of probably a nightlight in one of the upstairs bedrooms. Then something like the wisp of a faint shadow of someone, moved right to left across the room and the nightlight went out! I pulled into the driveway slowly and stopped, shut off the engine, and reached down for my ankle .32. I'd been carrying since the day after I moved to the city. Even at six five, idiots still try me in broad daylight. People there get stupid and have some serious entitlement issues. Twice the situation almost warranted my toy, but my farm boy fists were closer, faster and did the job just fine. Besides, I didn't want to kill anyone, unless it really came down to that. Being cautious is always a better option.

Someone was definitely on that second floor! This house had one of those remote security buttons you put on your keychain. Push the button and the entire house, inside and out, lights up like an airport. I counted ten seconds then unlocked the front door and cautiously let myself in.

A rather cool rush of gooseflesh covered me from head to toe, but it was still too early for me to start making assumptions, rationalizing or putting two and two together relative to those goosebumps. I carefully checked each room and closet on the first floor, while keeping an eye on the staircase when I could; no one was on the first floor. Slowly, I crept up the stairs. First to the room where I saw the shadow. I went to one knee, a bit to the left of the door, and slowly slid it open. Nothing! almost. I know this was the room where I saw the light and shadow! But still I was cautious. I couldn't tell weather it was aftershave or perfume at first, but there was definitely a trace of something in that room. There was also a flare of goosebumps that moved across my face and neck.

I checked every nook and cranny in that room, nothing! But someone had definitely been in there, and only a moment or two before me! Okay, maybe it was the other room. I was on my way to the next room, but as I reached for the sliding door, a cold rush of gooseflesh covered the entire back of my body. I dropped to one knee and spun around, the pistol again pointing into an empty room, my eyes intently searching every part of the room! Then a curtain across the room began gently waving, like there was a light breeze coming through the window, or someone had just brushed against it. Easy Charlie! You don't' want to start putting holes in your new house already! There was definitely no one in the room to be seen, yet the gooseflesh remained on my right arm, shoulder and back the whole time. I stood up and went to check the window; it was closed and locked! What the hell? As I checked the window, I could have sworn I heard someone breathing very close to my right shoulder in the total silence of that room. Spooky! Again I spun around, but saw no one. A lot of homes, even new ones, have traces or remnants of those that have passed. Either from the house itself, or the ground they were built on. You either learn to live with these things, or 'you' leave, not them! And even if they do leave, it's on their terms! This could be interesting; maybe I have a real ghost in my house! Come on Charlie, you're a little too old to be believing in ghosts don't you think? Not being completely serious about the situation at hand, I checked the rest of the rooms on the second floor; nothing! Okay, so what had I seen, and what was that smell? What made the curtains move? And what had caused all the gooseflesh? *Want to take a guess Charlie?* After I finished checking the rest of the house, I went out through the kitchen door into the garage and pushed the remote.

The big garage door slid open like silk, with almost no sound at all. Back out to the car, I drove into the garage. The kitchen is conveniently located just inside the garage door so you don't have to carry all your groceries that far. As I opened the kitchen door, there was more than a chill to the warm air coming out of the kitchen, and again came the goosebumps all over my face in a rush! This time they were all over my face, neck and chest. And again there was that slight trace of the scent of what I had smelled upstairs. Oh shit! There was no doubt in my bewildered mind now that someone was standing there in the doorway looking right at me! That was more than unnerving! There is definitely something, or should I say, 'someone' else, in this house!

"Excuse me," I said just to be courteous. I couldn't see whoever it was and didn't want to run into them as I made my way into the kitchen. After I put the groceries away, I made a pot of coffee, constantly looking around. Not sure what I was looking for, maybe something to move so I could tell where they were. Carefully, I listened for anything out of the ordinary, but nothing happened, but the gooseflesh remained. While the coffee was gurgling away in the pot, I made a couple of my favorite weird peanut butter, spam and cheese sandwiches and collected the paperwork the realtor had given me. It was time to learn a little about my new house. Maybe there was something about a ghost in the stats.

So, the stats say the house was designed, and the construction supervised by a man named Xhong Jun. His name implied he was Chinese. Okay; that explained all of the oriental things I saw, in and out of the house. The house was finished in 2002 and Mr. Xhong Jun, his Japanese wife and family took up residents here. But then they relocated back to China in October of 2004. What the hell; they only lived here two years? Weird! In November 2004, the Buckhurst family acquired the property. Then they too left, and moved to Coronado Island in southern California, in October of 2007. In November of 2007, a Mr. and Mrs. Dalton acquired the property. This was the guy that added the shops in the south part of the garage. But they too moved out to Palm Springs in October of 2010. Those two families had lived here for only three years each. How odd. That's when the house was taken off the market, refurbished and redecorated. There was no mention in the drawings of an attic, which I hadn't visited yet, until the refurbishing. Still, all of it was redone with the same oriental theme in mind.

Yet that theme seemed to be split in two ways, Japanese and Chinese, in and out of the house. The entire interior of the house was also a mix of Chinese and Japanese cultures. Both cultures were delicately woven and the result was magnificently beautiful! Then something odd occurred to me, and caught my attention at the same time. <u>The dates</u>!? Look at those dates again Charlie! No one has lived in this house for more than three years. Two of the three occupants had moved to a warmer climate. But the fact they all had left in the month of October seemed just a bit more than odd. Maybe winter comes early up here, or its colder up here than I thought. I guess there could have been many reasons, but one had to connect the three.

I was just about to finish the last bite of my second sandwich, and was still looking at my paperwork, when the air about the kitchen again became cooler, and the goosebumps returned to my right side. Somethings coming Charlie! There were two light knocks on the other end of the counter top! Then I thought I saw a wispy motion out of the corner of my right eye as I was turning my head. Almost at the same instant, the distinct soft scent of a sandalwood fragrance gently descended all around me! It was like I had just lit a stick of incense. By the lovely smell of the soft incense, I could now assume my new companion 'might' be a female. Great, now I'm thinking I have a female ghost in my house!

"Hello," I said quietly, looking in the direction of the movement I thought I had seen. But there was no reply; sorta! Then ever so slowly, the stool at the other end of the counter began moving backwards away from the island counter! Yup, I definitely have a ghost in my new house! It appeared I was going to have to eat my own words; "You either learn to live with them or 'you' leave!" And I had no intentions of leaving, at least not yet. Still, there would be a couple of situations I knew that would make me a little nervous; sleeping and the bathroom!

"Hello; You're welcome in my home," I said awkwardly and quietly, trying to establish some sort of contact. Who was she? And after the refurbishment, why was she still here? Then it hit me! The dates, the short stays and sudden moves of the residents; the ghost had scared them away! This female is from Mr. Xhong Jun's family. But the paper said the husband and wife both moved back to China?! Oh my God! This was his daughter! What the hell had happened?! Time frames Charlie. She must have died in September or October, and I'm willing to bet that damn fence out back has something to do with it.

I spent the rest of the evening trying to coax her into saying or doing something, so I would know where she was with no luck. But I knew she was there watching, cause the goosebumps kept coming back. Still, I didn't feel uncomfortable with my guest, and there were no more encounters that night, at least none that I was aware of. *But from that day, Charlie was never alone!*

The next morning I was at the city library as soon as they opened their doors. There are some things in life, even though your curious about them, deep down inside you really don't want to know what happened, or hope its not as bad as you're thinking, and this was one of them. But I had to know!

I was going through the obituaries for September of 2004. Oh my God, there it was! Her name is Shai shin! I don't know if that name means anything, but its a pretty name. She was only twelve years old when she was killed by a bear in the back yard of her home; my home! Oh my God! Obviously the reason for the electrified fence! How horribly terrifying that must have been for her parents. They must have been grief stricken, the reason they went back to China. Damn! What I was looking at drained me so much, I just sat there in a daze, dumbfounded! That was terrible! When I finally got some control of my emotions, I drove back to the house with a heaviness you wouldn't believe. I knew absolutely nothing about this family or these ghostly things. Still, I don't think they needed any kind of light to move around with. At any rate, I thought I was willing to learn something about this one. I wanted to help her find her way home, if that was at all possible; but how?

I had to cross one of my boundaries and wound up going to places I didn't belong in, and asking strange people, in strange places about strange things I knew nothing about. I did some snooping around with people in the part of town I didn't belong in, and found out about an older lady, Ms. Elda, that lived at the edge of town into the woods a bit. Supposedly she was some kind of a witch. I didn't know there was more than one kind. Still, I was told to be polite.

When I pulled up in front of her little shack, made of corrugated metal sheets and mud. She was standing expectantly just in front of her door with a stone looking expression on her face. Obviously, someone had told her I was coming. I got out of the car and walked up to her.

"Hello," I said as cordially as I could, but her expression didn't change.

"I'm Charlie, are you Ms. Elda?" I asked.

"I am, please come inside," she said softly. This all seemed more than a bit spooky to me. I don't know how to put it, but this lady seemed more than a little strange. But for what she was said to be, and does, it is probably quite normal. By my left forearm, she gently led me into her shanty, and to a table in the middle of what I think is her living room, and asked me to be seated. She sat directly across from me. First her right hand crossed over a little black glass container that had a candle in it, and the candle lit, as did several others in the room! Okay, that's different!? I thought.

The flickering flame of the candle in the glass container danced in the reflections of Ms. Elda's jet black eyes, that seemed to be looking right through mine. For almost a whole minute she just sat staring at me, then she spoke. In that short time, the room became cooler.

"You are here on behalf of the Lady Shai shin are you not?" she asked almost slyly, glancing just slightly to her right. Now how would she know that?

"Her name is pronounced 'Shay shin,'" she added. Lady? I thought.

"Yes; I am, I think. I want to help her get back to her family if that's possible. Do you know of this girl, Shay shin?" I asked. Again Elda became silent and closed those penetrating dark eyes.

"Shay shin wishes to stay with you Mr. Aldermon," Elda said.

Then her eyes literally popped open and she was looking at the chair to her right, and was silent for a few more seconds. How did she know my name?

"Shay shin has not spoken directly of this, but I see there seems to be a caring of you about her Mr. Aldermon," Elda said softly.

"No; no, I'm way to old for her. She's only twelve years old and should be with her mother and father, or ancestor's, or wherever it is that people like her should be. But, she is welcome to stay in the house as long as she wants to. But isn't she supposed to be somewhere else?" I asked nervously.

Again Elda was silent. Why did I get the feeling she was somehow actually talking to Shay shin?

"She is no longer a girl of twelve years, but a young woman and does not want to leave that house, or you! She means you no harm or inconvenience. Still, she wants to share 'her' home with you," Elda said. *'Her home?' Yes Charlie, that house is as much her home as it is yours! Ah, maybe more hers than yours!* And if she's not twelve, that would explain the perfume and her taunting. Remember your own words Charlie; put up or ship out.

What the hell, if I could manage a corporation site, I sure as hell should be able to manage a house with one ghost, or whatever it is that's in it. I had been told to give Ms. Elda some money when she was done, but how would I know when that was? I laid a hundred dollar bill on the table and started to get up to leave, but Elda said;

"Wait; there is one thing more; be vigil of the attic, there is something there she wants you to see," she said. In my distress, depression, frustration and confusion, I wasn't thinking clearly and didn't pay much attention to our parting words. On the way back to the house, it was like I knew I had heard Elda say something, but it hadn't quite sunk in, amidst everything else I was thinking. Still I carried that heavy feeling, a feeling of pity, sorrow, and confusion. A pain of empathy for what this girl and her parents had gone through. It was so heavy on my mind, when I got home I decided to take a nap. The potentiality of the horrors she must have gone through drained me mentally and physically. It was only ten thirty in the morning, but I needed to unwind. I needed to reboot, realign my files, sort out unneeded information and put the reality of me back in place. I took off my shoes, jacket and tie, and collapsed on the bed. God that must have been terrible!

But there was no solitude in the darkness of my wayward mind. Of my sleep there came a strange dream. That of a big angry bear and a building on fire, and above the bear and the fire, always there were two sets of eyes watching; but only one could be seen at a time. The eyes to the left were passionate, intense, confused, then angry. The other set of eyes were humble, wanting, and sad. But what were they watching, and why? The bear came closer, until it was right in front of me, and from out of the fire its right claw swiped at my face, its nails shredding the left side of my head and face, leaving the bloody flesh hanging to my chest! The eyes above the fire glared at me, that I should do something! That dream brought me upright in my bed in a cold sweat! Damn that seemed real! But a couple things in my bedroom were also real and more than a bit different from when I had laid down.

The first thing I noticed was a beautiful blue, red and gold silk comforter that covered me and the entire bed! I guess I should have paid a bit more attention to the designs on that comforter, not that I would have understood what they meant. It was so soft and warm, I hugged it close to me. And then from out of the comforter came that delicate trace of sandalwood!

That was starting to be an indicator of Shay shin's presence, if I paid attention. The second thing that really got my attention was I only had on my underwear! Someone had undressed me! Where the hell were my clothes? Then I saw them, neatly folded and hung on a chair across the room next to the bathroom door.

Now how the hell did they get over there? Dumb question. Shay shin! She had to be the answer to both questions. I glanced at my watch, 12:15. Okay; coffee; I really needed a cup of coffee. I grabbed my robe off the hook on the bathroom door and headed for the kitchen. I made a fresh pot of coffee and a bologna and cheese sandwich. Suddenly I could smell the scent of sandalwood! It was here, I mean *she was here;* somewhere! I looked in the direction of the chair that had moved before and said;

"Shay shin, thank you for taking care of me," I said as if I could actually see her. But there was no reply, but still the trace of the sandalwood remained. This was frustrating, but acceptable I guess for the situation I was in. Like I said, I know nothing about these things, but I was sure hoping to be able to at least hear her say something, anything!

"Shay shin, I now know just a little bit about you, and I'm sorry for what happened to you. Your welcome to stay here as long as you like, but it would be helpful if I could see you, so I don't accidently run into you. I know you're here; I just don't know where you are," I said a bit impatiently. Still there was no reply on her part, nor a movement of any kind. All that day I made attempts to coax her to say something or move something to no avail. Frustrated, that night I sat patiently in front of the fireplace until about 10:30, hoping she would move something, or say something so I would know where she was, but that didn't happen. Still that trace of sandalwood lingered near by. I had to go to work the next morning, and five a. m. comes early enough, so I trudged off to bed, feeling alone, empty, kind of rejected, and something else that seemed confusing; there was a wanting maybe, a bit of caring for her that I didn't understand. This time I took off my own clothes and wrapped myself up in my beautiful soft warm comforter and fell asleep. I slept better that night then I had since I came up from the city, with no dreams or nightmares. But as sleep caught up with me, so did that delicate misty trace of sandalwood. Like the wispy apparition she is, Shay shin's ghostly being affectionately caressed and protectively embraced Charlie's body and his dreamless passions, as she would from this night on.

The first three weeks after opening the facility were kind of hectic. Everyone was still learning their jobs, where things went, and who did what. But the staff worked like a well oiled team, keeping everything moving, and headed in the right direction. Shelly had her unit downstairs set up like a progressive production line.

Obviously she had done a bit of time and motion study management somewhere in her career or in college. With the number of people she had, it was fascinating to see how efficiently and quietly things worked down here. Wonder if we could do that upstairs? When I went over to her office to commend her, I suddenly thought to make a quick detour, but she saw me coming! She tilted her head a little to the left, and the look in her blue green eyes was scary;

"Come here boss man, let me show you how smooth I can really be," they said. It was all over her face. She wanted to play! Right here, right now! Run Charlie! Too late! Still, I commended her on her operation as she stood and came out from behind her desk to stand very close in front of me. The palms of her hands lightly glided over my chest and up to my tie, just incase someone was watching. Literally I was saved by the bell! My phone rang.

The guy from the building signs wanted to know if I was ready to put the signs up? I said we were, and they got there about two thirty with a crane, and the signs were put up. One on the front of the building and one on the back. That was better; now we looked somewhat official; sorta. Then I had another idea. I went to a shop in downtown Wilton, and had some business cards and postcards made up for distribution. They had a picture of the front of the building and a little blurp about our functions on the back. The next week I sent some out to the architect gurus in Vegas, Frisco, LA, Dallas, and Florida. I even sent a few to Japan and Hong Kong. Then I had another idea and headed for Corinth. I had the name of the contractors that built my house and got a copy of the prints. Immediately, even at a glance, something didn't look right. There was no attic on the original prints! It must have been an add on that came about during the refurbishment of the home, but at the request of whom? I left that set of prints in the car so I wouldn't forget to take them home.

Back in the office, I got a phone call from a gruff sounding guy that had heard via a town council member, about me looking for a franchise just off corporate property. He wanted to know if we were serious about the idea. I said I was, and setup a meeting in the conference room for Wednesday morning. I wanted Blake, Shelly and Marrket, along with Tristan and Gibbs to be there. I called Foster for his input.

"Make it happen Mr. Aldermon," he said affirmatively. This was truly to be my first business venture with company funding, and I wanted everything to come out right. Then it was time for a bit of homework. First; how far did I want to get from corporate property? I actually wanted the restaurant within walking distance from the office building if possible. Second; where was the halfway point between highway 87 and the corporate property? I was thinking of other things that we might be able to add out there in that field. Third; who owned that property out there, and how much of it, and how much would they sell it for, if they would sell at all? There were the zoning codes for that area to consider, but that was no big deal. Shelly mentioned the fact there was a college just to the north of Wilton that might bring a fair amount of daytime and maybe evening input to the restaurant. Then Marrket came up with a hammer.

"What kind of impact is this restaurant going to have on the restaurants in Wilton, and are we going to be putting a crimp on someone else's business there?" he asked. Good question; I didn't want to go stepping on somebodies toes already. Then I threw out a few other ideas, like a breakfast bar, multicultural foods, and maybe a gas station to draw patrons from the highway. Then something hit me like a wall that I didn't mention to anyone. I was making an excessive amount of money that was just sitting in the bank. If the price of that property wasn't to high, what if I bought this site with my own money and gave this franchise guy a lease to build? What if I invested some of that money in stocks, or just outright bought a couple of the local restaurants like a merger, and let those people work for me at the new restaurant? That would give me something to build on, and another income. It would take time to build my little empire, but it would be better than throwing all that money away or letting it sit idle in some bank, leaving those people without a job. Now I was excited! Again, most of the income for the restaurant would be during breakfast and lunch from our office, and maybe the college, with dinner income maybe coming from the college and the freeway. I needed to look into a sign or billboard along the highway, maybe two, to let passersby know where the restaurant and the facility was. Blake and I went out snooping around the potential location that turned out to be almost in the middle of what used to be a huge open wheat field. Hell, I could build a whole town on this site.

But it was obvious from looking at the soil that was caked and cracked, this ground hadn't been worked in years. That made me wonder why? Was it in a flood zone, or infested with insects or a fire hazard? I mean we're talking an area of possibly eight miles long and two and a half to three miles wide. That would have been a decent yield for a farmer. The longer we looked at the property, the more possibilities came to mind. But at the moment, I needed to stay with the original plan of feeding the facilities workers. Still there were a lot of other options I wanted to keep open.

Wednesday came and the meeting with the franchise owner was brought to order. I had one of the secretaries that could take shorthand there as well. Even before the meeting started, something didn't feel right. I didn't like the looks of this guy or his attitude. He was a lot like those people down in the city. The franchise owner was a bit grubby in appearance and seemed a bit skittish; he seemed to be up to something, I could feel it. Then came the dead giveaway when he asked about a "joint" venture. That meant he would be only partially into the operation of the restaurant, and wouldn't lose a lot if he backed out. I looked at Blake and hit the brakes. I told him we'd think about it. I didn't like the idea of buying into something that might turn into an obligation of some kind later on, not even a little one.

The next morning I called Blake and asked him to take the helm until I got back, and headed for town. First I went to the Chamber of commerce, then the Town Council, then the BBB. Turns out the guy who owned the property was getting up there in age, had some medical issues, and wasn't able to work that field anymore. His family had no interest in the property, and I had showed up at just the right time. He was willing to let the field go for a hundred grand. One of the guys on the city council mentioned the fact there was a pig farmer that accepted food stuffs from other restaurant's in town, and asked me if I'd be interested in that sort of thing. I saw two openings at the same time and said I would be. The farmer would supply his own containers and would pick them up twice a day, and we would get a discount on pork products. At the BBB, I asked about the guy with the franchise. He turned out to be a potential risk with a police record. It fit! Then I was off to the bank. I had a long candid conversation with the bank manager. For the price of the property that included the right of way, water and mineral right's, I could buy it myself with just a little backing from the corporation.

I had that much in my savings, but I only put down seventy five thousand, so I wouldn't drain my savings totally. With my new CEO paychecks, I could pay off the loan in five months. The transaction went like silk. The bank paid off the owner and put a lean on the property, with an investment option for me to build on it in the meantime. Mr. Foster was apparently keeping closer tabs on me than I thought, and I got a phone call from him the next morning.

"Mr. Aldermon, why are you spending your own money to support company personnel?" he asked slyly. I suddenly had a lump in my throat!

"Well sir, they are my people as much as yours. An opportunity presented itself along with two other options, so I took it to hurry things along. I hope that's not against any rules," I said a bit nervously; hoping I didn't just buy a field and loose my job in one decision. Turns out he knew every step I had taken to acquire the property.

"Apparently you are more business minded and enthusiastic about your job and your people than I gave you credit for, Mr. Aldermon. I'm going to reimburse your endeavor and increase your accounts a bit, just in case you run into another opportunity. Following your past and present ambitions, I'm sure you know what's required to move this project along. Have your drafters start on the building design and prints as soon as possible? I'll be down next month to see the progress. Your even more than I hoped for Mr. Aldermon. You have my complete backing in your endeavors. Keep up the good work. Be seeing ya," he said and hung up. I went in and told Blake what just happened, and to have two drafters start on the designs for the restaurant building, and to be sure to include a dumbwaiter from the kitchen to the second floor, a sizable parking lot, and a drive thru. Frank took on the electrical, gas, water and sewer. The plumbing and sewer drains would lateral into the corporate building drains. I wanted everything well above code, underground, and double insulated well below the frost line because of the weather up here, and I wanted it all to last forever. We had all the codes and knew what was required, and would be well above them, so that part was not a problem. I wanted it easily accessible for simi truck deliveries and garbage trucks as well, with potential access for the option of the gas station and a motel. I called Shelly and Blake upstairs to the conference room and the three of us kicked around some more ideas.

That evening we went out to dinner at the hotel to kind of celebrate Foster's backing. During the course of dinner, it became evident Blake was more than a little interested in Shelly for obvious and whatever reasons. But Shelly is a strong minded aggressive woman, and at the moment, Blake was not on her drawing board. And even though he reluctantly took the hint, he wasn't giving up. After dinner back at the office parking lot, Blake pulled out first. I waited for Shelly to pass me, but she was waiting on something. What the hell was she up to? As soon as I left the parking lot, it became obvious; she was following me! My heart started pounding. Calm Charlie, you only think you know what she wants, but that don't mean she's in love with you. You know what a woman like that can do to your mind; she just wants to play a little. Anyway, what makes you think you can handle a woman like that anyway?

She stayed right behind me all the way to the house. I pulled into the driveway and pushed the remote. The whole place lit up like an airport and the garage door slid open. She pulled into the garage right next to me. Oh shit! My heart is pounding like thunder in my ears, and it feels like my adrenalin, hell, my whole body is on steroids. It was now more than obvious she wasn't a tease, and probably wouldn't take no for an answer. I hadn't felt like this in a long time. Does she want what I think she wants? I wasn't aware I'd given her any reason or cause for her to act like this, what the hell had brought it on? That's the last time I offered her lobster and asparagus in the same meal. The garage door closed and she slowly sautéed those curves around the back of my car in a tease, like "do you like what you see boss man? How about a little sample?" and she was right up to me. I sure as hell didn't have to ask what was on her mind now. Licentiously she unbuttoned my jacket, rubbing her forearms and hands slowly over my chest. Her arms slid around me under my jacket. Holy shit, this is not a woman; this is an animal! She was mine; or was I hers?

"Do you mind Charlie?" she purred, making a slow motion intentional full body contact. You have got to be kidding I thought. She was warm and firmly pressed against me, standing on her toes. The warmth of her breath was now just under my chin, then suddenly her mouth was on my throat just under my left ear, and her tentacles were all over me, all at once! Oh hell yeah, this is a real woman that wants what she wants, and she's not the least bit bashful about how she gets it!

"No, I don't mind, not at all," I sort of whimpered, feeling like a schoolboy on his first date with his biology teacher! She's going to turn you into hamburger Charlie! She pressed her whole body hard against mine, pushing me into the door frame. I was working hard on getting the key into the lock, but it was taking forever to get the damn door unlocked, because my mind was in a lot of places it shouldn't have been. Finally the key was in the lock and I turned it. But I didn't get a chance to reach the door knob before the kitchen door opened, by itself! The sensuous scent of Shay shin's sandalwood perfume swirled out of that kitchen like a nor easterner, around Shelly and I! Suddenly I had a feeling I was in some kind of real trouble! Shelly looked up into my eyes, and hers said it all.

"Would you mind opening the garage door Mr. Aldermon?" she questioned softly. I pushed the remote and as the big door slid open, she planted a full lip lock on me trying to swallow my tongue, as she pulled her fingers out of the depths below my belt.

"It could have been fun Charlie," she purred; then saucily sashayed around the back of her car, got in and backed out onto the road and drove off. Whoa! She had wound me up, and let me go! I let out a heavy sigh and turned toward the kitchen door. The cool gooseflesh covered me! Shay shin had been waiting for me! Why? Was I missing something here, again, or still not paying attention? Shay shin's perfume had said more and faster than I could think, and Shelly caught it all! Nope, this is definitely not a twelve year old girl! At the moment I was thinking Shay shin was as unpredictable as Shelly. Now I'm also thinking, Shelly and Shay shin were both up to something; the same thing! But why did I feel so guilty? I felt like I had brought my secretary home and was met at the door by my wife! **Caught you bad boy!** And why did I feel like I had to justify any part of this situation to either one of them anyway? I'm not going steady, engaged, or married to Shay shin or Shelly! I hadn't taken Elda's words seriously enough. You need to start paying attention Charles! So, now what was Shay shin up to? Hell, I haven't even seen her, and never know where she is. Just that she's someplace near, and at the moment, I kind of figured she was somewhere just inside that kitchen door, right in front of me!

Oh well, it was time for a hot shower, or was it a cold one?! But first I started a pot of coffee and put one of those magnificently nutritious TV dinners in the little oven and set the timer.

As I crossed the living room, to the bedroom, the essence of Shay shin's sandalwood gently swirled about me. Okay, is she here, or is she there? Is she in front of me or at my side?

"Hello Shay shin," I said in the direction of the perfume that was definitely sandalwood, but now just a little different. It now had a very sensuous scent to it. This was starting to get frustrating, and more than a bit comical at times. Oh well, I went into the bedroom, dropped my clothes on the bed, slid out of my underwear, dropped them in the hamper and headed for the shower in my birthday suit! Shay shin is a ghost right? I can't see any part of her, her emotions or reactions to me, so in my mind it didn't matter; that made it okay in my mind for me to run around the house naked. I sure as hell wouldn't have gotten away with that around Shelly!

Under the pounding pulsating thunder of the shower water on my head, I felt a release, a freedom, a relief from life's complications that I was doing well in my endeavors. For about fifteen minutes I was in my own little world. No office or business concerns, only the pacification of my pounding waterfall. I'd had another good day, and it was time to relax.

Chapter 4

Then seemingly for no reason, my pounding waterfall went from pulse to a soft spray and the air about me cooled! Everything in my being said, "Don't even think about moving Charlie, she's here, somewhere very near in the shower, and she's up to something!" There was just a trace of her scent, but enough for me to know Shay shin was getting closer, *a lot closer than I could have ever imagined.* I felt no reason to be afraid, but still I felt a need to be cautious. I still had no idea what these things were capable of. And she came! I actually felt her presence before she touched me, kind of like a vibration or something. Don't move dummy! There came a wanting of her that was so powerful my body was shaking, even though I was attempting to remain very still. Why did I want her so? Something about being a guy I guess. Even so, what are you going to do with a ghost anyway dummy? I don't even know what she looks like, and she's a real ghost, but for some reason that didn't seem to matter to my deranged brain at the moment.

Then came her touch. Ohh my! how can she do that? I didn't think a ghost could physically touch you, let alone do what she was doing to me at the moment. I guess I still had a lot to learn about these things. I could actually feel her velvety fingertips; delicate and gentle, with just a hint of mischief, as they slid slowly over the back of my left hip. Of course the mischief part was probably just my imagination thinking, or maybe hoping! There was only the sound and warmth of the showers soft rain like water falling all about us.

Then her left hand slowly moved up my hip, and her delicate fingertips were now gently resting just below the front of my waist. Her right hand then slowly moved up the muscles of my back. My anxiety level went ecstatic, and it became difficult to breathe! Then came the tender softness of both of her palms and forearms, ever so gently slipping over my arms and shoulders, then both of her hands moved to the front and across my chest. Gently she pulled herself snugly against me. Holy shit! I could actually feel her breasts against my back, and her thighs as her left leg wrapped around the back of mine. Then came the softness of her cheeks, then her lips just below my left shoulder. She had to be at least five eight or so. Elda was right, this was definitely not a twelve year old!

With all her delicate fury, she was holding me as close to her as she could get, or so I thought. What more could a man possibly ask for? Well, besides that! I know I'm awake, yet this seems so much like a sensual dream. I just stood there trying to be humble, trying to subdue my animalistic desires from exploding, and being very still. Let her do whatever she wants. I was so afraid my lust would suddenly burst out of control and I'd do something stupid and this encounter wouldn't just disappear. Well Charlie, at least you know where she is, but do I dare turn around to get a look at her? Was she just an illusion, or was she for real, or could she possibly be both? Shay shin had put my desires, and Shelly wrapped around me at the kitchen door together, and came up with her own version of making my loss of Shelly's affection worthwhile. I didn't understand how I could feel her touch though, she's not supposed to be real; but it feels like she is!? This was going to drive me crazy. I really wanted to turn around and get sensuously mushy with her, but then she might disappear! I didn't think the timing or situation was right. How could I make love to a ghost anyway? Thirty minutes in that shower with her, and I was totally relaxed, or was it exhausted? Elda had been right, Shay shin did care, a lot! Even a dummy like me could feel it! The realization of that caring was coming slowly, but it was coming! I could feel her tender caring, her wants, and the power of her passion, but as of yet I still couldn't see her. Then she backed away like I had farted. Damnit! What the hell had happened? No I didn't fart! I suddenly felt an emptiness of my entire being, a longing for her touch. So what had I done wrong?

Once my composure calmed down, I dried myself off and went back towards the bed. I felt rejected and heavy, with an unfulfilled desire and craving. Even at my age, I still didn't handle rejection very well, and this wasn't helping my esteem one bit. I also felt I needed to start being a bit neater. Again my clothes were folded neatly on the chair. I wish she would quit doing that, she's not my maid or my wife. I don't know if a wife would even care about such things. She'd probably tell me to pick up after myself! I put on a clean pair of shorts, snagged my robe off the bathroom door and headed for the kitchen for my dinner and a much needed cup of coffee. Now what was I supposed to do? My situation wasn't out of control; it is just out there, someplace! Why did I have this longing and need for her? This is almost like being in …! I don't want to say it.

I know as much about that as I do Shay shin; nothing! I couldn't see her, and didn't know anything about her. I couldn't even imagine how I could make things work with Shelly and Shay shin together in the same house. I was positive that was one twosome I could not handle! And other than what happened with Shay shin in the shower, and with Shelly in the garage, neither one of them has given me a reason to really care for them. As far as I could tell, Shelly just wanted to play, but Shay shin was starting to be a very different story. Sure as hell it was going to come down to choosing one or the other. Then there was Lacey, my secretary that was starting to act like she wanted to be a whole lot more than just my secretary! The two pairs of eyes I had seen in my dream were now clear; one had to have been Shelly, the other had to have been Shay shin! Oh my God! If that part of my dream was real…!

After my fabulous dinner, I took my coffee and sat in front of the fireplace, alone, well, sorta. Between me and the flames, there was the occasional flutter of a wispy thing from right to left, and with it came the scent of Shay shin's sandalwood perfume, and the coolness Shay shin brought. I tried talking to her, but that was as far as it went, me talking to myself. She didn't reply or move anything so I still didn't know where she was.

The next morning on my way to work, I stopped at a gun shop and picked up a .444 mag and a box of ammo. I didn't want another part of that dream to come true and not be ready. You might say I had been warned! When I got to the office, I was crossing the lobby to the stairs and here she comes. Shelly looked exceedingly beautiful this morning, and smelled oh so good. She kind of swaggered up to me from her office, her eyes saying all kinds of things I wasn't ready to answer or do.

"You could have told me you had company waiting. I could've taken a hint," she said slyly in almost in a whisper, adjusting my tie, while rubbing the back of her hands and forearms against my chest.

"It's a long story you wouldn't believe or understand. And I had no idea you were going to follow me home, or that I already had company," I said with a smirk.

"Your not as innocent as you make yourself out to be Mr. Aldermon," she said with a giggle that suddenly turned into a frown, as she took two steps back and looked at me strangely.

There had been the sudden distinctive staunch fragrance of sandalwood between us. Still Shelly didn't give up and headed back to her office with that enticing rocking sway, teasing my animal instincts. What had just happened? Both Shelly and Shay shin were tempting as hell, *but this mix wasn't over yet.* How do I get myself into these situations? I just needed to get back to work and went upstairs to check in with Blake.

"Should I ask?" he said with a big grin as I stepped through his office door.

"You'd be asking the wrong person," I said with a smirk.

"How are the drawings for the restaurant coming?" I asked, breaking his train of thought. He walked me down to Gibbs office for a look at the structural layout drawings. Then we headed next door to Frank's office; he was handling all the utilities over a sketch of the structural layout.

"The guy with the franchise called again this morning. I didn't mention any of the new developments to him. I just told him we were still working on it," Blake said. After that we moseyed back towards Blake's office.

"You wearing a new cologne Charlie?" he quizzically asked as we were about to his office door.

"What does it smell like?" I asked.

"I don't know, something oriental; like incense, sandalwood maybe," he said quizzically sniffing the air.

"Well, that's probably what it is then," I said trying to avoid his stare. *But there was something else about Charlie neither Blake nor Charlie was aware of; how the origin of that scent came to be. It turns out Shay shin had another ability!*

"Which reminds me; you wouldn't be a little sweet on Shelly would you?" I queried.

"I'm not stepping on your toes am I Charlie?" he asked.

"Nah, I just don't want to get in the middle of something that's none of my business," I said.

"Well, after what I saw last night, I thought I was the one that was headed in the wrong direction," he said with a grin.

"Blake…," I started, then changed my mind. I wanted to tell him about Shay shin, maybe, but for some reason quickly decided it wasn't time, not yet.

Besides, I couldn't prove her presence other than the sent of her perfume and the coolness that came with it. We were headed into a four day weekend and were putting a few loose ends together. Lacey, one of the now two second floor secretaries tapped on my door.

"Please; come in," I said inviting her into my office and standing to take the four large tubes she was juggling.

"UPS just brought these in the mail sir," she said softly, trying not to drop any of them. I stepped up to her to accept the tubes before she lost any of them. As she handed them to me, the back of her left hand brushed firmly but gently against my chest. Then she tilted her head forward and to the left a bit, and those big brown eyes said, "Give me a chance boss man, even a little one." Yup, the mix just became a bit more complicated. The look she gave me jolted me somewhat, and I barely caught myself.

"Thank you Lacey, I'll take care of these," I said trying to look busy with the tubes. Then she did one of Shelly's numbers. She was about five steps away when she gracefully turned her head and shoulders to the left, swinging all that wavey long silky brunet hair over her right shoulder, and looked back to see if I was still looking at the merchandise. Close your mouth dummy, I said to myself; she caught you looking! The rest of her gate across the office lobby was a slow liquid gyration, an exaggerated tease, enticing my animalistic instincts. What's wrong with men? We see those curves move a certain way and our morals go right out the window, or we act like we have none at all. But this one I had to be careful with, she did have that mommy look to her. One wrong word or move with Lacey and it would be mommy and daddy! Again the scent of sandalwood made itself known, and my system mellowed somewhat. Where was that fragrance coming from? This is all kind of weird I thought. I never got this kind of attention in the city, not even from Shelly, or maybe I just wasn't paying attention. I'm thinking its my new position; or maybe they're all in heat, or looking for a nest, or both!

51

An old man once told me; "Charlie, nothing, absolutely nothing lasts forever!" *Well, that'll give you something to think about.* They'll get over whatever it is, and I'll be just another guy on the street they can snub.

It was quarter to seven. Yeah, we were running a little late getting out of there tonight, but everything had to be just so before we left the building for the long weekend. Except for the main trio, everyone else was long gone. Blake and I did a careful walkaround of each office, fire doors, bathrooms, thermostats, vaults, lights, and security systems. All the contracts and records, along with the tubes of prints and drawings were kept in fire proof vaults that we sealed every night. Shelly had her own vault for personal files and important stuff downstairs, and was doing the same thing down on the first floor. Then we were all out the front door. I locked the door and set the double alarm, then stepped out onto the walkway, turned around and was looking at 'my' building.

"Come on Charlie, that building is not going anywhere, and you can't take it home with you," Blake said with a chuckle. Shelly was halfway between Blake and I, waiting for me. Oh shit, here it comes I thought.

"Do you have plans for the long weekend Charlie, or is your 'other' still keeping you company?" she asked.

"Not that I'm aware of, but you saw what happened last night," I said.

"Your letting an opportunity slip through your fingers Charlie, I hope you know that," she purred smugly, now with both her palms on my chest.

"At the moment I'm a little involved you might say, but I'm not blind Shelly. Let me sort this out. I'm sure you'll know if a change comes," I said, and right on cue, a strong scent of sandalwood presented itself and Shelly backed up a couple of steps and gave me a surprised look. I was really starting to wonder why I felt the need to explain myself to her, and walked her over to her car.

"You know how to reach me if that change comes around Charlie," she said slyly and drove off.

The next morning I was sitting at the counter with my coffee and the business section of the Corinth Tribune. For no reason in particular I looked at my wristwatch. Friday, November 11, 2011, and it was 11:11 am (11:11:11/11:11)! Hum … That had to mean something; a something that wouldn't happen again in my lifetime.

"*Charlie...,*" came a delicate angelic voice, with just a smidge of echo. I raised my head. That's the same voice I had heard in my hotel room!

But now I was pretty sure it was Shay shin even though it was kind of noonish, but where was she? Curious as to where her voice came from, I got off the stool and went to the kitchen door looking into the living room.

"Oh my God!" fell out of my mouth. The entire living room, stairway and balcony has a strange shimmering glow to it that twinkled here and there. There was a waterfall of a ghostly white and gray mist, cascading through the poles of the balcony, and another flowing gently down the staircase. Wonder what the occasion is? I'm sure not worth all this, I thought to myself. Then I saw her! I could actually see her! At least I thought it was her. This had to be Shay shin! Like an image of royalty she came; dressed in a silky Chinese gown, silently, one delicate step at a time. She had a tempting smile of mischief, and her sparkling eyes never left mine. This looked like a wedding ceremony more than anything else. *Charlie, I think your situation just took a gigantic leap!* The motion she created beneath that gown with the gentle sway of her hips, brought to mind that night in the shower. But with her, I thought even this occasion would have its limitations as well. What could she possibly be up to or want? I'm not, and can't be any part of her world unless I'm dead. And I was pretty sure I didn't have anything she could possibly want. But then again, maybe she just wanted her house back, without me in it! Looking at this magnificent being coming towards me, again the question came to mind; Is she real or am I staring at an illusion? Or is it possible she can be both? Finally she was standing almost right against my chest. Way too close! She was a first generation Chinese and Japanese mix, with long dark chestnut hair, that almost looked black. She had thick dark eyebrows, long eyelashes, deep light golden sandy brown eyes, a perfect mouth, and light cherry pink lips I suddenly wanted to kiss. Would that be a dumb thing to try? Would it make her disappear again? Whoa big guy, give the girl a chance to state her intentions. My God, she is absolutely beautiful!

"Charlie; if you want me, I am yours," she said in that delicate whisper that made me weak all over. I was finding it difficult to breathe, and stay in that spot. What does she mean "If I want her?" Who or what else could I possibly want? But she's a ghost! Or is she real?

"From now on Charlie, I will be as you are. You will be able to see and hear and feel me, but only when we are alone with each other, or if I choose something other.

For a time, our relationship will not be as a man and woman bound by vows. But, of your mortal life, I vow to never leave you Charlie. I have seen for myself the temptuous lures of others you face daily. I understand the desires and temptations men must cope with away from their homes. It is a powerful urge some foolishly think they can control. But if I cannot please you with all I am Charlie, and you still desire a change for a time, then she, or another may subside your wants, needs and desires. I will not interfere or stand in your way, *as long as you come back to me!*" she said softly. *Did you catch that Charlie?!* I knew the 'she', Shay shin was referring to, well, at least one of them for sure. Come on Charlie, wake up and pay attention. If what I was thinking was even partially accurate, I was being bonded to Shay shin! Kind of like getting married, but not. I'm not sure if I'm really ready for this, or maybe it was past that point? Actually, I guess I've been ready for some time now, I just didn't think I had found Miss Right, or had the balls to take that first step and ask. Hell, I'm not even sure what love is. Sex, yeah; love? well, I kind of thought that happened slowly over time. But just maybe that time had caught up with me, the reason I was getting so much attention. I don't think I look all that different from when I lived in the city, and I'm still just me. Maybe it's the new deodorant or aftershave lotion?! Shay shin took my left wrist and put the palm of my hand on her waist. Oh my God, I could actually feel the curve of her waist beneath her gown! She is definitely real! I mean, a lot more real than I imagined these things were supposed to be. She was absolutely beautiful, and God, she smelled so good!

"Shay shin honey, I don't honestly believe I deserve anyone as wonderful as you, so I have to ask; why do you want to be with me? Is it the house you want? And why do you think you care for me? I'm no different than any other man, I'm nobody special, I'm just me. I don't have anything to offer you, you don't already have Shay shin, nothing but me," I said hopelessly.

"Charlie, this is your home! I am here by choice, and because I want to be with you. So, no, I don't want the house, that's yours," she said quietly.

"I have been with you when you have been challenged by the temptations of others, when your animalistic desires have surfaced, and twice I thought I would loose you. The one called Shelly, is persistent and is still determined to be with you.

She does not give up easy and will keep trying, but only until she gets what she wants. But even in your stress of her, I became of your thoughts and I knew then, I surely cared for you just because of the way you are Charlie. You don't pretend to be someone you're not; you treat others fairly, and your truthful even if it hurts you. In your own way, you have been gentle and caring with me. This you have shown with your kindness and patients of my being, even with the uncertainty of what is, and that to come, yet still you are here! I can be as human as the one that came here to bring you only pleasure. She does not care of your heart as I do. I can do as she does, but she will leave you, and I will not!" she said this looking straight into my eyes with intent. That look was almost scary!

"Don't be afraid Charlie, no harm will come to you while I'm with you," she said softly. Then those beautiful eyes began to close in slow motion as she leaned into me. Slowly, as not to create a fear in me of what she truly is, she came. Still I was more than a bit nervous. Too many scary movies I think. She's a real ghost Charlie!

"It's okay, don't be afraid Charlie, I'm right here and won't leave you," she said so softly it was almost a whisper. As in the shower, my body was again like a vibrator all over, but it wasn't from fear. Very slowly her lips delicately touched to mine. Ummm; soft, moist, and delicate. Her breath was like honey comb, and warm. Oh yeah, she was real! I don't know what I did in the shower that made her leave me, so now I was extra careful. Please don't leave me again, came my thoughts as I gently slipped my arms around her, and carefully pulled her to me; she was still there! I was thinking maybe she might snuggle into my chest, and she did, sorta! But what she did do, was a big surprise! Most of her body absorbed right into mine! The part of her within me was so warm, and there was no weight to her at all. How could this be happening? How could she do this? Then came the realization; Charlie, she's been in you before, at the office! One second she can be real, the next she's a ghost again, or at least a part of her is; you know; what I assumed a ghost is!? I needed to make another trip to the library. Then came the question. Was it really possible for a regular person like me to fall in love with a ghost! Damnit, what was love anyway? But if this wasn't it, I probably wouldn't know it if it hit me right between my eyes. Suddenly I didn't care about any of that stuff, I just wanted her in everyway my imagination allowed me to.

But what I was contemplating, had nothing to do with love, it was pure unadulterated lust, or so I thought. But in reality, it seems there is a very fine line between the two. Its difficult to have one without being infatuated with the other. Right now I just wanted her in my arms! We just stood there in each others arms in total contentment. I was holding this precious being in my arms, my lips pressed down on the top of her head. "My God Shay shin, I love you!" I didn't say that, but that's what I was thinking, and within me, body and soul I did! I honestly don't believe Shelly with all that she is, could make me feel the contentment I do at this moment. But of course she has an excuse, she's human. Then I thought I heard something. Softly, Shay shin began humming an oriental song, and her hold on me tightened just a bit. Yup, she was as content as I was. Okay, this has to be what love feels like, two people content and at peace with each other. But how can this be? I'm alive and she's …..! I was starting to dislike that word very much. I took her hand, kissed it gently, and led her down into the living room. We sat on the love seat in front of the fireplace in each others arms, holding onto each other for about two and half hours, like nothing else in the world existed. Then those misty gold brown eyes looked into mine. With her lips barely touching mine she whispered;

"Charlie...," she purred in a whimper. Oh, oh! I knew what that look meant, and what was on her mind! But she's a ghost! Can she do that?! Still, I was thinking we should relocate to the bedroom because I didn't think we could do those kinds of things on that small love seat; but yeah, you can! You just gotta be agile and kind of acrobatic, and Shay shin was also clever. Whenever I would get close to a climax, she would slowly back off to make everything last longer. She also pulled a couple of tricks with her ghostly talents Shelly no way in hell could have accomplished. But we still wound up on the floor, snuggled in a very thick white blanket. Don't let anyone tell you the tunnel of love is in some amusement park! Still, content with Shay shin in my arms, I fell into a peaceful dreamless sleep.

It wasn't until early the next morning when I woke up, that I found her exactly where she had been when I fell asleep, looking into my eyes with that beautiful smile. That's when I realized something. She doesn't have to sleep, or eat, or go to the bathroom or any of several things I have to do to stay alive. And now I was pretty sure where the scent of her perfume came from at the office.

When Blake had asked me about my cologne, and when Shelly and I were talking inside and outside the office. She really had been with me all the time! I pulled on my slacks and took her hand and we headed for the kitchen. I had to have her near me all the time; touching her, smelling her hair and her body, why was that? I think I had just got hit between the eyes! I made a pot of coffee while she stood next to me, staring at me with that mischievous smile, propped up on one elbow. Then I gently wrapped my arms around her, picked her up and took her to the bathroom and into the shower. In the warmth of the shower water, she leaned into me, pressing me against the wall, and that's the way we stayed for almost an hour. Yup, this had to be what love felt like! I didn't want to move an inch without taking every bit of her with me. I wanted to hear her voice; touch and smell her hair, look into her eyes and hold her close to me all the time! Then ever so lightly I patted her dry with a towel, but only after my lips had kissed away every drop of water on her body. Then she took the towel from me and turned me into a crazy man!

After our shower, from the bathroom we were headed back to the kitchen, but we only got as far as the bed until lunch time, and we damn near didn't make it out of there then. But this honeymoon couldn't go on forever, and we finally did make it to the kitchen. I heated up one of those TV dinners, but she only nibbled on it just to visually appease me. How was I ever going to be able to go to work Tuesday morning? But like she said, "I vow to never leave you," and she meant that, literally! For the next two days we were never more than an arms length from each other, if it was that far. She was naughty and I loved it. We were getting to know every inch of each other, intimately! I was totally mesmerized, intoxicated, and infatuated with every part of her. I didn't want to go to sleep at night, because that would be a time seemingly without her. But like I said, she would always be exactly right where she was when I fell asleep, her sparkling eyes looking right into mine, then she would ever so softly kiss me with all her passion, like she meant it, and the honeymoon would start all over again.

Unfortunately, Tuesday morning did come, and way too soon. But Shay shin kept her word, she didn't leave me! I got as far as the kitchen door into the garage, wrapped my arms around her and held her close and kissed her with all my heart. Her arms went around me and her body nestled into mine. As I kissed her lips, then the top of her head, her body absorbed into mine.

She was a warm comfortable feeling, yet without distractions or temptations. So this is how she did that! Lookout ladies, I've got a bodyguard; literally! At the office, Blake, Shelly and I went into the conference room to go over a few things for the coming four day week. At about 9:30, the guy with the franchise rudely showed up, and we all got a surprise! Blake, Shelly and I took him into the conference room. The guy seemed agitated and a bit pushy this morning. I also didn't care for the way he was acting with Shelly or the language he was using in her presence. He said we were wasting his time, and that if we weren't serious about the deal, he was going to look elsewhere. Now, Blake, Shelly and I were at one end of the long conference table and this guy is at the other end, but all of a sudden, in the midst of his anger, it sure as hell looked like somebody hit him in the face, hard! He rocked back in the chair that rolled him almost to the wall. He got up and went out slamming the door! Blake and I looked at each other, and Blake gave me a very strange look.

"Did you just throw something at him Charlie?" he asked quietly.

"I wanted to, but no, I didn't," I said. Then everything went blank! My body became calm and still, and I heard Shay shin say;

"He's a bad man Charlie, and intends to harm you in someway." Then everything went back to normal. Blake and Shelly were staring at me quizzically.

"You okay Charlie?" Shelly asked. My mind was flying. 'The dream!' The building on fire! Again I had been warned. That afternoon I went to the Shirreff's office and asked if he could put a couple of officers out back of the building for a couple of nights. He asked me why, and I told him about the guy with the franchise. He knew of this guy and said he would put a tail on him. Because of what the Shirreff's tail on this guy saw him doing, they beefed up the stakeout and things went from bad to worse! That very night, the guy with the franchise paid my office building a visit. He brought a box of Molotov cocktails in the back of his pickup and a .357 mag. With the .357 he took out two of the big windows on the first floor at the front of the building. Then he sat the box of Molotov cocktails just in front of the broken windows and lit one! All of a sudden, the road leading into the facility had two more police cars on it, blocking his way out.

At that same instant, six police officers with drawn pistols converged on him. Three from either side, and back of the building, while he was standing there with the lit bomb still in his hand. With his left hand he drew the .357 and pointed it at one of the officers. Everything went to hell from there! He fired two shots at the officers. Two of the officers returned fire and hit the guy in the shoulder. The cocktail in his hand fell into the box with the rest of them. The guy would have survived with the shoulder wound he received, but he fell right next to twelve exploding Molotov cocktails that turned him into Jell-O! I got the Sheriff's call at about 10:45 that night. He said I should come down to the office as soon as I could. I knew it was going to be bad from the way Shay shin was pacing the floor. I called Blake and asked him to meet me at the office. When I opened the garage door, I could see a lot of flashing red and blue lights down in front of the office building. When I got down there, two fire trucks, an ambulance, a coroners van and eight police cars were there.

"What the hell happened," Blake asked.

"The Sheriff says the guy with the franchise showed up and had shot out two of the big windows on the first floor of the middle section, then took a couple shots at his deputies. Because the explosion was so close to the building, it took out two more windows on the first floor, and shattered two on the second floor," I said. I called Foster. He said he was on his way! It only took about an hour before his chopper landed in the midst of a flood of glaring red and blue flashing lights near the pad, and out front. There wasn't a lot of real damage inside the building, other than a few burned papers here and there. Three or four of the desks had been blown across the room colliding with other furniture and a coffee machine. Blake and I carefully examined the exterior walls for cracks. We found one vertical and one lateral crack in the same wall panel right where the box of Molotov cocktails had been. Mr. Foster stayed busy on the phone the entire time. Then he found the Sheriff and talked to him for about twenty minutes, then came back to me.

"Bring your staff in and call your employees. Their all on paid emergency leave until we can fully repair this building," he said assertively. Blake was on his phone to the staff. Another chopper landed in the parking lot out in front of the south wing about an hour later, more big shots. Two of them took a company car and went somewhere.

Chapter 5

All night and into the next morning, different kinds of trucks and a lot of workers were in and out of the building doing different jobs. There were a lot of workers working on taking out the broken windows, but they didn't replace them yet, and still Foster did not leave the scene. It was quickly becoming obvious how this man had became the VP of this corporation. He was coordinating multiple situations with two telephones, and four assistants who were also on phones.

By noon, an oversize lowboy slowly maneuvered a crane into position in front of the building. The empty lowboy that brought the crane in, took out the cracked panels that came apart in three pieces laterally and vertically when they tried to pick it up the next morning. By four p.m., another lowboy with a new prefab panel was there. At six pm, Foster shut everything down. All the workers and drivers were taken to town, fed and put up in hotels and motels for the night with breakfast the next morning. Foster paid for everything. The hotel he had put me up in became his headquarters during the repair operation. The hotel staff treated him like a God. This guy was not only solid gold, he had a heart to go with it! Ruthless, untiring and dedicated to his people and his job. Me, I got to go home to Shay shin each day. She had been right about the franchise guy, and as I said before, she was smart!

"Charlie, there's an open franchise now, can you afford it?" she asked quietly. By the end of the next weekend, we were back in business. Hell, that last day we all looked more like construction workers instead of business men. The staff got on their phones and brought everyone back to work. Mr. Foster was at the back door getting ready to leave then turned and looked me over.

"Mr. Aldermon, you could sure as hell use some new clothes, a long hot shower, and about twelve hours of sleep! I have firsthand witnessed your management abilities, initiative, fortitude and stamina during this crises. I want you at corporate level within the month. You sure as hell deserve it. But I want you to tell me if that's what you want? It would be a hell of a pay raise you know; what do you think?" he asked, his chin raised a bit, staring up into my eyes expectantly. I didn't have to think.

"Sir, this might change how you think about me, but my job is here, here with our people and the work that needs to be done here. I'm not one for leaving things half done. I very much appreciate your offer sir, but I hope you understand why I would rather decline it. What I have to do here is more important than prestige or money. Please accept my apologies," I said looking down at the floor.

His glare never waivered, but for almost a whole minute he was silent. Then his eyes became glassy. Damn, it looked like he was crying deep inside. What had I done or said to cause that?

"Very well, Mr. Aldermon; keep up the good work," he said without a flinch, then shook my hand. The man had the grip of a giant. But he wasn't finished with me yet, not by any means! He had a mind like a steel trap and just as quick, and it just slammed shut! His chopper lifted off the pad out back, and slowly hovered up and just over the building into the parking lot out front next to the second chopper. His four assistants got into his chopper and they left. The second chopper lifted out of the parking lot out front and came over the building and landed on the pad outback.

"What the hell," Blake murmured as we watched the chopper touch down. I was just as confused as he was. The pilot came in the back door and walked right up to me.

"Steven Hunter at your disposal sir," he said with a slight bow of his head. Blake and I looked at each other with the same surprised shock!

"Excuse me," I began. "I don't understand?!" I said.

"Mr. Foster says I am now your pilot and employee, on twenty four hour call sir," he said. He gave me a card with his name, number, call sign and the tail number of his chopper. Wow! What the hell had just happened?

"Blake?!"

"Charlie, what have you done?"

"I don't know," I said dumbfounded, shrugging my shoulders.

"Steven, where is your family?" I asked my new pilot.

"Mr. Foster's pilots have no families sir," he said politely.

"I have permanent reservations at the hotel and a company car.

I am available at anytime, day or night to take you anywhere you would like to go," he said politely, but assertively. I looked at Blake, then back at Steven.

"Well Steven, its been a bit of a stressful week. Uh, I'll give you a call if I need you; yeah, and thank you," I said a bit astounded.

"Yes sir," he said and headed out the front door to a waiting car. I was starting to feel and get caught up in the effects of one of Mr. Foster's traits; he was impulsive and he thought and did everything quickly! Holy shit, what had I done to deserve this?

Blake and I had made it to the bottom of the stairs and my phone rang; it was the bank.

"Mr. Aldermon, I was just advised to inform you that your corporation account is now fifty million dollars," the manager said.

"Thank you sir," I said and hung up. I wobbled a bit and Blake caught me by my shoulders and sat me into a chair. Wow! What the hell is happening? I suddenly felt I had to become part of this madman's rat race or I was going to get lost in the shuffle. My thoughts were hectic. It was like I was working against the clock. I got back up to my office and pushed Shelly's call button.

"Shelly, would you please come up here; I have a special task for you, and do not say 'yes sir!" I said, and pushed Blake's call button, then undid it. I got up and went to Blake's office on my way to Marrket's. I stuck my head in Blake's office and said, "Come on Blake," and did the same in Marrket's office. We were headed for the conference room just as Shelly got to the top of the stairs. In the conference room I started out straight forward as soon as they were seated.

"Marrket, I need you to fill in for Shelly for a few days. Shelly, I need you to take some time off, sorta. I need you to get the skinny on that hotel everyone has been staying at. Heat things up and find out who owns it, and insure them they want to sell it for whatever. Call me with the price and I'll give you a yay or nay right then. Blake, I need you to find out what happened to the dead man's franchise, and buy it. Then find me two of the best accountants, a CPA, and a tax consultant that money can buy. Any questions?" All I got was the expected blank look I got from each of them.

63

"Okay then, let's get to work," I said, stood up and left the room, knowing the questions that would be asked behind that door.

I went down to Gibbs office to check on the drawings for the restaurant. He was very close to completing his part of the blueprints. Then I went into another office to check on the blueprints for a couple other structures. One in Manhattan, and one in Corinth that looked sort of like a warehouse, but not. Thursday morning, a contractor showed up in my office with orders from Foster to put another helo pad out back. Now what? Foster was up to something, again! Nothing that man did was without reason or was on a small scale. The contractor and I went out back and selected a location behind the south wing. A work crew was there in an hour and began prepping the site that lasted through the night. They wanted that site ready for the cement trucks the next afternoon. Shelly called me just after lunch.

"Twenty million," she said softly as if someone was listening.

"Take it! Stay with the process until its ours. Don't let them squirm one inch. Let me know when your ready for my signature. Get the account and routing and let me know when to transfer the money," I said flatly, and she hung up. Blake was on call waiting.

"They want three hundred thousand Charlie, what do you think? I got a weird feeling about this one, but said;

"Take it, and basically told him the same thing I had just told Shelly. By the time I got home that night I was exhausted, and Shay shin knew it. But still she gently took my hand and led me to the office upstairs. Behind a bookshelf was the ladder access to the attic.

"Come Charlie," she said softly as she touched a hidden button on the wall, making sure I knew where that spot was, and down came the steps that led to the attic. I followed her up the ladder wondering what was so important I had to see up there. Of course I was looking up her dress! Two steps in front, and at the top of the ladder, was a heavy black lace veil curtain. Shay shin gently took my hand and led me through the curtain, constantly looking into my eyes. "Holy shit," came my thoughts. What the hell was all this? The entire attic was a shrine of some kind! I'd seen one of those things on the floor in a book once, but not in such an elaborate setup as this. But what was it doing in my house? Like the soul of an apparition, a shimmer fluttered over the curvature of the pentagram. Is this thing alive?! I thought.

This must have been what Elda was talking about at her place when I wasn't paying all that much attention. Shay shin watched my eyes and facial expressions intently. I had a hundred questions, but I kind of figured if I needed to know something, she'd explain what was before us sooner or later, so I held my questions. In the center of the room on the floor, were three circles and a star; this was a full fledged working pentagram with all the trimmings and then some! *And it knew I was there!* The star and its circle was made of black matted brass and was curved up off of the floor about four inches at the center. There was a circle of copper around it, and a circle of solid silver around that. There was an elaborate altar at the bottom of the silver circle just in front of me, covered in silk, with a lot of strange looking symbols or writings of sorts. I had no idea what I was looking at, but it all seemed pretty impressive, and just a bit evil. Then from behind and just to my left side, Shay shin came and spoke.

"Charlie, I want you to wear this. This is your talisman, an amulet, something to keep you safe, for me," she said, as she put a necklace around my neck. It was a heavy gold braided chain with one of those screw on binders, holding an exact image of the pentagram before me. Then she came around and stood in front of me, and looked into my eyes.

"If for some reason I am not with you, and you feel you are in trouble or danger, wrap your hand around the talisman on the chain and think "help"; it will protect you! The power for your talisman comes from your thoughts and this pentagram here in this house. It will use whatever energies are available about you wherever you are; be ready for that help to come Charlie," she said and sincerely kissed the talisman and placed it against my chest; it was warm. Again the shimmer crossed the star; *to acknowledge my presence and the acceptance of its power.* But there was something else about the talisman and that pentagram Shay shin neglected to tell me. Talk about feeling just a little strange.

"If you feel troubled about something, you can come up here, even without me, and sit there," she said pointing to the area in front of the altar.

"Think about your problem and the answer will come to you," she said. Two days later, Shelly called.

"Its yours boss man," she said with a quiet giggle.

"I'd like to agree with you Shelly, but it belongs to the corporation," I said with a little laugh. We finished going over some of the details, and our conversation ended, then I was on my way to town. The empire building had started, and there was no going back now. I had to do this and now! I visited the town council and set up a meeting with two restaurant owners in town. The plan was to buy them out and have them and their people run our new restaurant. I'd find out what the town needed and open another store where those restaurants were, creating a few more jobs in those buildings. It would be a win, win situation for everyone. Blake lined up the two accountants, the CPA, and the tax consultant. One of the accountants came out of Frisco, the CPA and the other accountant came out of NY city. The tax guy was a referral from the bank manager in Corinth. We set up the accountant's and CPA in an office of their own on the second floor, with their own vault. I explained my expectations to them for the hotel, the new restaurant, and incorporated our facility, along with a possible multitude of things to come, then asked Shelly to QC their ledgers every other month. With all that was going on, I stiil managed to keep track of incoming contracts, and quality control the outgoing blueprints that were taken out by two of my engineers. I expected construction to slow down a bit because of the snow and nasty weather, but proposals for spring building still came in on a pretty regular schedule. My old boss in California found out where I was working and what I was doing. He offered me a hell of a deal if I'd do there, what I was doing here. But that would take me completely out of the kind of work that I really loved, drawing buildings. Besides I was comfortable here with Shay shin and growing my empire.

Then Mr. Foster called and asked if I'd come down to his office in Kingston for a visit. Now what was he up to? Naturally Shay shin was to go with me. I feel so empty and alone without her, and I can't think of nothing else but her when she's not with me. Now I was sure I was in love with her and I wanted the world to know it. I called Steve and he was there in twenty minutes. When I got to Foster's office, the reception was a bit overwhelming. I was royally escorted by two gentlemen from the helo pad, and delivered into Foster's office building like a dignitary, then to his glassed in conference room, where he was with two other gentlemen who left as soon as they saw me coming.

"Charlie," he said as I was ushered through a set of double glass doors by two lovely ladies.

"Hello Danial," I said, testing the water so to speak. He had used my first name and I countered just to see what it would bring.

"How's my favorite corporate chief doing today?" he asked.

"Or should I address you as Mayor Aldermon?" he said with a chuckle.

"Excuse me?" I questioned.

"Charlie, you need to step outside your box to see what I see going on up there. Your progress in leaps and bounds is phenomenal. So much so, that it's sometimes even difficult for me to keep up with you. However, you have my complete backing in all that you do. You're headed in the right direction and I will not hinder the swiftness and aggressiveness of your progress in the least; although at times it seems a might vicious. Just don't forget how you got there, where you are, and why you're there. Take care of your people and be compassionate with those you deal with. The hotel was something I thought about a long time ago, I just didn't see the need for it until now. You did well with that, and I'll replenish your funds," he said, then his demeanor changed.

"Charlie, the reason I asked you to come here is, I have some serious concerns, and some questions I'd like to ask you. I would like to know your heartfelt intentions and desires for Wilton, Corinth, and the corporation. Because it sure as hell appears you're on to something even I hadn't foreseen," he said with a bit of concern in his voice.

"Well sir; I'm taking things pretty much as they come for the time being. But seemingly with each opportunity that's presented, comes another. If the second one is feasible and worthwhile, I'd rather not let the potential pass us by. I want to keep the foundation of the corporation in sight, not just for me, but also that the people of Corinth and Wilton can see that we are keeping their best interests in mind. I don't want this to seem like a bad merger to them. If anything, I want to put more people to work, not out of work! I dare say my endeavors are to make the corporation looked up to by this town and city. I want to assist them productively, as well as financially, even though the corporation may wind up owning a large portion of both. I hope I haven't over stepped your boundaries somewhere," I said feeling just a bit guilty. Foster sat quietly for two or three minutes.

"Wow; you know Mr. Aldermon, looking and listening to you and what you've managed to accomplish thus far, and in the period of time you've done it in, is phenomenal. A simple blue collar drafter, taking an empty building in the middle of nowhere, and in three months, turn it into one of the most important productive parts of this corporation.

I see another me in you when I was much younger, but with more courage, drive and the balls to seize a business opportunity, and make something out of it, even when it seems out of reach. Often I waited too long, thus the hectic pace I now work at. Your foresight, aggressiveness and intuitiveness, and the manner in which your people function, and the quality of your output, says it all Charlie. And if I have anything to say about this corporations future at all; you Mr. Aldermon, will be sitting in this chair when I retire! I couldn't imagine leaving this responsibility to anyone else," he said assertively. I just sat there in shock! I couldn't speak or think, I just sat there in a daze. What could I possibly say to something like that? What had I done in my life to deserve something like this? *(Remember the wish Charlie!)* Maybe he's thinking about someone else?

"Sir, I seriously think your looking at the wrong portfolio. I'm just a regular guy trying to do my job the best I can, with what you've given me. I don't want your job, or to be at this level," I said a bit frustrated.

"Your getting closer to this chair with every word that comes out of your mouth Charlie. Now, I had a bundle of tubes loaded in your chopper that need to be attended to. Sorry to have caused you any grief or anxiety, but come hell or highwater, you 'will' be the next VP of this corporation! Now, I'll let you get back to work," he said, stood up and shook my hand. I could hardly stand; my legs were so wobbly. You really did it this time Charlie! I thought as I left his office. I was escorted back to my chopper with the elegance that Foster himself would have received. Steven started the engines and the chopper was ready to go a few seconds after he saw me coming through the lobby. "Home Steven," I said, and he replied "Yes sir," and we were off the ground, or should I say the top of the building. Its only about a thirty five minute ride from the corporate office in Kingston back to Wilton. But it was good to be on our way home. Home, and into the loving arms of my Shay shin. Oh how I needed to hold her physical being in my arms!

Blake came out to the pad to meet me with Marrket, who collected the print tubes and took them to the conference room upstairs to sort them out.

"How'd it go," Blake asked, but I was still in a daze, and lost for words.

"We need to talk my friend," I said as he quietly followed me to my office. I sat down behind my desk and buzzed Lacey and asked her to hold all my calls and visitors, and asked Blake to have a seat.

"Okay, what's going on boss man, your up to something," Blake asked with a big sigh.

"Well Blake, you and I have worked together for a little over seven years now, and I have nothing but good things to say about you, your work and your supervision over your responsibilities. But, as your boss, I'd like to hear your opinion. First of yourself, and then of your job, and where you think you would like to go from here," I said, and sat back in my chair. I kind of expected the silent look of confusion and surprise he gave me, and then he started.

"Well, I think I'm not that bad of a person, I'm fairly level headed, I don't have any eccentric habits. But like you, I can be impulsive, assertive, even aggressive if the situation warrants it. I think I'm sociable enough to mix with just about anyone, and I think I get along well with others for the most part. Like you, my friends are few and far between. As you've guessed, I'm kind of fond of Shelly. But the mutuality of that situation may not be the same on both sides of the fence, at least at the moment, but I'm working on it. Watching you and Mr. Foster, I've kind of got caught up in the quick pace of handling things, and a foresight I don't think I had before. It's broadened my horizons more than a bit, and I see things and opportunities I never thought of looking for before. Once I was satisfied with just being an architect, but watching you, I can see there's more possibilities out there for me and my work than I once saw. I still like what I do a lot, and think I'm pretty good at it, but I sure don't see where your going with this?" he said quizzically.

"What exactly are you looking for Charlie?" he continued.

"I'll tell you in a few minutes, but first, where do you think you'd like to go from here?" I asked. Blake sat silently for almost a minute thinking.

"Why do I get the feeling what you just asked me is a loaded question?" Blake asked.

"Am I underfoot, or not doing as good as I think I am, or am I about to be transferred?" he asked looking a bit worried.

"None of those," I said, sitting up to the desk. "I just don't want to wait until the last minute to decide who's going to be sitting in this chair if I have to leave," I said quietly.

"Charlie! What the hell happened down there?" he asked. I picked up a pencil and messed with it for a few seconds, then I told him exactly what happened, and what Mr. Foster had said.

"It will probably be some time before anything happens, but I as well as Mr. Foster, would like to know this part of the corporation is in good hands. I chose you to be my exec when we were moved up here for that purpose, but I no way in hell thought Foster had the same idea for me. Truly I'd rather you go there than me, but the way he does things, he may not give us much of a choice. You've proven you can run this place as well as I can. I'd just like to know your heart is in it, and where your loyalty in the corporation lies," I said kind of flatly.

"Oh my God Charlie! I'm, well, I don't think I'm ready to step into your shoes, but with a little tutoring, I'd like to continue on with what you've started," he said.

"That's what I wanted to hear!" I said.

"And none of this is to get to Shelly, you hear; at least for the time being. Now get your ass back to work," I chuckled and pushed Lacey's button.

"Yes sir," they simultaneously replied.

"Okay Lacey, I'm back on line," I said. "Yes sir," she replied. Well, that was settled. Now I just had to figure out how to keep Shay shin's house and my job at the same time. I checked around to find out who the best general would be to run the building of the restaurant, and what construction company he was with. I wound up with a list of six individuals. I didn't want any shortcuts on any of our projects, and chose the best of the best. Just for P's & Q's, I had our own engineer go over the drawings before the blueprints were actually made. He made a couple of minor suggestions that Blake and I took into consideration. When we decided who we wanted as the general, I called him and asked him to come to the office. When he got there about tenish, I had him go over the blueprints with Blake and I in the conference room.

I was animate about the coordination and timing of subcontractors and the delivery and quality of their materials, as well as the safety of their workers. It would be specified in writing, that he would incur the costs outside of set amounts, and be responsible for the product quality and timing in the contracts, to include the subs. That there would be no substandard or substitute products or materials used in the construction of this facility. The foundations for loadbearing walls were to be given an extra twenty four hours of drying time above code, as were the concrete floors. The building itself was to be fireproof.

That I would have one of my engineers on sight the entire time to note construction methods, wasted time and materials, and OSHA standards that were not met. I wanted the general to have his ducks in a row and understand the consequences before the first shovel of dirt was cast. If things didn't go right, he would forfeit intended funding, his bonus and his job. The entire property for the restaurant, was to be elevated three feet and graded six degrees from the entrance road that led to our facility. The parking lot and drive through were to have underground heating for snow and ice control. With all that said, I asked him if he wanted the job. The general accepted the job, and agreed on the terms and conditions.

The excavation for the foundations, the incased sewer, gas, water and underground power lines started right on schedule. Piles of rebar started showing up over the next week, along with reels of various kinds of wiring. Pads for the central air, trash, garbage, and another pad for a backup generator were laid. Three days later, pipes of many kinds and sizes began to arrive. The lateral into our main was laid and capped, and everything went from there. The designs of everything laid into the ground was more than a bit above code, but like I said, I wanted this place to last forever. The exterior too was off scale as far as codes were concerned. The inside of the prefab walls was to be covered with interlocked cinderblocks, filled with a cement made with fly ash and a special sand. The outsides of the prefab walls were to be covered with a rubberized plastic coating and brick. As I said, everything was over done, but that's the way I wanted it! I don't care for micro managing someone that's supposed to know what their doing, but between Blake, Marrket and myself, and the engineer, we kept pretty close tabs on what was going on, on the construction site. I needed to find the trust factor for this general before I really turned him loose.

At home Shay shin would divert my thoughts of work back to her. It was like going from a laborious hectic pace, to the calm slow warmth of her passionate mode. In about an hour or less, she could wipe out all the stress, and turn me into a handful of silly putty. She knew Shelly was still trying, but made it emphatically clear who I am in love with. Her touch teased and tempted and tortured my mind and body in ways I never knew were possible. Her strength was incredible, the likes of three men. Still, she was delicately gentle, then aggressive and occasionally animalistic. With her chin just below my belly button she whispered my name; *"Charlie..."*

Then came a deep throaty growl that rumbled softly, then bellowed into a crescendo that vibrated the tissues in my lungs. Her nails raked little red, occasionally bloody trails into the flesh of my chest, stomach and thighs. Still I'd seen nothing of her true savageness, or the full potential of her abilities, not to mention the cynical side of what she truly was. All over the house she played her game of 'here I'm not', while her nude apparition teased me with an occasional touch that drove me out of my mind with her lustful taunting. She was making absolutely sure my mind was on her alone, and not anyone else or my job.

Then something terrible happened! In the shower, though just for an instant, somehow Shelly crossed my mind, and something was immediately different! From behind my left shoulder came Shay shin's soft voice.

"You're still curious of her wants. But soon you will understand the difference of her and me. Still the test must be of more than one, to know which you truly want to be with," she whispered softly next to my left ear, and she was gone!

"Shay shin….? Honey? Where are you?" I called, but there was no reply. "Shay shin?!" There was no trace of her perfume, no sound of her breath or vision of her in any manner. She was gone! But to where? I literally felt lost! That was the loneliest feeling I've had in a long time. How could a woman affect me like this? From that day on I was lost! I became easily irritated, and my trust in women vanished. Shelly and Lacey became enemies on a battlefield I couldn't see, and didn't understand. I could only imagine, like Shay shin, they too would leave me empty and lost.

Chapter 6

In the sixth week of construction, even in the snow, the prefab walls and cinder blocks began showing up. Two cranes were busy the whole week putting up the walls, steel beams and the interior galvanized roofing panels, along with the insulation for the four pitch heated roof. Then a sub brought in the soundproof metal exterior roofing panels. All the interior of the prefab walls were cinderblock, glass block or fire brick depending on the location. More than a bit overdone, but I had my reasons for all of it. All the plumbing and electrical work was right on schedule. The general, Blake and our engineer was staying right on top of things. Then Blake, Shelly, Marrket and I started working on some designs for a dozen or so landscaping sketches for the spring. Blake and Shelly kept looking at me like something was obviously wrong. I turned around and checked my fly. Nothing in my teeth, and my breath wasn't that bad.

"What are you two looking at?" I asked.

"Something is different Charlie. I can't put my finger on it, but something about you is definitely different," Blake said quizzically. Then came *mistake No. 1*. As soon as Blake finished his sentence, Shelly's head snapped in my direction and I saw the twinkle in her eyes. She became poised, but didn't move or add to Blake's thoughts. She was going to wait till we were alone and come on in her own way. Unknowingly, with Shay shin's help, I was playing right into Shelly's hands. *Mistake No 2.*

"You guys want to go to the hotel for dinner?" I asked just after Lacey had stepped up to our trio, and Shelly's eyes lit up. It was like her entire being ignited! She put me not going home for dinner as the change she had been waiting for! Something must have been very different, because Lacey had that same look in her eyes, and was now standing very close to my right shoulder. What the hell was going on? *Mistake No 3.* Just trying to be nice, I asked Lacey if she would like to join us for dinner; really big mistake! She said "I'd love to," and wrapped her arm into mine and pressed into my shoulder. I thought Shelly was going to get violent, but instead she took Blake's arm and the four of us walked out to the car like civilized people.

Lacey was riding shotgun, and I couldn't help notice her already short skirt was now more than teasing, and she knew it! But I was still having issues about Shay shin and wasn't paying all that much attention to either one of them. When we got to the restaurant, things got even crazier. The waitress that came to our table was another supermodel. She was about twenty four or five, six feet tall and some, and had long large blond wavy curls, beautiful green eyes and a mouth that gave your brain a long list of naughty things that left you breathless. She also had a skirt that was so short, she didn't dare lean forward to expose the unrestrained cleavage beneath an open blouse that left nothing to the imagination. Her perfume made me relax and weak all over, and she was more than looking at me. She took a pose right next to me and asked;

"Is there anything I can do for you Mr. Aldermon?" Waited a few seconds, then gave that come on look to Blake;

"Are you ready for me to take your order sir," she purred. I glanced over at Shelly. She was smoking! She looked like a wife whose husband was being taunted by a goddess. Blake too was in total lust, almost to the point of drooling, and couldn't look away from the velvety cream colored thighs that extended from beneath that pink micro mini skirt. Shelly and Lacey were throwing daggers at the competition that was paying absolutely no attention to them. Her concentration was now totally on me. During dinner, everyone stayed socially polite. Still, it was obvious from her slanted remarks, Shelly more than preferred to be where Lacey was, right next to me.

After dinner, we got back in the car and somehow Lacey's skirt had gotten even shorter. We went back to the office where I dropped Blake and Shelly off at their cars, but Lacey stayed put. She had that loving come on mommy smile, and her eyes sparkled in the dash lights. If I didn't put the brakes on right now, this situation was going to get out of hand real quick!

"Ah, Lacey, I really should let you off here too, it wouldn't look proper for you to be hanging out with an animal like me," I said sheepishly. Her look became sad. Still she slowly leaned over the console exposing more than her thighs, closed her eyes and kissed me ever so softly . Oh my God I wanted to reach out and take her in my arms. Right! Then what would you do with her Charlie?!

"Thank you for a wonderful dinner Charlie," she said, her lips still almost touching mine. Then she methodically got out of the car making sure I didn't miss anything. I waited till she got in her car and was pulling out of the parking lot before I even moved. In my rearview mirror, a set of parking lights came on! I didn't even have to think who that was; Shelly! That woman is persistent and aggressive! Again she followed me to the house but this time she stopped in the driveway. I walked around to her drivers side door and stood there.

"What are you doing Shelly?" I asked.

"Protecting what I believe to be mine from the rest of the competition. Should I leave, or are you going to invite me in Charlie?" she asked assertively.

"I don't know if my friend is here or not, so it would probably be best if you left this time. I'm not sure what's going on here, but I'll let you know in a couple of days," I said and backed away from her car.

"I won't give up Charlie. I want to make you happy, and you know I can, if you'd just give me a chance," she said softly, then gave me a little wave and backed out of the driveway. I was fairly sure Shay shin was not in the house, but not 'positively' sure! It was back to being just me and my job. Women were too complicated and confusing, and I really didn't want to have to make a choice. In the house there was no trace of Shay shin's perfume and it was just as well, I was frustrated and in no mood for playing games. I made a pot of coffee, put a TV dinner in the oven and went to take a shower, alone! I wasn't all that hungry after the hotel restaurant, but eating would give me something to do, barely redirecting my thoughts from Shay shin. In the pulsating shower I waited in vain for something to happen, but nothing did. After my shower I started looking for signs of Shay shin being in the house, but my clothes were right where I dropped them, and the comforter wasn't on the bed anymore. I picked up my coffee and TV dinner and went down and sat in front of the fireplace till about ten thirty, then headed for the bedroom. God, I was lost without that girl, and full of the pain of loneliness. I went off to bed frustrated and depressed.

No dreams or nightmares, just sleep. *But Charlie wasn't sleeping alone! Shay shin's love for Charlie was just as strong as his for her.* At five a.m., I was wide awake and went through my morning routine, then trudged off to the office.

Passing the restaurant construction site, I couldn't help notice things seemed to be coming together faster, now that the walls, roof, and windows were in place to keep out the cold air. Winter up here did seem colder than the city. From my office I called the two restaurant owners in Wilton to get their input about the restaurant. I didn't want to bring in outside people if I could help it. Then to affirm the situation, I went out to pay them a visit and make my offer in person. One restaurant owner was an older gentleman with a mom and pop operation that had probably been in Wilton since the town was born, I think. He wanted to maintain his restaurant for the college kids; I guess that was understandable. The other restaurant was owned by an Italian gentleman that was interested in the idea I had to offer. I was to buy his building, and move him and his people to the new restaurant. He would have the money from his building for a retirement account, and still have the same type of job and income he was use to, and doing it with the same people. This would give the corporation the new restaurant and the property they had reimbursed me for, and the franchise. I would have the old restaurant building for another endeavor, that turned out to be a hardware store with everything you could imagine, operated by fourteen local entrepreneurs. This put my accountants to work fulltime for awhile. I called the general and my engineer into the office for an update. I wanted to know the approximate date to have the building inspected, turn on the utilities, order supplies, and bring in the new workers. Both agreed the inspection could take place in three weeks. We kept the name of the old restaurant for several reasons. I talked with the new manager and told him what to expect in the way of patrons so he could schedule his work force. The franchise was pretty much limited to fast food and would take up only a small part of the restaurant. I asked the new manager if he could incorporate full meals for three meals a day in addition to the franchise? He said that wouldn't be a problem and showed me some menus that looked just fine.

Today Blake and I went to dinner at the hotel, alone! I wanted to talk to him about a few things and I didn't want the distractions of Shelly and Lacey warping my mind anymore than it already was. We were escorted to the upper dining room where all the waiters were guys in uniforms.

But something was different?! It took me a few minutes to realize we now had our own little separate dining room that seated twelve people. This was also the cubby hole Mr. Foster used when he was here.

We had our own head waiter with four servant's that would be there just for Mr. Foster, Blake or myself and our guests. After we were situated and had placed our orders, I sat back in my chair and started.

"Blake, there's something I'd like to tell you; something I need to get off my chest, and this is the perfect time and place," I said seriously.

"You're the one person in that facility I believe I can trust totally, and for the time being, you're as far as any of this goes, understand?!" I said looking right at him.

"Understood," he replied with a wrinkled forehead and a strange look on his face.

"Blake, I took this job, and came up here to start my life over again, literally! And for the most part, things have been going even better than I could have hoped for, until a few days ago. Obviously you and Shelly noticed the difference. Since then, I've been dragging my sorry ass around like a whipped dog. I can't think, I can't concentrate, I feel lost and empty. This is not me, and it's the reason of that difference you see, that I'd rather not keep hidden any longer. What I'm about to tell you is not something I've made up, it's very real and it's serious. It's about the house I live in Blake. Well, not so much the house as what's in it, or I should say, who's in it! Someone else lives in that house with me Blake, and is the reason Shelly stays frustrated with me. The person that shares my home is a girl; a young woman who was killed by a bear in the backyard of that house in 2004. I was thinking that would make her nineteen or twenty. But a lady in the know, says she is much older than that. She's a ghost Blake! I have a real ghost that lives in my house!" I said looking right into his eyes to see his reaction.

"Charlie, are you sure you haven't created this ghost out of loneliness?" he asked seriously.

"Yeah, I can understand why you would ask that; but no I didn't make her up. She's the reason for my loneliness. She was in the house before I got there, and is the daughter of the Jun family, the man who designed and had that house built. Indirectly, you've met her twice, sorta. The day you asked me if I had a new cologne, that was her. When the franchise owner was hit in the face, that was her too. Shelly has run into her twice as well. Her name is Shay shin. She is a magnificently beautiful oriental girl, and the first woman I think I have ever truly loved.

But she's trying to teach me a lesson in relationships. She's just a little possessive, which brings out the jealous side of her. The only thing I think I know about these things is that they can be very dangerous if you push the wrong button. She knows about Shelly and Lacey and any woman that looks at me for more than a minute. She's only let me see her a few times when we were alone. But a few days ago, she left me! I wanted you and Shelly to meet her face to face, so you would both kind of understand what's going on with the ups and downs in my life. Women are so weird. Even when they're not real, they can drive you out of your mind. Now, I'm not sure how she would take having Shelly in the house, or Lacey for that matter. But if either of them got possessive of me, I'm pretty sure Shay shin's reaction might be a bit painful for them. I did a little research on the subject of these things and got another surprise. According to the books in the library, Shay shin is more like a 'transmute' than a ghost, in that she can become physically real and more than touch you, and I can touch her, and that she can become anything she wants to be. You saw what she did to the franchise guy. That was her way of protecting me. But that was nothing compared to what she's really capable of. I feel like I'm stuck between a rock and a hard place, but I'm open for suggestions," I said flatly.

Our dinner showed up just then, but I really didn't have the appetite to eat what was in front of me, and wound up pretty much playing with my food.

"Charlie, how do you know she's not here? Right here, right now? That you just can't see her?" Blake asked.

"There's no trace of her perfume, which is usually how I know she's with me, or I can feel her inside me," I said. We both just looked at each other blankly.

"Well, maybe she wants you to make love to Shelly or Lacey to see which one of the three you really prefer. Then maybe she'll come back to see if it's her, or one of them you really want," he said quietly.

"I also think that's the only way your going to get Shelly and Lacey out of your system, and know for sure if Shay shin is the one you're really in love with or want," he added. Damn, that was almost exactly what Shay shin had said in different words.

"Blake, you know where your mind and brain goes when you're having sex; I don't trust myself with another woman. Not only would I be doing it because I had to, but I might get stupid and give in to one of them just because I feel I owe it to them. It wouldn't be the same as it is with Shay shin. In my head I want her near me all the time. I don't feel like a whole person without her," I said dishearted.

"Hell, I could have sex with a hundred girls just for the gratification of it, but that wouldn't mean I love any of them," I said.

"Maybe that's exactly what Shay shin wants you to do, so she will know its her you really want. If you can have sex with Shelly and Lacey and it doesn't mean anything, and you still want Shay shin, that will prove you love her and not them, he said quietly.

"But the next time I make love to Shay shin, she'll think I'm thinking about them instead of her, you know how that happens," I said frustrated.

"Well, you can't help that. That's what drives our instincts," he said still trying to keep his voice down.

"What your saying is probably true Blake, but I don't know what's on Shelly and Lacey's mind? Would they be satisfied with a one night stand, or are they in it for the long haul? I'm thinking Shelly is just curious, and with her I might be able to get away with a one night stand. But Lacey? I don't think so. She's the mommy type, and is looking for a daddy! As I said before, the line between love and sex is really thin, and thinking like Shay shin, Lacey wants to cross that line," I said. I got frustrated with my food, so Blake and I went back to the office and his car. As he pulled away, another set of headlights came on about four car lengths behind me. Oh my God! Don't that woman ever give up?! That had to be Shelly! Again she followed me to the house, pulled into the driveway and into the garage beside me. I had a feeling she wasn't going to take "no" for an answer this time, no matter what I said or did! My heart wasn't in this. This time there was no thrill, no excitement, only a guilt and frustration I couldn't let go of. My adrenaline was flat lined, and my heart could care less. It was more like something I was going to have to do, or never find out what Shay shin was looking for. A woman can present an alluring illusion when they're on the make. Its not only their makeup, what they wear or the perfume, or the way they manipulate and move their bodies.

Their skin texture changes, their eyes brighten, and their smile becomes an inviting lure fools like me can't look away from. Men's perceptive intuition is so blinded by their own animalistic instincts, and the desire of past exposures of the feeling and texture of a females flesh, it causes a psychosomatic psychosis, a lustful urge of a brain rewarded gratification. The determined want of what we want and 'think' we're going to get; its what blinds us to the point we don't see the deception of the trap until we're in it. We're such easily deceived fools because of what we want!

As soon as I opened the kitchen door, even Shelly knew something wasn't right and clung to me as if she was just a bit afraid. Even though the outside of the house is lit up like Fort Knox, there were no lights on anywhere inside the house. The inside of the house is dismal and almost as dark as the night outside, adding to the anxiety of an already bad situation. Besides a dingy black and gray, there is no color to anything in the house; how is that possible? The air in the house is still and almost as cold as it is outside. I turned on some lights, only to find a thin layer of gray haze throughout the first floor of the house. Shay shin was here; somewhere, but I didn't tell Shelly that! I lit the fireplace that sucked out most of the mist in a short time, then turned up the thermostats to make the temperature more hospitable. Somehow Shelly knew that what I was going to do wasn't of my choosing. But this woman is persistent of her wants, and was going to get what she wanted at any cost! We both knew we were going to go through the motions to accomplish our gratifications, without meaning, without feelings, and without the emotions of passion that love brings. There was no foreplay, only dishearted sex, and we did just that. Don't get me wrong, Shelly is a gorgeous woman, even without her clothes, and she felt so good. But my heart was not in this, and as near as I could tell, she wasn't even close to being satisfied with my performance. I didn't know if Shay shin was there to judge the outcome, so again I felt it was all for nothing.

At the office the next morning, I saw Shelly talking to Lacey who coolly glanced in my direction. For the rest of the day, Lacey kept her distance formal, or away from me altogether. Shelly had got what she wanted and Lacey now knew that. As far as they were concerned, I wasn't anything special anymore, and was back to being a regular guy on the street they wouldn't give the time of day to. And that was fine with me, I didn't need their distractions.

Blake and I went down to the restaurant to see how things were going. They were ready for the building inspection and furnishings. I had the new restaurant manager come over and start making lists of what he needed and wanted, and what I wanted. Then I called the franchise dealer and told him we were ready for them to deliver the basics. The inspections came first. Building safety and codes, then the fumigators and Health Dept.. The city delivered two dumpsters and the guy from the pig farm brought four containers over. The general was staying with the program, and more subs came in with furnishings and the breakfast bar.

There was the kitchen equipment, like stainless steel sinks, tables, pots and pans, a grill and a dishwasher, large utensils, and then the dishes and silverware arrived. The décor came in slowly a little at a time. The new manager and his people began their setup of things. I asked him to let me know when he was in full operation. Food stuff began showing up along with the franchise stuff. Ricardo, the new manager, didn't seem happy with the franchise part. He said the quality of the food was bad and disportioned. I asked him if he could do without it? He said "Yes!" I called Blake and had him shut off the franchise. There would be a penalty I was sure, but I didn't care. I told Ricardo he was fully on his own and he said he would make it work, and he did! It was another week before he called and asked if I would come to the restaurant. Even though the restaurant was right at the boundaries of the facility parking lot, and within walking distance, I had the staff pile into three cars and we paid Ricardo a visit. The place was absolutely perfect. I called the sign company that I had already made arrangements with, and the sign, "Rico's" was installed that afternoon. Ricardo was very happy with the sign. I called Foster to let him know the restaurant was ready and he was here an hour later. Foster was pleased with Ricardo's ingenuity regarding the franchise, and extremely impressed with the new restaurant. Shelly called the college to let them know the new location was open for business, and the kids poured into the place, happy to see their old friend again. Ricardo made a lot of meals from scratch, and they were all delicious! He had the full support of all the people in our facility from that day on. They made over $14,000.00 the first day they were open, and it went up from there. Word travels fast about good food, and Rico's had a lot of visitors from Corinth and Wilton, as well as out of town customers.

I had Blake look into what we needed to put a couple of signs up for the restaurant and our facility near the Wilton turnoff of Hwy. 87, and he got that going.

I went to Wilton to check on the hardware store and stopped by the town council to see if there were any other perspectives, and what was available at the moment. It was time to start doing what I told Foster I was up to. Busy day. Then only because I was wore out, I headed for the house. I still didn't want to be there without Shay shin. Surprise! Blake's car was sitting on the street in front of the house. This should be interesting I thought. What would Shay shin do in his presence, if anything? As I pulled into the garage, he got out of his car and followed me in. I walked around the car and met him.

"Okay boss, now I feel like I live in a tent compared to this," he said laughing.

"This is a fantastic house Charlie," he said.

"Wait till you see the inside," I said. The garage door closed and I opened the kitchen door. He was speechless! This was definitely not what Shelly had seen. All he could do was look and gasp!

"Wow, wow, wow!" was all that came out of his mouth. I took him on a tour of the house and "Wow!" was all I could get out of him. I made us some coffee and we were finally sitting on the upper ring of the three tier sunken living room across from each other with our coffee.

"Charlie, this is the most incredibly fantastic house I have ever seen! And it's in New York! It just doesn't look real," he said excitedly.

"It's like a larger version of a very special doll house," he added.

"Blake," I said coldly. "Close your eyes. Don't say anything, just close your eyes and listen," I said, and he did. I gave him about a full minute before I said anything.

"What do you hear Blake?" I asked.

"Absolute total silence, nothing," he said.

"And how long do you think you could put up with that silence until it drove you batty?" I asked, coming to the edge of the sofa.

"Oh, I see what you're getting at. Have you tried talking to her?" he asked.

"Yeah, but she won't answer me. If she doesn't come back, I'm thinking seriously about taking Foster up on his offer, and moving to Kingston, and you can have this place for free," I said totally depressed.

"Jesus Charlie, you can't be serious! You can't give this place up; this is every man's dream house!" he said assertively.

"Without her, that's all it is Blake, a house, an empty house, with an empty man in it," I said without care.

"Charlie, if I heard you correctly at the hotel, you said, Shay shin said, "more than one." What about Lacey?" he asked.

"That one scares me Blake. She's a real woman looking for real love. She would try twice as hard as Shelly. Lacey wants into my heart not just my pants. I don't want to hurt her. If I brought her here, even for one night, to her that would be an invitation to my heart, not just sex. She thinks differently than Shelly. To tell her it was just a test the next morning would shatter her heart, and I won't do that," I said flatly.

"No, it's Shay shin or no one! But if she walked out on me once, she'll do it again. Without Shay shin I'm nothing! How did I let myself get this way? Even down in the city with no one, I was mentally more stable than I am right now. In this house, I can't be without her. If this is what love does to you, I don't want any part of it," I told him. I really was ready to call Foster and ask him what my options were. I couldn't live like this, not without her. Then I had an idea but I didn't mention it to Blake. It was pretty much shop talk from there. Then he said he had a date and had to go. I didn't ask with who. I gave him ten minutes then I headed for Corinth. I just couldn't stay in that house without her!

In Corinth, I checked into a different hotel, then checked out my room. Then I went downstairs to the restaurant to have dinner. That's when I discovered it wasn't the house; hell, even here I felt lost without her. I was sitting there waiting for my order, then from across the dining room, I saw a woman staring at me. Did I know her? Her expression was stone cold, with no facial or body language to read. She seemed more than still, with no one else at her table; she just sat there staring at me.

Strange! I tried to evade her stare by drawing on a napkin, but still I could feel those penetrating eyes staring at me. It was just like Ms. Elda staring at me! I looked down at my drawing and she was there, standing right next to me! I never saw her leave her table.

"May I," she asked quietly, standing right next to me. I stood up and pulled out the chair across the table from mine and she sat down. Now what are you going to get yourself into Charlie?! Why did she come to my table? Who is she? She looked to be in her mid fifties, a decent figure in a light tan suit, and a hat that had a little veil over her eyes, and she was unmistakably oriental! Maybe she was the boss of an escort service for high class hookers, looking for a trick for one of her girls. She just sat there for a moment not saying anything, just looking into my eyes.

"May I offer you dinner?" I asked, starting to feel more than a bit uneasy and nervous.

"Thank you, Mr. Aldermon, but I've already eaten," she said in a dialect accent that definitely sounded Asian, then glanced at the chair to her left.

"I know who you are Mr. Aldermon, and I'm a bit surprised your not at your own hotel, but even more surprised your not at home. I read that you moved into the 'Jun' residence. That's a large home even for two people.

If I may be so bold, have you acquired a house keeper and cook as of yet Mr. Aldermon?" she asked softly. I hadn't thought about that yet. What did she mean by "two" people? Maybe the tabloids thought Shelly and I were ... .! Or did she somehow know about Shay shin? For reasons I didn't understand, this woman was making me very nervous.

"I visited that magnificent home with a realtor a few years ago. That house would require at least two people to maintain it," she said again softly, still staring into my eyes. Spooky! This woman was almost as unnerving as Ms. Elda. Strangely they seemed from the same mold.

"I happen to know two reputable aspiring young ladies that would be perfect for the care of you and your home, if you wish it so," she said softly. Oh, oh! This was starting to sound like one of those human trafficking deals I'd heard of.

"They just arrived here from China Town in San Francisco four days ago. My brother asked if I might assist them in seeking employment. They are presently staying in my home, and attend the college near your home in Wilton.

They are traditional Chinese women, and are very respectful, and well mannered," she said with a nod of her head toward the chair on her left. That nod must be an Asian thing, because Shay shin does it a lot too. What the hell, they would bring some real life to the house, and probably keep it a lot cleaner than I do.

"When would they be able to start?" I asked.

"Whenever you are ready for them sir. And their salary would be up to you, based on the quality of their accomplishments, care and service," she said. As I watched, she wrote her phone number on a napkin and slowly slid it across the table to me. It was a Corinth number.

"Well, if you've been there, you know, there are several bedrooms upstairs. I have very little or no company. They could actually live there for nothing," I said, and again she bowed her head, got up and went back to her table. *But as Charlie spoke, he 'was' indeed having company, unexpected company!* That was strange I thought. I went up to my hotel room and spent a lonely night there, tortured by my own self indulgence of Shay shin's memories. Damn; it was no different here than being alone in that house.

At that very moment, a car slowly pulled up curbside, and parked in front of Charlies house. For a moment it just sat there, then the headlights went off, and Shelly got out of the car.

There were several lights on in the house downstairs, a fair indication Charlie was home, alone she hoped. She went up to the front door and pushed the doorbell. Throughout the house, little oriental chimes rang out and all the lights went out. A few seconds later, the front door slowly opened, but seemingly without assistance! Shelly took that as an invitation and cautiously stepped through the threshold. "Charlie?" But there was no response. She found a light switch with her telephone, but no sooner had she turned it on and looked away, it went off again!

"Charlie? Is that you, Charlie?" she called softly. But the answer she received this time was not even close to what she expected! Shay shin's ghostly wispy apparition was suddenly before her! There was the fiendish loud scream of a banshee from the apparition! Needless to say, Shelly also screamed, and was out of there, running back to her car!

The next day at the office, Blake asked;

"How did it go last night?" he asked.

"Oh, I didn't stay at the house last night. I can't stand being in that house alone without her," I said shaking my head.

"Well, Gibbs has something he wants you to look at. He thinks there's a structural fault or a problem with the drawing in the Cimmerman building proposal," Blake stated.

"Okay, lets have a look, I said, and snagged one of my engineers on the way. It took the engineer only a few minutes to find the problem. It was also obvious to me that the drawing had probably moved on the board, but more than likely, it had somehow moved in the print machine. The eight main vertical support beams, and twelve of the lateral support beams had been overdrawn in the proposal. Marrket called the contractor and took control of the situation. I didn't know why, but Shelly seemed very nervous about something and kept her distance from me the entire day. At about four thirty, I asked Blake to see if he could find out what was wrong. Shelly explained to Blake what had happened last night, that there was something horrific in that house, and Blake came right back to me.

"Charlie; Shay shin is still in that house, and she scared the living hell out of Shelly last night," he said flatly.

"She what?! Last night?! What the hell was Shelly doing at my place?" I questioned.

"You know her, she don't give up so easy," he said.

"My God, Shay shin is still there!" I said in a mild shock. I asked Blake to lock up and I left the office headed for the house. Okay, if Shay shin was still in the house, and had scared the shit out of Shelly, what was going to happen when the two house maids showed up? I thought. I parked in the driveway and hurriedly went in through the front door. Just inside the door I stopped! What the hell! Again the inside of the house was dreary and dismal, and almost as dark as night. There was no color to anything and the air was almost as cold inside the house as it was outside.

"Shay shin?! Honey? Where are you baby?" I called softly.

"Shay shin, I know you're here, please come and talk to me," I said, and waited. For sometime nothing changed. I turned on the fireplace and stood in front of it.

Facing the center of the living room, from my left, out of the guest bedroom, slowly only the wispy trace of an apparition hesitantly appeared and moved towards me; that had to be her! She looked just like one of those floating wispy ghosts you see on TV, parts of her clothes and hair blowing in a gentle breeze that didn't seem to exist.

"Shay shin, you know that I love you baby, why are you acting like this? You said you'd never leave me, but you did," I said a bit more than assertively.

"No Charlie, I never did leave you," she said with a tinge of echo.

"I've been with you the whole time. I was with you and Blake at the hotel restaurant, and I was with you at the other hotel where you met that lady, and she knew it. She is much like Ms. Elda, but different. The two young maids she spoke of are as she said, and are welcome in our home. I visited with them for a short time. The two of them have already been given minimal instructions in the basic care of your mortal needs, desires, and the house, if they still want the job. I slept beside you in that lonely room Charlie. I'm so sorry I made you sad. I'm sorry I scared your friend Shelly, but I didn't want her in the house without you being here. Please say you still want me Charlie?" she begged in a whimper that sounded like she was about to cry.

"Want you?! Damnit Shay shin, I can't live without you! Of course I want you baby, and you know it," I said somewhat relieved at her presence, and started towards her. I was about half the distance to her and stopped! She hadn't changed from her apparitional form in the least.

"Charlie, you must know this is what I truly am; this is what I truly look like. I appear to you as your thoughts wish for me to be. You are in love with the illusion I present to you. Can you truly love something like this now before you Charlie?" she asked in a whimper.

"Shay shin, baby, I want you just the way you are, right now, or the illusion you present, or anything else you want to be baby. I'm in love with you Shay shin, the part of you that cares for me with all your heart. Honey, if this is what you must be, or want to be, then so be it, I don't care. I know that whatever you look like, or whatever you are, you care as much for me as I do for you.

My God I love you Shay shin!" I said and continued toward her. Instantly she became the beautiful mortal looking woman I truly loved. We fell into each others arms and I held her tightly, her lips pressed onto mine.

"I will always love you Charlie," she softly whispered in an echo. That's all I needed to hear, even though that echo sounded very much like something from the past. Yeah, in her ghostly form, she did look a bit scary, but the warmth of her loving soul was mine. The interior of the house also began changing back into what it had been just like Shay shin, magnificently beautiful. I made up my mind that the next day, things at the office were going to be more than interesting. I was going to introduce Shay shin to Blake and Shelly. Whatever happens, happens!

The next morning, I had Lacey hold any calls for Blake and myself for at least an hour. I called Shelly and Blake, and asked them to meet me in the conference room upstairs. When they were in the room, I locked the door. That noticeably got Shelly's attention, but she didn't say anything. I had them sit side by side in the middle of the long side of the table, and I sat opposite of them.

"What's this all about Charlie?" Blake asked leaning onto the table.

"She's back Blake! And this is something I've been wanting to do for some time now. Maybe, just maybe, this will ease some of the tension and frustrations I have been causing both of you. You are both not only my employees, you are also my close friends. Shelly, I am about to introduce you to the reason I have attempted to keep you at bay, so to speak. Both of you have had indirect contact with the person you are about to meet. Blake knows who she is, but has never seen her," I said, and stood just behind my chair. Blake sat up straight in his chair.

"You both might be a bit surprised as to what occurs in the next few seconds, but that too, is part of why I want you to see her. I would like to present to both of you, the woman I love so dearly! Shay shin, if you will please honor us with your presence my dear," I said proudly. Immediately from my left side, Shay shin materialized and stood very close to me, holding onto my arm! Shelly gasped audibly at Shay shin's appearance from my body, and Blake's jaw fell!

"Shay shin, these are my friends, Blake Arnold and Shelly Balintyne. Blake and Shelly, this is Shay shin!" I said proudly taking her hand, as both of their mouths fell open.

Shay shin was wearing a short dark burgundy, silk form fitting Chinese dress, sparsely decorated with flowers, and a slit up the left side of her dress to her hip. Her bangs were barely above her thick eyebrows, and her straight long dark hair hung to the middle of her back.

"Hello," Shay shin said shyly in that accented voice that made me weak, bowing her head just a bit. Shelly was flabbergasted at Shay shin's beauty as much as where she had appeared from. Blake was literally drooling.

"As you have seen, and probably have surmised, Shay shin is a transmute, a ghost, and not mortal. But as you can see, she can be very real, and is very much alive in human form," I said softly. Shelly was in total shock and just sat there staring at Shay shin in absolute amazement, and still with her mouth open.

"Shay shin is always with me, in the way you have just seen her appear," I said, and Shelly turned a bright red, and Blake blushed.

"Is there anything either of you would like to ask Shay shin? she speaks perfect English," I asked our two astonished guests.

"Ah, are you two somewhat married?" Blake asked quietly.

"Not officially, but yes, you could say that. But if Shay shin will have me, I really would love for her to be my wife," I said looking love struck into her eyes. Right in front of Blake and Shelly, Shay shin turned to face me and slipped her arms around my neck. Her eyes met mine, then she ever so passionately and gently kissed my lips. The room literally vibrated. Okay, something else is at work here!

"I accept Charlie," Shay shin said softly, lying the side of her face against my chest looking straight at Shelly.

"Then, that, that was you I saw at the door the night I went to Charlie's?!" Shelly sort of stuttered. Then Shay shin did something none of us had thought of. She changed into her apparitional form right in front of us! Blake's chair scooted back away from the table, and Shelly grabbed Blake's arm and turned her face into Blake's shoulder. When she finally got the nerve to look at Shay shin she said in a stutter;

"That's what I saw!" she said pointing at Shay shin. Still in her wispy apparitional form, Shay shin apologized;

"I'm sorry I scared you Shelly," Shay shin said turning back into her human form. The look on both of them was precious.

"Okay then; if there are no more questions, I guess we should probably return to our duties before we are missed," I said. Blake and Shelly were slow to get up as they headed for the door, still looking at Shay shin, who gave them a little wave, and Shelly waved back. I think at that moment, I was the proudest man on this earth. I was thinking they wanted to see if she would disappear again, but Shay shin waited until they were gone before she did so. But not before I got to hold Shay shin in my arms and kiss her. When I came out of the conference room, Shelly and Lacey were having a conversation. Now I can't imagine what they would be talking about!? Back in my office I buzzed Lacey and told her I was back on line. Shelly went back down stairs and Blake was standing in my doorway.

"Come in Blake," I said cordially.

"Charlie, that was absolutely perfect! A bit unnerving, and spooky, but perfect. I don't know how you manage it, but you seem to have the knack for accomplishing several things at once, and that took care of a lot of them all at one time," he said.

"Shelly's a bit disappointed that you're off the market now, but couldn't get over how beautiful Shay shin is, and not to mention how openly passionate she is. That was incredible. By the way, you were right about the Cimmerman job. The drafter tried to save some time by using an overlay, but it had moved during the print stage," he added.

"What are we doing for lunch," he asked.

"Rico's of course," I said, and he was on his way back to his office. We grabbed Shelly, Marrket an Lacey and headed out the front door of the building and headed out across the parking lot. At Rico's everyone is on the same level, and I liked that.

I was treated 'almost' the same as everyone else, and the place was always full, but still fairly quiet. Ricardo met us at the door and said he had a table upstairs for us. Shelly was now fully attached to Blake, something else I had to keep in mind. They made a good couple.

Ricardo asked if we would like to try his pepper steak and rice, and we all said yes. Oh my gosh it's mouth watering delicious! Marrket and Lacey were starting to hook up, and that too was good. Lacey hung on to him for dear life, delicate and passionately, and he treated her like a queen. I was right, she is the mommy type and she had found her daddy. They made such a cute couple. I often wanted Shay shin to be at my side like that; to hold her hand, but she said it wouldn't look right for her to sit at the table and not eat anything. So I was content knowing she was with me in another way. But we always made up for it when we got home. She really made my life worth living.

That evening while Shay shin and I were in each others arms, sitting in front of the fireplace, Shay shin suddenly sat up straight seemingly in a daze, then her head began turning slowly towards me like she wanted to say something, but was listening to something else. She slowly put her left hand on my knee and was now looking right at me.

"That's a scary look your giving me honey," I said, also sitting up.

"What is it baby," I asked a bit worried, as she stared into my eyes.

"Someone that knows of you is going to join me," she said quietly. but I don't know who he is. A man, an older man. He came to me just now, and then went back. He told me of things you would do. He said he would call you, that's all," she said almost in a whisper.

"Was it Foster?" I asked.

"No, it wasn't him, but it is someone in your company," she added.

"What do you mean he's going to join you? Is he going to die?" I asked.

"Yes! He has a problem with his heart, but he's okay for now. But he said he will come to me soon," she said.

The next morning I got a strange call from Mr. Foster. He said he wanted me to come down and spend two or three days at his office in Kingston. Damn, I could feel it coming! I was his excuse to retire, and I was sure that's what this was all about. Shay shin and I did not want to move to Kingston and leave our home. Shay shin said this would be a good time for me to visit the attic. I'm not a religious person, and I don't have a lot of faith in things I can't see or touch, but Foster was closing in on me; I had to try something!

When Shay shin and I got into the attic, like before, a glitter shimmered over the pentagram that made me think this thing was alive. It was as if it knew we were there. Shay shin sat next to me but did not touch me, but she was looking at me.

" Think Charlie; first of the problem, and then of what you want, and then ask what to do," she said softly. So, I thought about the situation I was sure that was about to happen with Foster, and what it probably entailed, and waited. I did not want to lose this house. I don't know what I thought was suppose to happen, but that shimmer fluttered over the pentagram again and it began to change color, a dull reddish color. It stayed that way for about two minutes then faded back to its original black color. I guess that meant it was doing whatever. Shay shin then gently took my hand.

"It will come to you Charlie," she said almost in a whisper, then we went back down stairs.

Coffee time. Shay shin mentioned I should call the lady I had met at the hotel about the two girls, so I did. I asked her to have the girls ready to move to my place about noon, and got her address. I never did know that lady's name and she never mentioned it. Then I called for a small moving van to go to her house and pick up whatever there was of the girls stuff. Shay shin and I went over to pick up the girls in my car. The lady met us at the front door of her home. Our meeting was more than a bit strange. The instant the lady saw Shay shin, her body noticeably shook violently and she turned her head to the right and stumbled backwards a few steps! Her hands went up in front of her face, then she bowed at the waist until Shay shin said something in Chinese. It was more than obvious the lady was for some reason in fear of Shay shin! When she stood up straight she kept her hands over her face to avoid looking into Shay shin's eyes.

"Shay shin, what the hell is going on?!" I asked, a bit confused.

"She knows what and who I am, and she fears those of the spirit world," she said. We weren't invited into the lady's house, but that was okay by me. The lady called out to the girls to come to the door and stood behind them as they were introduced. They were a set of twenty three year old, first generation Chinese identical twin sisters, and they were magnificently beautiful. Just looking into their eyes made all kinds of things go through your mind. I'm glad Shay shin came back before these two came to the house or I could have had all kinds of problems!

91

Lenin Tao and Leunig Tao, bowed gracefully; first to Shay shin then to the lady of the house, then to me. The two girls didn't seem to share the fear of the elder lady. Some how, Shay shin had already spoken to them, and for the moment, their fear must have been in disguise. They were both dressed in dark blue jackets, skirts and blouses that looked like school uniforms. I told the lady a small truck was on its way to pick up the girls things. Shay shin and I brought the girls back to our house in my car with Shay shin physically sitting next to me in the front passenger seat. I loved having her next to me, but with these bucket seats it's a little difficult. So we just held hands on top of the console. The girls in the back seat didn't say a word all the way home, but Lenin watched me in the rearview mirror. Just before we got to the house, Shay shin asked me to stop on the street in front of our house, and asked me to stay in the car, so I did. I thought the next few minutes more than interesting and a bit odd, but I watched carefully.

The three women got out of the car and some kind of traditional ritual began. For a few seconds the three stood side by side in the blowing snow, then bowed from the waist to the house. I looked at the house; but there's nobody there?! Then the two girls turned and bowed from the waist to Shay shin. Then both girls went to their knees in the snow and again bowed to the house. What the hell?

What was I missing? Then I think I figured it out, maybe?! Although it didn't show, the two girls 'did' in fact fear to a degree, or were at least leery of what Shay shin truly is. They had obviously been told by the lady from the hotel about Shay shin, and the circumstances of her death! That meant they knew she was a ghost! Or what I called a transmute. The girls were paying their respects to Shay shin's family and home; then to Shay shin; then to her house of death! Then they stood and bowed to Shay shin again. Well, I think that's what was going on?! Whatever it was looked very respectful on the twins part. They then followed Shay shin to the front door that opened untouched just before they got to it. Spooky! Shay shin took the girls upstairs to their rooms. Then I heard Shay shin say;

"You can put the car in the garage now Charlie," and it sounded like she was right next to me, even though I couldn't see her. The van was only about forty five minutes behind us with what little the girls had. The movers brought the girls stuff in the house and took it upstairs. Shay shin asked them to put the boxes in the middle of the hallway outside the girls rooms.

After the girls put their stuff away, and changed clothes, Shay shin took them on a detailed tour of the house. I only caught glimpses of the tour as they were going from room to room. They were instructed as to what was to take place there. There was a conversation near the ladder to the attic, but they didn't go up there. Then Shay shin asked me to sit in a chair in the living room. The girls were facing halfway between me and Shay shin, and listening to Shay shin speaking in Chinese. This conversation lasted at least thirty to forty five minutes and as I said, it was all in Chinese. To me, her speech seemed quick and gruff. Then the girls bowed to Shay shin, then turned to face me, stood from their chairs and went to their knees, and bowed all the way to the floor. I didn't have a clue as to what was going on, but they didn't have to bow to me, I'm American. Then I heard Shay shin's thoughts;

"From this moment, you are their Lord and master Charlie. Please accept their humble offering of praise and respect," she said bowing her head a bit. Then it was my turn.

"Shay shin, I'm just a man honey, they are welcome in our home, but I'm nobody's master, and I'm definitely not a Lord," my thoughts went back to her. There was no reply, she just smiled.

Shay shin made out a shopping list for the kitchen and the rest of the house. Then we, all four of us, went shopping, which filled up the trunk. When we were back in the car, Shay shin looked at me questionably. Verbally she didn't say a word, but I heard her as if she had.

"Charlie, can you afford to get these young ladies some clothes?" she asked. I started to speak, but her finger touched my lips. "Think it," came her thoughts in a whisper. It always took a minute for me to figure out how to do this, but I did manage.

"You can get them anything you or they want, anything!" I thought. She told me where she wanted me to go and how to get there. Then again we went shopping; well, they did, I just sat looking at a magazine until they were done and paid the bill. I don't know what they got for four thousand dollars, and it didn't matter. When we got home, the girls excitedly took their stuff upstairs and Shay shin and I unloaded the trunk, mostly into the kitchen. That's when I realized I didn't really have two refrigerators; one of them turned out to be a standup freezer. Then I found cabinets I didn't know existed. All those little panels look the same, but some of them were actually drawers. Then Shay shin disappeared.

The house was quite quiet for about an hour or so, then Shay shin called me from one of the girls rooms mentally and asked if I would take the girls to dinner at the hotel restaurant? "Certainly," I said.

I was sitting in front of the fireplace when the girls were finally ready. Ever so slowly they came down the stairs in a slow rocking sway, with Shay shin one step behind them. My hormones went out of control! The twins were absolutely stunning, and seductively tempting as hell! My love for Shay shin just got jolted, or was it my lust? Was I ever in for a surprise! They were wearing very short, form fitting Chinese silk dresses, one in red and one in gold, both were slit to where the panty line should have been. And the way they moved; oh lord, no worm could wiggle like that! There goes that male thing again. This was going to be a very interesting evening I could tell already. At the hotel restaurant we were escorted to my special dining room. Two waiters trying to be gentlemen, rushed over to help the girls out of their fur coats and pulled out their chairs. But then something I thought a little strange happened. Instead of them sitting, one girl came and stood to either side of my chair.

"Shay shin honey," I thought; "What are they doing?"

"You are their master and they are your servants, and that is their place of honor, my dear," came her thoughts to me.

"Okay; now tell them to sit down," I said a bit awed by the situation. The attention these two girls attracted was almost hilarious. Their manners were so finesse and pristine, they made everyone else look like barbarians. The place was suddenly a buzz of gawking conversationists. Then it started! The girls got their first mental instructions from Shay shin that I was aware of. They came to the table and sat directly across from each other, one chair from mine. The waiters were having a hell of a time concentrating on their job at the table, they just wanted to look at what could be seen of the girls, and I couldn't blame them. Then some guy from downstairs got brave enough to push his luck; bad idea!

"How much for one of them," he asked quietly, then froze. I didn't have time to give him a sarcastic answer it happened so quick. I could tell from his bulging eyes, Shay shin did, or was doing something to him. The guy collapsed to his knees on the floor in total shock or pain, or both!

When he was finally able to stand, he slowly stood and went back down stairs without a word, and was asked by the manager to leave the restaurant. Obviously he thought I was someone or something else, a pimp probably.

The hotel manager hurriedly came to apologize. It hadn't dawned on me till then, that Mr. Foster was always accompanied by a minimum of two other gentlemen. Bodyguards! Humm…. Well, I had one too!

When we got home I managed to get out of my suit and into a pair of genes and a t-shirt, barely! But I hadn't completely got away clean. From in front of the fireplace I heard Shay shin call.

"Charlie, come," came Shay shin's angelic voice from our bedroom. Okay I thought, she wants to play. No way in hell could anyone have made me understand what was about to happen, nor would I have believed them. The two girls were standing one to either side of Shay shin, dressed in sheer, open silk gowns, and nothing else! My composure went to hell!

"Charlie, these young ladies are to be much more than just your house maids, they are also your mistresses," she said softly, but assertively.

"In meticulous detail, they have been instructed on how to care for you, and your mortal needs and animalistic desires," she said assertively. Both girls slowly came to me and bowed. Each one delicately wrapping an arm around my forearms, one to either side of me, they smiled and their eyes never left mine. Once their hands touched me, they didn't leave my body until I was methodically undressed and blushing in my birthday suit. I was then escorted into the shower.

I went from shy, to more than a bit bashful, then oh my God!

"Shay shin, what are they doing honey?!" I thought.

"In our culture, you are no less than a Lord, and will be treated as such. Love, trust and devotion exceeds that of jealousy and contempt. I will not interfere with their duties and compassion for their Lord and master Charlie," she said in a whisper. And then both girls removed their robes.

"Oh my God! Shay shin!" and it came out loud and clear.

"Calm my love, they will not harm you. They are just following their instructions. They will please you in any manner they can, to fulfill your innermost desires," she said with a little giggle.

Then they started messing with my head; both of them! One in front of me and the other from behind, as they slowly pressed me snuggly between them.

"Don't blame me for what's about to happen Shay shin, I thought.

"Calm Charlie, I know you love only me; allow them to fulfill your mortal lustful desires; then they will bring you to me, and I will love you unto the depths of your soul," she whispered.

"Okay!" I said, and it started. I'm a bad boy! Oh my God was I naughty. And they were both naughty girls. Here I am, pressed between two nymphomaniacs, and a third waiting in the bedroom! After the twins drained my body and mind in the shower, they started drying me off with the towels, but they weren't' finished with me yet, and we wound up back in the shower again, towels and all! When the girls were finally finished with me, they delivered me to Shay shin in the bedroom. This shouldn't happen to a king. Lying there in her silky satin gown, Shay shin held me in her arms and next to my ear hummed an oriental lullaby that put me off into lala land. I didn't know or care what happened after that.

But after being with Shay shin for only about twenty minutes, there was an explosive crash and two horrific screams that brought me out of that bed in a run! It came from the kitchen! Deep inside I knew what it had to be! I spun through the kitchen door, opened the drawer, pulled out the .444 mag, aimed, and emptied it through the already shattered glass of the back door!

"Shay shin, is that the one?!" I growled.

"Yes, Charlie!" she cried as I dumped the empty shells and quickly reloaded the pistol. Then I took Shay shin's wrist and opened the back door. I put the pistol in her right hand and wrapped both of my hands around hers, locked my elbows and pointed the pistol at the bears head.

"Pull the trigger Shay shin! BANG! Again Shay shin! BANG! Again, I hollered, and again until the gun was empty! Then I took her in my arms and held her tight. She cried hysterically for the better part of thirty minutes, while the two girls and I were trying to comfort her. I called the sheriff and told him what had just happened and he and four deputies came. After I explained what had happened to Shay shin, no more was said. They put the bear in a pickup and took it away. That evening I gave both the girls instructions on how to use that pistol and how to be safe with it.

I had each one of them fire three rounds from it, then I showed them how to reload it, then I put it back in the drawer. I called a guy to repair the back door and had it replaced with a steel door and bullet proof glass. Until the door was replaced the next morning, Shay shin and the twins were a nervous wreck, and no one got any sleep for the rest of the night.

Chapter 7

At the office the next morning, the call from Foster I had been dreading came. I called Steven, my pilot, then went in to tell Blake to hold down the fort for a few days. Shay shin had left the girls in charge of the house and came with me. When I got to Kingston, it was exactly what I thought it would be. Mr. Foster had made his decision to retire. He took me on a slow methodical tour of his entire facility. It was big, but not as big as any part of the one in Wilton. I had to ask for another notepad, cause I filled my first one in about an hour. It turns out the president and owner of the corporation resides at another facility in Pittsburgh, PA. For two entire days, I calculated, measured and contemplated space, equipment, people and occupied areas inside and out of the building. Then it hit me, the wings! Oh my God! Foster had been planning his retirement when he asked me to design our facility five years ago. That sneaky old man! He had already planned to retire before he moved me up here. He knew then I was going to move to Wilton, and I'm thinking he knew what I was going to do before I ever got here. It was now going to be my job to move every desk, person and piece of paper from Kingston to Wilton, including all of the monetary accounts and every other account Foster had. Wow, that ought to ruffle somebody's feathers. The gears started turning, timing would be critical. I'd shutdown this facility and put it on the market for sale. But as monstrous as the job seemed at the moment, methodically it was all feasible. Then Foster added a twist, we were going to see the 'man'! Holy shit; if I was ever going to lose my job, this would probably be the day!

I called Blake and told him my intentions about moving the Kingston operation to Wilton. I was pretty sure the big man wasn't going to be too happy about my decision. I told Blake to be prepared to take the helm as the CEO of the Wilton facility permanently, one way or another! Either way, if I got fired by the big honcho or became the VP, he would be the new CEO of the Wilton operation.

Then Mr. Foster and I got in Steven's chopper and headed for PA, and the main corporate office. I knew I wasn't going to like this part. A politician I'm not, and I don't deal well with showboats, stupidity and blatant authority, regardless of who they are, or think they are! They cop an attitude and things will go bad; I don't care how big a boss they think they are! I had already wound myself up.

We landed on what looked like a taxiway amidst several other business choppers and a business jet. Then Foster and I got a royal escort to the big boss's office, and he was waiting. His attitude was already more than visible and he didn't look happy with the situation! Standing in front of his desk, Foster made the introductions. The boss man stood and shook Mr. Foster's hand, but didn't offer me the same.

"Mr. Holdin this is Charles Aldermon, the CEO I told you about from our Wilton facility. Charlie, this is your boss; the owner and president of the corporation, Mr. Holdin," Mr. Foster said almost cautiously. Holdin's eyes were like lasers, staring into mine, and I stared right back.

"Daniel," the boss man said in greeting, then again looked me right in the eye, and sat down.

"So; Mr. Aldermon, do you really think you're ready, or even qualified to step into the shoes of one of the greatest architectural engineers in the continental United States?" he asked. He was trying not to be too sarcastic, but not trying very hard. No holds barred, I don't care who this guy is, I didn't like him already, and I let him have it!

"No sir, as a matter of fact I don't. And you sir, have the option of selecting someone else to fill those shoes if you so desire," I said returning his glare.

"Do you know who you're talking to young man?" he blurted, pushing his body against his desk.

"Yes sir, I do! I'm talking to a man who is about to lose one of the greatest architectural engineers in the continental United States; that's being replaced by a younger man you don't know, but have already passed judgement on. And you will care even less of that individual when you find out he's going to move the Kingston establishment to Wilton," I said aggressively. Mr. Foster intervened.

"I told you he's a powerhouse and doesn't backdown from anyone," Mr. Foster said quietly. Mr. Holdin just stared at me for a few seconds, and started turning red, unbelieving he was being challenged by a nobody. Here it comes Charlie, you just lost your job! I was sure he wanted to come around from behind that desk and get himself laid out for being stupid. But he clenched his fists and stood his ground for the moment.

"Why would you want to destroy a part of the corporation I built into a multibillion dollar business?" he replied back aggressively.

"Because Mr. Holdin, even if I can't fill his shoes, I would at least like to continue in Mr. Foster's footsteps. My facility is more than adequate and capable of incorporating both operations and then some. We will be saving proceeds and make a profit from Mr. Foster's facility in the sale, without losing one employee, piece of furniture or piece of paper. In addition, a process has been initiated to enhance the city of Corinth, and the town of Wilton, that will bring profits not presently visible to the corporation. However, if you wish me to leave, I'll be more than happy to tell you what you can do with your corporation," I stated almost aggressively. Mr. Holdin quickly stood, his fists pounding into the top of his desk. His neck and face were now a bright red, but he was smart enough not to come around that desk.

"I understand your dilemma sir, but that doesn't mean you should take it out on someone you don't know, and got off on the wrong foot with," I said a bit more calmly. Foster made a gesture across his face with his hands looking down at the floor, but didn't say anything. If I was going to take Fosters job, this guy had to know the meat of who he was dealing with as well. I had no fear of speaking my mind, and he just got a taste of that! This was it for me and we both knew it. Either I stood my ground with this very economically powerful man, or he would make it so I couldn't get a drafting job anywhere on the US continent, and I would get smeared right off the map. Still, in a lighter shade of red, Holdin slowly sat back down into his chair, but still his fists were clenched, and still he glared at me like he really wanted to do something stupid. After a good two minutes of silence, it was like the whole meeting and conversation started over, but with a minor change of his attitude.

"Your proposed time frame for this move is?" he asked calmly.

"As you know, our people are the foundation of this corporation. Without them, you and I are no more than figureheads of an establishment. Their displacement must be taken into consideration first and foremost. As soon as I have that situation under control, and not until, will I start the move. It should go smooth enough that you won't know its happening. Once it starts, I'm calculating a month and twenty days to complete, right down to the last piece of paper and account.

And still, in the process of that move, we will maintain the corporate working structure, etiquette and professionalism we have at the moment. And it will be without any inconveniences to our contractors, construction sites, our print quality, or the lax in quality of supervision for our staff or customers," I said as cordially as I could manage, attempting to calm the situation somewhat.

"Very well Mr. Aldermon. I expect to be kept informed of your progress in this matter; thank you for coming. Mr. Foster will be with you momentarily," he said cordially. I took the hint and headed for the door and the chopper. I could only imagine the conversation after I left that room. I called Blake and told him I was still alive and he was about to become the new CEO of Foster IND., and that Marrket was to be his exec, if he approved. Steven flew us back to Foster's facility, and then me back to Wilton; home! I was thinking Shay shin would be exhausted, but she became herself as soon as we got home.

"My goodness Charlie, you had me worried for a minute or two. I had no idea you could become so aggressive. But I told you it would come to you," she said with a big smile and kissed me softly.

"I love you Shay shin, I really do baby," I said.

"Charlie; that was the man that came to see me," she said softly.

"Holdin?!" He's the one that's going to die?" I asked.

"Yes," she said quietly. Holy shit! What a bucket of worms that will open up I thought!

Lenin and Leunig, the twins, were going to take more than a little getting used to. I didn't want their chores in the house to interfere with their studies at the college and their upcoming graduation. They already knew how to drive, so I bought them a little SUV they could drive back and forth to school. I made sure both had everything they needed for their studies at home and at the college, including a tutor if they needed one.

I opened a savings and checking account for each of them. I decided to deposit fifteen hundred dollars in each account for each of them each month. I told Shay shin if they needed anything above that, all they had to do was ask. Their manners were impeccably polite, until my bath time! Then their mild mannered illusional pretense turned into a couple of saucy nymphomaniacs, even in the presence of Shay shin. Once in the shower, in Shay shin's presence, I thought I noticed something about her and the twins.

It was the way she was looking at the girls in the shower, but I thought I was keeping this thought to myself for the time being. I told Shay shin, I would preferer to take my morning showers by myself, or I'd never get to work on time. Both girls were excellent cooks and worked as a team in the kitchen, and keeping the entire house immaculate. You would think both of them had OCD issues. If I sat something down in the wrong place, one of them would be right behind me to pick it up and put it 'exactly' where it belonged. They were also emphatically meticulous of the appearance of my hair, suit and shoes before I went to work and the fact I had clean finger nails. When I got home from work, they would undress me, hang up my suit, wash and iron my shirt, and made sure my shoes were clean and shiny for the next morning. There was even an oriental barber that showed up every two weeks in the laundry room, that gave me a straight razor shave, and made sure I didn't have a hair out of place. I thought a lot of what they did was overdone, but like Shay shin, I didn't interfere with what she had obviously instructed them to do.

It was time to start planning the move. Foster's facility had two hundred and twelve people in it. I paid the town council a visit and we talked about a rapid influx of two hundred people and their families. We did some checking with realtors to see how many homes were available and their price ranges. I didn't want the new people to be taken advantage of, and was working on a couple of backup plans. Then we checked on the impact these families would have on the schools, stores, hospital, electrical, gas and water services, and mail service. I was sure there would be glitches here and there I'd have to work out. Anytime you involve 'people' in anything, there always is! I asked Foster when he thought he would like to retire. This guy was slick; he saw right through me.

"Alright Charlie, you have one year from today to do whatever is up your sleeve, and not a day longer," he said slyly. Okay, here we go Charlie! But Foster was still giving orders. The very next morning, the contractor that had built the second helo pad, came in with orders for another pad that would hold six choppers, two hangers and a refueling unit. I'm thinking he picked up a couple of ideas at the PA office. That took about three hours to finalize, and again the contractors workers were there in about an hour to start on the job site. I had our chopper moved to the south corner of the front parking lot to keep it out of harms way. Then I had a conference with Shelly, Blake, and Marrket.

Shelly and Blake were to fly to the Kingston corporation building to ask every individual in person, by name, their preference in moving, and how many owned their own homes. How many lived in apartments, how much they paid a month for their residence, married, married with children, single, medical issues, and anything else that would assist in their placement into the Wilton community. It took almost two weeks for Blake and Shelly to gather the info I wanted. When they got back, we began the correlation of that information. I then had the new drafters start work on my backup plan, a housing tract with seventy five low maintenance homes and one hundred and twenty five apartments. I had Marrket draw up three different lot plans for the housing tract to include electricity, water, gas, sewer, fire hydrons, street lights, a C store, school bus stops, and a corporate shuttle bus that would also stop at Rico's. A dry cleaners and laundromat, and anything else he could think of that the people might need. The rent money would be a small portion of the residents wages they were being paid, and that money would go right back to the corporation. Then a thought came to mind; we were basically building a small town, and I had the perfect name for it; "Fosterville!" I was now thinking the wings on our building had been Foster's secret future plans. I couldn't believe Holdin didn't know what Foster was up to. And now, I too had a secret plan. Two hundred homes that would put company money back into the company. That big field was about to come in handy, and I was going to make good use of it. Then I called the realtor that had showed me my house and asked him if he could stop by the office. When he got there, I took him into the conference room for a little chat and had Shelly and Blake come in there too. David Spencer, the realtor, looked a bit nervous, but held any remarks he might have had.

"Mr. Spencer, how would you like a new job?" I asked with my loaded question. Shelly was taking notes.

"What did you have in mind," he asked quizzically.

"How long have you been a realtor?" I asked flatly.

"Going on twelve years now, I think," he replied quietly.

"You've dealt with a lot of people and a lot of homes in that time I assume?" I said.

"Yes," he replied.

"The job I have open will take someone like you who has delt with homes and people, a manager of a housing tract that will take good care of my people. You will be employed by this corporation; your pay will be set, along with a semiannual bonus, based on the occupants response rating of your care for their needs and homes, some two hundred of them. Because it's quite an endeavor, I don't expect your reply right away, but I'd like to know your thoughts on the issue," I said thoughtfully. He seemed a bit taken back, either by the offer or the size of it, and was thoughtfully silent for about three minutes.

"The rent for these homes is already set; your job would amount to contracting quality maintenance when required, bookkeeping and personally interviewing each and every home or occupancy every three months to insure there are no issues with the homes, none! These are my people, corporation people, and I will not allow them to be screwed over in any fashion," I said flatly.

"When would you like me to start Mr. Aldermon?" he asked quietly.

"I expect the first tenets in six months, so, you let me know when your ready to start and we'll go from there, I said assertively.

"Give me three or four weeks to wrap up this job and I'll be ready," he said.

"Very well, I'll expect to see you then," I said and we stood up and shook hands across the table. As soon as he was out the door, Blake unrolled the three different layout sample drafts of the tract and we went over them.

"Shelly, would you get a hold of the general that did the restaurant and have him come here as soon as he can, please," I said, and went back to the drawings. She was out the door. I called Gibbs and Frank into the conference room to talk about the designs for two hundred homes and what they were for. I asked them to monitor the new guys close and push them along a bit and to quality control their proposals. The general Shelly called, said he could come out tomorrow, and I said that would be fine. Blake went to Rico's and picked up a bunch of sandwiches and sodas for Shelly and the upstairs crew. These guys didn't want to stop what they were doing. Dedication; I love it!

I think Shay shin was starting to trust either me or Shelly a bit more I guess, because she stayed with the girls a little more now.

It was getting close to their graduation, but there might have been more to that too then I was looking at. That damn bear shook her up pretty bad. When the girls go to school she would come to me and I'd take time to make time with her for a few minutes. It is wonderful to have her with me if only for a little while. But she'd be home by the time the girls got there. Their homework is more important to me than the house work, and Shay shin knew that. But still, they made sure I was taken care of in the manner of Shay shin's instructions.

The general contractor showed up the next day and we went over my plans for the housing tract. It was going to be a mammoth job, and I had a time limit to deal with. Then I asked him if he wanted the job. He said 'Yes." Then I asked him how many apartments and how many homes he thought he could have ready for occupancy in six months. He went over the tract layout twice, slowly, then the home and apartment designs carefully. I was very surprised when he said he could have half of each if we used insulated prefab walls with six pitch insulated metal roofing. I told him to do it; and like the restaurant I wanted everything insulated and underground. I took him to the drafters offices and showed him what they presently had finished for the three different homes and two different styles of apartments. Then we went over the tract layouts again. He went over the building plans and the tract layout three times, which made me think something was wrong. Then he backed up against the wall and stared at me.

"You said you had one year to move those people. If you can foot the bill, we can have everything done in a year" he said coldly. I stared at him in disbelief.

"Are you sure?!" I asked almost aggressively in question. And he said "yes."

"I'm going to hold you to that sir!" I said aggressively this time.

"You know my rules, no shortcuts anywhere, no shoddy materials of any kind, and time and safety is of the essence. If you accomplish this project in 'one year' from today sir, you'll be able to retire on your bonus," I said assertively.

"Well, Mr. Aldermon, its going to look like a battlefield out there for about four months, but you have my word, it will be completed to your standards in one year," he said assertively.

The contracts were drawn up, the blueprints were ready and the tract layout was done, and all of it started the very next day! I had two engineers on the site twenty four hours a day, because the general had people working night and day on three shifts, and they never shut down. Ricardo immediately put on a night crew for the workers and was making a mint, a third of which went back into the corporation to fund the housing project. I put another two hundred thousand on Rico's account so he could order enough supplies to keep up with the work crews. Everything but the weather was cooperating, but the general plowed on like it didn't matter. The excavation crews were closely followed by sewer, electrical, water and gas lines, laid deep and insulated.

In three weeks, there where at least four cranes on the site on the southern end of the tract. Then the insulated prefab walls started showing up in a constant flow into the tract, one truck behind the other. Subs too, brought in the windows, doors, roofing, water heaters, central air units, lighting and electrical fixtures, cabinets, and carpets in the same manner. It looked like they were finishing three houses and five apartments every three weeks. The number of workers and equipment was phenomenal. I made sure they had the money and a little extra, to do what was needed to be done, and they too kept that ball of fire rolling. It was time to bring the 'wings' to life!

The taxiway out back now incorporated the other two pads and was complete in three weeks. Then they started on a short runway for the business jet. A second chopper landed out back and we had another pilot. This one was for Blake. Now we each had one. The pace Mr. Foster had set was PDQ, and Blake and I kept that pace rolling. I had Shelly hunt down a business realtor that handled large buildings like the facility in Kingston, and to give them an acceptance time frame of one year. But it didn't take that long to sell. In a month and a half, an outfit out of NYC made an offer of two hundred million for it, and we took it. Apparently Foster or Holdin had leaked the move, or someone in that company knew Foster, and that the facility would be coming on the market very soon, and they grabbed it before it could be advertised.

I put a hundred thousand in Shelly's next paycheck in appreciation for her work. That was almost a mistake, and I had to have Blake rescue me. Damn that woman is persistent! The next task would require a lot of coordination, and the timing had to be on the money.

I had Shelley locate two east coast moving companies with a large fleet of trucks. One that moved people and one that moved material. I situated Blake and Shelly in a hotel in Kingston. Marrket and Lacey would handle the Fosterville end of things. This was going to be tricky and hectic, but the four of them were an aggressive synchronized team! As the homes and apartments became available and in full operation, the coordination of certain people with certain jobs in the Kingston facility were moved to Fosterville. The incoming part of the Kingston operation would be situated in the north wing. The wings turned out to be larger than I thought. I was probably only thinking about one floor in each wing, when in fact there were two floors and a basement in each wing. But the plan came together like it was made to happen that way. In the next six months that flew by, we had half of the Kingston facility situated at our facility and hadn't put a dent on the main floor space in the north wing of our building. The peoples jobs didn't change. Even the arrangement of their desks was the same, only their physical location to this facility had changed. Those with homes were paid top dollar prior to the move. Mr. Spencer, the realtor, stayed right on top of things, making sure the incoming occupants had everything they needed, right down to a cup of coffee that a catering service provided. He also assisted them with community assets and establishments, like schools, medical facilities, churches and specific shopping locations and auto shops. I think I made a good decision putting him in that job when I did. Mail service started right on time because we had notified the postmaster ahead of time, and again as the people moved in. Change of address had been one of Blake and Shelly's tasks.

When the last person was moved from the Kingston facility, and the doors were locked, Blake and Shelly came home with them. They were one happy couple. Not sure why, but I felt a wedding coming on. Another two hundred thousand went to each of their accounts for a job well done. When all was said and done, we were back in full operation a month ahead of schedule and everything was working smooth as silk. The bank wound up hiring five more people just to keep up with our new accounts. A couple weeks prior to that, Mr. Holdin had called Foster.

"Daniel, how the hell do you keep track of Aldermon? He's harder to keep up with than you are. Have you any idea of what that guys accomplished in the last eleven months?

Not to mention he slipped two hundred million plus back into the corporation, along with the flow of rent money from his little project up there in Wilton," he asked Foster.

"Well, sir, I warned you about him. He loves his job and cares about his people, our people! Just don't piss him off. You push your luck or your position in his face and he becomes a bit more than aggressive, as you almost found out in your office. I'm thinking a pat on the back, a raise in his account and paycheck, might show a bit of confidence in his work and worth on your part, don't you think?" Foster said smiling.

"Well, I guess I'm going to have to swallow my pride. He was right ya know, we did get off on the wrong foot, and I'm going to apologize to him in person. How about you and I paying him a visit next week, say Wednesday?" he asked.

"I'd like that," Foster said slyly. And they did. Wednesday morning at about ten a.m., a white executive chopper landed on the pad outback. That could only be one person; Mr. Holdin! And Foster was with him, along with four body guards. Blake and I met them just outside the back door. Mr. Holdin walked right up to me and started speaking.

"Mr. Aldermon, before anything is said, allow me to apologize for my rudeness in our first meeting," he said and put out his hand.

"Accepted," I said and shook his hand, then shook Mr. Foster's hand.

"Gentlemen, welcome to Holdin industries and Fosterville. Yeah, I changed the name on the office building. It seemed more appropriate to the cause. This is Blake Arnold sir, the new CEO of this facility. Beware, he's just as honoree as I am," I said with a chuckle.

"Blake, this is the owner and president of our corporation, and your boss, Mr. Holdin." Then I introduced Mr. Holdin to Shelly.

"As with all men sir, there is the mainstay of a woman behind it all. Mr. Holdin, this is Ms. Shelly Balintyne, the dedicated mainstay of this facility, who was more than a prominent drive in the transformation of the two facilities," I said with pride.

"It is a pleasure to finally meet you young lady. Mr. Foster and Mr. Aldermon speak highly of you always," Holdin said and shook her hand warmly. Shelly blushed and looked a bit shy.

"Blake," I said quietly.

"Sir, allow Shelly and I to take you on a grand tour of our facility and Fosterville," Blake said, and led them on a tour of our operating wing and the hub of the facility. Then we got in two limo's and made a tour of Fosterville.

"I am so honored Charlie," Daniel said as we passed under a large arched sign that said 'Fosterville'.

"This sir, is where almost all the people, our people, that work in this facility live, and their rent, as you know, goes right back into the corporation," I said as we made our way back to the entrance of the tract. Shelly had called Ricardo as soon as the tour in the facility had started. He and several of his waiters were waiting, and met us at the door. I introduced Mr. Holdin to Ricardo. They shook hands and Ricardo escorted us upstairs where six more waiters in uniforms were waiting. The Italian dinner was absolutely fabulous. Once we were situated at our combined tables, I began.

"Mr. Holdin; this Mr. Holdin; this facility, this restaurant and the housing tract; all of this, is what you have accomplished with a little bit of help from the people sitting at this table. It couldn't have been accomplished without each and every one of them. The people that work and live here are your people, they are the corporation. As I said before, without them, you and I are no different than any other man on the street," I said assertively. Holdin bowed his head and was silent for about two minutes then spoke.

"Mr. Aldermon; with foresight, intuitiveness, ingenuity and aggressive guts, you, Mr. Aldermon, created all of this. Outside of the funding, I lay no claim to any of it. I feel inadequate for words to express my appreciation for your dedication and devotion to the people at this table, and the people of this corporation. Thank you; thank you all for your hard work and dedication," he said bowing his head. Shelly and Lacey were in tears and there was a round of applause.

"Now, if you'll forgive me, I must get back to my job before Mr. Aldermon takes that away from me too," he said with a chuckle, and everybody stood and applauded.

Holdin personally found Ricardo and thanked him for the wonderful meal, his service and his management efforts; and gave Ricardo and each of the waiters a hundred dollar bill.

Back at the office building, as Mr. Holdin's chopper lifted off the pad, I felt a proud sense of accomplishment, a pride in everyone that had partaken in the effort to bring this massive task to fruition. Myself, I'm still no more than just a man. A man that had come a long ways from the schoolboy in Olathe Kansas, with a dream and a wish of just becoming a really good architect. I've learned as an architect; I'm only one of the pieces on the chess board. It takes all the pieces and often sacrifices to win the game. I had sacrificed a lot of time away from Shay shin's affection, and it was time to make up for her patients, devotion and a love that kept me going when I thought I was faltering and couldn't go on. As I told Holdin, the driving force of a mans will, is the unseen woman that stands by him through all his trials. I may be the vice president of this massive corporation, but I'm still just a man, and its time to start acting like one! I decided this man needed his woman, the woman I loved so very, very much!

Chapter 8

It was the weekend after everything, the restaurant, the housing tract and the movement of the facility from Kingston. Shay shin and I were sitting in front of the fireplace, holding on to each other like the rest of the world didn't matter. I had to do this! I got down on my knees in front of her.

"Charlie?! Charlie, what are you doing?"

"Shay shin honey, will you marry me?" I asked as gently as I could. There was a very surprised look on her face.

"Charlie, why would you want to marry what I am?" and she changed back to her wispy skeletal apparition. Wow, did she ever look scary! But I didn't care, I loved her with all I am!

"Charlie, is this what you want to call your wife?" she asked with just a tinge of echo. Needless to say, yeah, I was a bit shocked at the sudden change, but even that didn't change how I felt about her.

"Charlie," she said, gently placing her skeletal hands on the cheeks of my face and looking into my eyes.

"We have all of each other that we can, the way we are. Being married will not change any of that. We don't own each other, but I will always be a part of you, and you will always be mine, weather we're married or not," she said so softly, and changed back to the Shay shin I was more familiar with.

"I know you love me very much Charlie. But the license, the vows and the ring can't make us love each other more than we already do, even though it would sound nice to call you my husband.

There are no words to speak of, that I can tell you how much it means to me that you still want me, knowing what I am and what I truly look like. In the realm of death, a living persons feelings such as yours is not uncommon for one such as I, but very rare. But it has, and did happen in another place not far from here. Strange it be, that mortals name was also Charlie!

Lenin and Leunig 'were' your mistresses, but I'm afraid that's as close as you came to having a real wife," she said quietly. Then it hit me!

"What do you mean were?!" I asked, and the phone rang.

"Aldermon," I said.

"Mr. Aldermon, you need to come down to the highway patrol dispatch office sir; I'm afraid there's been a tragic accident sir," he said solemnly. The phone fell out of my hand, my knees buckled and I fell into a chair. I was devastated! Shay shin knew! The twins car had been sideswiped into a deep fast river. They never had a chance. After the funeral, I was still totally devastated and depressed. I didn't feel like doing anything. I could barely move because I felt so heavy with despair. I was going to work but couldn't concentrate on what I was looking at. When I got home there was an indescribable loneliness in the house and me. Shay shin could see my thoughts of what my mind was seeing.

"You are not at fault Charlie; it was an accident. You should go to the attic," she said quietly. But in the attic, something came over my thoughts and the evil of my soul surfaced. At my side, Shay shin looked at me, more than a bit shocked!

"No Charlie," she said frantically.

"You can't do that!" she scolded, grabbing my hand and turning my face to hers.

"This is too powerful for revenge, please don't do this!" she said assertively. But it was too late. The demon of my inner self had been released! The pentagram turned a bright red and a bolt of lightning seared right through the ceiling into the center of the star. That got my attention! When I got back downstairs, something was very different, something very evil now lurked in all my thoughts. I was overcome with hate! And hate begets hate! Then suddenly, I was tightly enveloped in a thick haze that was more than restraining, it was holding me down in one spot.

"I can't allow you to do this Charlie!" came a deep growling echo from Shay shin's apparition. I struggled to free myself to no avail and finally gave up in despair. I felt totally useless, worthless and without the energy to do anything. I had bought them that damn car. They might have still been alive today if I hadn't! They had died because they were in that car, and there wasn't a damn thing this bigshot could do about it!

"Why Shay shin? Why did they have to die?" I asked in despair.

"Look at me Charlie; I was only twelve. My father screamed the same question.

It seems death comes often without reason or timing, but those that live must live, or they too will die in the pain and despair of their emotional agony of the ones lost," she said sorrowfully. The life in our home was gone. I missed their sounds, their attention, their mannerisms and dedication. I was sure I'd never get used to them not being here. It was the better part of two weeks or more before I finally started feeling somewhat normal, if you can call this dreadful feeling normal. But the pain of the twins loss, always brought on my guilt, that I had bought them that car. And then there was the hate for the person that caused the accident that still more than simmered in my mind, and the demon of me would not let go of that. I wanted them to pay with their life for what they had done! *Of the living, when one wants or wishes for something or someone with persistent intent, even of their thoughts, it will come! There's an old saying; "Be careful what you wish for. For always there is a price; and it too shall come!"* When you have what you think you wanted, then what?! Is that what you really wanted? Are you satisfied and ready to pay the price for the want of that wish? Have you ever thought about trying to 'undue' a wish? It is possible, but its not as easy as making that wish. *Wishing is a form of a spell, a hex or a curse; and some spells have repercussions times three.*

It was the end of February with business as usual. Foster had retired to a huge mountain cabin in Montana. A double wedding was planned to come in June for Blake and Shelly, and Marrket and Lacey. I was still down in the dumps about Lenin and Leunig, but I was getting better. I hadn't touched anything in their rooms. In my mind it was like they had just gone somewhere and would be back soon. I was hoping they would somehow come back and everything would be as it was.

It was about four days after Valentines Day, that something in the house changed. It was near the middle of February, but the house seemed much cooler than normal. Wonder what Shay shin was up to? If it hadn't been for her, I probably would have done something really stupid by now. I probably would have hunted down the person responsible for the accident and ….. Then came Shay shin's voice;

"Charlie, I have a surprise for you," she said quietly from the top of the staircase. As I looked up to the top of the stairs, my knees buckled and I went into a mild shock!

"It can't be; they're ….!"All three of them, Lenin, Leunig and Shay shin were in that wispy apparitional form at the top of the stairs!

"Oh my God," I exclaimed, jumping up from the sofa and headed for the stairs excitedly. Then all three of them at the same time, changed into mortal or human form. The two girls hurried down the stairs to the main floor, stopped and bowed, then threw their arms around me. I just reached out and hugged both of them. I didn't know what to say?!

"Shay shin; how, how is this possible?" I asked happily, holding onto both girls.

"They had to 'check in' so to speak, then made their way back here," she said with a smile.

"How is it they can change like you," I asked.

"It took a bit of coaching, but they catch on quickly," she said with a giggle. Now I had three happy ghosts in my house and one bewildered human! That evening, the four of us cuddled in front of the fireplace. The relief to my system of their presence was incredible! They were all here and I was elated! That night all four of us slept in that huge white blanket on the floor in front of the fireplace. But the next morning it was back to the same old routine. The girls fussed over me just as before, making sure I looked like an impeccably dressed business man. I couldn't resist giving them both a hug, then went to Shay shin and kissed her. We were back to being one happy family again, sorta.

My elation must have been clearly visible, because Blake asked what was going on. When I explained it to him, he dropped down in a chair and said;

"Oh my God! That has got to be the scariest house in all of New York!" he said humorously.

"Not really, you should come over for a visit some time," I said.

"Come by yourself though, because if you bring Shelly, she'll see how beautiful all three of them are, and Shelly will never let you come over again," I said with a laugh.

I called Mr. Spencer, my tract manager and asked him to stop by. Then I had the bank cut a million dollar check for the general contractor. We also increased the buying account for Ricardo and gave him a twenty five thousand dollar bonus. We now had more drafters and engineers, but weren't as busy as I thought we would be. I had Shelly look into a worldwide advertisement campaign of a sort. Then it was off to Wilton to check in with the town council. I wanted to find out about the impact we were having in the community, and to see if there were any more prospects available. The council said we had boosted the economy of Wilton considerably.

That there was a guy that owned a bakery just down the street that was calling it quits. I bought the place, put one of his lead employees in charge and kept the rest of his workers employed. Then I did the same thing with a grocery store in the middle of town. I Checked in with the electrical, gas and water companies pertaining to the housing tracts draw on their systems. Everything there was fine. One of the council members asked if we could assist the fire department with a donation to rebuild the old firehouse. I took out my phone and called the general and asked if he had retired yet.

"For you sir, I'd come out of retirement this afternoon," he said.

"When can we meet?" I asked.

"You name the time and place and I'll be there," he replied. I looked at the council member and said;

"We're going to build you a new fire house and update your equipment a bit to make sure we have coverage for the new housing development. I put Blake and Marrket to work on that job. Tristin coordinated with the fire chief of their needs to include the new housing tract and we went from there. But in the back of my mind, something else was brewing, something just a bit bigger! Then I visited the Board of Education while Shelly paid the college a visit to see if there was anything we could do there. I had money to burn and was going to put it to good use. Holdin Industries was becoming a household name in Wilton, and that was fine by me. The places I bought in Wilton all had 'Aldermon' on them, then whatever kind of store or business it was across the front of the building except for the fire station.

After we had helped where we could, I went a bit introvert. I made it a point for Blake, Marrket and Shelly to take the spot light if it was needed. I just kind of guided them along from behind the scenes. Shelly became the colleges prime contact for updating their facility and job placements into our corporation, and for any other facilities in town we acquired. We stretched out into Corinth, and bought several businesses there to keep their people working and that worked out well. We also did the prints for twenty two more buildings there.

My old boss down in the city started putting his nose in places it didn't belong and got mixed up with one of the secretary's, but Holdin fired him before I could get to him. I took Blake and Marrket with me to visit our old office. They were in a mess!

I did the same thing with that office that I did with the Kingston facility, and we came out a million ahead in that deal, with satisfied employees that were moved to Fosterville, which by the way had a new gas station, twenty five new homes and fifty more apartments. The Wilton facility was now pushing two and a half billion dollars a year in business. A large part of that was coming out of California, Denver, Dallas, Vegas, Chicago, and Atlanta. We even received four proposals from Japan.

Then I got a call from Holdin. I knew as soon as I heard his voice this was not going to go well. "Well Mr. Aldermon, I think its time you paid me one last visit. The sooner the better if you please," and he hung up. It was 9:15 am. I called Steven and he came right away. I took Blake and Shelly with me and asked Marrket to hold down the fort. Then I told Steven to push it! When we landed at the main office in PA, we were put straightaway into a limo and driven out to the hospital. This was worse than I thought. This had to be what Shay shin was telling me about. In his hospital room, I went to his side and held his hand. Holdin looked pathetic lying there in that bed. The lawyers had all the paperwork signed and ready on a table. He was barely hanging onto the feeble life he had left. There were two lawyers there, with Holdin's chief CEO, who showed no emotional sentiment to the situation at all; and there were no family members there, not one!

"Charlie, thank you for coming so quickly. I wanted to witness you signing these papers. You are to take complete control of the entire estate of Holdin Industries. You are now the president, and owner of Holdin Ind.!

It's all yours my son," he said feebly. I was shocked! I started signing the papers and the lawyers were stacking them. I was in a daze of distress and disbelief that something like this could happen, even though Shay shin had warned me. I had only just become the VP, and now this!

"Be strong my love, very soon he will join me, but together we will guide you," Shay shin's thoughts came empathetically. Blake was holding Shelly, who was already in tears in anticipation of the coming moments. I signed the last page and went back to his side, and held his hand tightly.

"Its done sir," I said. His feeble hand squeezed mine in a shake then went limp! An instant later, the monitor blared a single steady tone in the quiet room. I couldn't believe this was happening. Why him? Why now? Why me?!

"Be strong my love," again came Shay shin's thoughts.

"Mr. Aldermon, your requests sir," his chief CEO said coldly, seemingly without emotion. I just stared at him blankly. This bastard was cold as ice and all business, but I still wanted to hit him! Shelly came apart in Blake's arms. I was lost for words. But at the moment, a lot of people were depending on me to do something, right now! I needed Shay shin to hold me and tell me everything was going to be alright. For three days we waited, but no family came, not one! How does that saying go, "It's lonely at the top!" We laid Mr. Holdin to rest in the plot next to his wife, and flowered both graves. Foster made it the second day and stayed until it was all over. Still standing at his grave side, Shay shin's thoughts came softly.

"He says thank you for everything," she said softly. Now I had four body guards. Two at my side, and two more and the chief CEO tagging along behind Blake and Shelly. We were taken back to his facility and escorted to Holdin's office, where I asked to be left alone for a few minutes, with Blake and the two bodyguards just outside the door.

"Is he with you Shay shin?" I asked quietly, trying to act like I knew what I was doing, without being obvious.

"Yes Charlie, he's right here," came her thoughts.

"He wants you to sit in his chair and open the middle right hand drawer of his desk. Reach halfway back and push the button on the left side of the drawer wall," she said. So that's what I did. Like some kind of weird robot, a panel rose out of the center of the desk, a large computer screen showing the entire structure of the corporation, it was all there; locations, accounts, CEO's, earnings per location, and on it went.

"Charlie, he says there is a box of thumb drives in the bottom left hand drawer. He wants you to copy everything on the computer to the flash drives, then delete everything on the computer," she said with some urgency. I numbered the thumb drives as I loaded them. It took ten thumb drives to record everything, then I reset the computer to its factory settings and restarted it. It was now in factory configuration and the memory was totally blank. Then she said;

"Now go to the wall directly behind the desk, and take out the book titled 'Bits and Pieces'. The book is a remote.

Halfway inside the book you'll find a button, push it while looking at the floor under the desk," she instructed. I did as she said, and a floor panel under the desk rose and slid towards the front of the desk. There was a safe in the floor there. I wasn't sure I wanted to know what was in that safe, but at the moment I didn't have much of a choice. She gave me the combination to the safe.

"Take everything out of the safe. Double check the safe to make sure it's empty, then put everything from the safe into your briefcase. Close the safe; open the book, and push the button again; then put the book in your briefcase," she said.

"The white helicopter and its pilot are now yours, take them back to Wilton with you. Turn this facility over to my chief CEO for the time being. You can return here at your leisure to examine and do what you think is best for the facility. Now, return to Wilton, and thank you!" Shay shin said; softly, and that was the end of Holdin's instructions, for now. Holdin had to have known about Shay shin, but how! I sure as hell couldn't have found out about all this stuff on my own. The night Shay shin told me about the older man that would join her, it 'was' Holdin; he had had a heart attack! That had to be it!

Blake and Shelly flew back to Wilton in Steven's chopper. My flight back to Wilton that evening in that big white chopper was somber. Still, I needed to think. But the first thing that came to mind is, "Death can arrive in two colors; black or white!" Where the hell did that come from? When we got back to the facility, Blake came to my office door, and for a few seconds I just sat there looking at him, then motioned him to come in.

"Are we in a hell of a mess or what," he asked. I let out a heavy sigh, and for a minute just sat there. I was still lost for words. First Foster retires, then Holdin dies, and the time frame between those two events was only about thirteen months. The entire corporation was on a thread, and I needed to do something, or at least act like I knew what I was doing, and quick, but what?

"I'll let you know in the morning," I said, and patted him on the shoulder as I left my office. I knew what I had to do, and I had to do it now! It's strange how an experience can give you a belief in things I would have never believed in before. But that pentagram has made a believer out of me. It had become the answer to my wishes and prayers of many things.

And that's where I needed to go, right now! As soon as I got home something was different, everything was very formal like. The girls undressed me and helped me into my home clothes, but there was no fooling around. One of them brought me a cup of coffee. Shay shin became visible the instant we came through the kitchen door from the garage, and was watching my eyes and every move I made.

"This is the way of all on this world. Even for the most powerful, death has no mercy. It is the same for rich and poor, young and old. It makes no difference what you have or have not, or who you are. Your choice of advice is correct and should be done now," she said, heading for the staircase, and I followed. We were headed for the attic! But now there were four of us. The two girls sat just behind and to either side of me. Shay shin sat to my left and barely in front of me so she could watch me.

"First Charlie, ask forgiveness for your vengeance of the accident. That must be let go of before any good can come of your wishes. Then think of your situation and assistance needed in its closure," she said watching my eyes and hands. And I did what she said. The star turned a dull red, then went back to black. Then the circle around the star turned a dull red and the shimmer I had seen before crossed over the entire pentagram. Shay shin made a motion with her right hand and every candle in the room lit!

"This is for the guidance Mr. Holdin gave you, Charlie, and your empathy and remorse of his passing," she said quietly. Suddenly his image was right in front of me, but in that wispy mode, but clear as day. He bowed his head for a few seconds, yet without a word, looked into my eyes, then slowly disappeared. Shay shin made another wave of her hand and all the candles went out.

"It will come to you my love," she said softly, taking my hand and we went back downstairs. Downstairs it was back to eating by myself. The girls had made me a wonderful little dinner, and it was delicious. Still my mind was at full throttle. Blake had been pushed into the vice president's spot, with Marrket as CEO of this location. Then I had an idea.

The next morning I asked Marrket to have the chief CEO of Holdin's office to pay me a visit. I assigned two of my bodyguards to Blake. They were getting underfoot, but I wanted to keep them in reach.

About an hour and a half later a black chopper with the corporation logo landed out back, and was met by Marrket, who escorted the chief CEO to my office. I met him at the door and welcomed him in, shaking his hand. This was Donavan McCane. Right at about six foot, a bit baldish with blue eyes. I'm guessing in his late forties. Extremely well dressed, and was accompanied by a bodyguard who stood just outside my door.

"Mr. McCane, thank you for coming. I was a bit overwhelmed the day Mr. Holdin passed and his loss still leaves me awe struck. You would think a man like that should live forever. But his legacy must continue, and that's part of why I asked you to come here. After just becoming VP several months ago, and now, well, it's more than a munges undertaking. I was totally shocked by his choice because I had challenged him once and thought I would lose my job in the process that day. Needless to say, it was not my choice in the matter for this position. Mr. Holdin was a fantastic man in all respects. However, I think you understand the perplexity of the dilemma we have found ourselves in. And therefore, there are a few questions that need to be satisfied in my mind before I state my intentions. First, how long have you worked for Mr. Holdin?" I asked.

"I was transferred from the Kingston facility some eighteen years ago. I became Mr. Holdin's chief CEO ten years ago, to replace the CEO that was relocated to a quality control job at your California office. I've known about you ever since you were hired on down in the city. Mr. Holdin, through Mr. Foster had monitored your work from that point. I believe Mr. Holdin's choice was made when you designed this facility, so it was no real surprise to me that you were his choice. You are very much like him, only a bit more assertive in your methods to take care of your people and the corporation. I have been an architect by profession for twenty two years now. At present, I oversee designs, prints, proposals, and contracts, and disseminate the material coming in and out of three other of your facilities," he said affirmatively.

"I'm responsible for the multi billion dollar accounts for your people, facilities, property and aircraft in Pennsylvania, Florida, Colorado and California," he said quietly.

"And what do you see as your future Mr. McCane?" I asked quietly.

"I'm quite satisfied with my work and location Mr. Aldermon, but I will work wherever you need me to be sir," he said. My thoughts went to Shay shin.

"Tell me what you see of him my dear," I requested of Shay shin with my thoughts.

"He is a business man, though not a people person. He is a good man and truthful of his words. At the moment, he is worried about his family and their home, as you are of our home. He is in fear of your judgement of his position and responsibilities. Like you, he is responsible for, and to a lot of people, many yet unseen by you, yet still in your company. He understands his fate is in your hands, as is the entire company in five states," came her thoughts.

"Thank you Shay shin," I replied.

"Mr. McCane, obviously you have been a trusted employee of a very powerful man that was used to getting what he wanted without rebuttal. I work similarly to him. However, unlike him, I expect your input and ideas. I expect you to challenge my methods, decisions, and my ideas if you think they are incorrect, not beneficial or detrimental to the corporation. The employees of this company are our most important assets, and I expect them to be cared for. Now; very slowly I intend to relieve you of some of your burden of responsibilities, as I move parts of your facility to this location. In time, probably a long time from now, as this facility is much larger, it will become the main headquarters of this corporation. However, you and your family can rest assured there will be no change or relocation of your job, income, or your place of residence. You are now fully in charge of that facility unless, or until I tell you different. Therefore, I believe a substantial raise in pay is in order as well. I expect the same diligence and quality of performance you gave Mr. Holdin, and the customers we serve. You are still the Chief CEO for the four facilities of the corporation you have maintained to this time, and your position will be just under vice president Blake Arnold. As I stated, the changes to come will be minimal for the time being, and slow to come. However, if you see a needed change, please don't hesitate to make it known. Insure the quality of our workmanship to our customers is not hindered in any way by Mr. Holdin's loss. The corporation name and symbol will remain the same for several reasons. I intend to pay you a visit every three months at minimal. My first visit will be in two weeks, at which time I will expect a detailed complete tour of your facility, inside and out, and its people.

Then you and I are going to pay a visit to the other three locations. Now; I would like you to speak your mind and ask any questions you have, including any needs or adjustments we can make to improve our service to the communities, the customers we serve, and the people of this corporation. Also, any concerns you have of me, your position or staff," I concluded. He just sat there for three or four minutes before he said anything. I must have covered pretty much what he was thinking, or those he wasn't prepared for, but that was only an assumption.

"Thank you Mr. Aldermon," he said quietly in relief. He really had been worried about his job, family and home. But then, Shay shin is always correct in her foresight as well.

"If there's nothing else sir, thank you for the invitation, and I guess I'll see you in two weeks," he said, and got out of his chair. Blake and Marrket met us at the door and we all strolled downstairs and out to the pad. We all shook his hand at the back door. His chopper was already running and they lifted off. The sight of that white chopper in the open hanger across the ramp was intimidating as hell. It reminded me of the fear that Holdin put in people. I hoped I wasn't doing the same.

"Blake, do you see me as the likes of Holdin?" I asked.

"You have a hell of a responsibility Charlie, one that I don't believe either one of us saw coming, or ever thought about having in our entire careers. You might say it was dropped in our laps, in a hurry! And you have to remember Charlie, you backed him into a corner with nowhere to go. Obviously, word has got around, but your not like that with other people. He just pushed his authority and you told him what he could do with it," he said quietly. Listening to Blake I got to thinking, I don't want to seem like a tyrant. I just had to stand my ground that day or lose it. Then I had a terrible thought!

"Shay shin; honey was I responsible for Holdin's death?" The length of her silence was not something I wanted to hear. She was thinking of how she was going to sugarcoat this, even if it was the truth.

"Charlie; do not believe you were responsible for his death, any more than that of the twins; you were not! But as a light breeze teeters a feather from a table top, the traces of your anger of the accident, and your first visit with him lingered.

Chapter 9

Still, of your unfulfilled wish, was the assistance to make it final. Through your grievance, empathy and remorse, you have paid the price of that angry wish in full. No more should it be thought of. He has no ill feelings of you, and still stands at your side ready to assist you. The next attack would have killed him even without your assistance, and it was soon to come," she said softly. I took that as a yes, and no matter how trivial my part had been, I still felt guilty as hell. That thing in the attic was nothing to mess with. And still there was a lot more to that stuff I would never understand.

That evening, Blake and Shelly, Marrket and Lacey, and Shay shin and I, along with the twins had dinner at the hotel restaurant. I was thinking this should rid us of the gloom of the last couple of weeks; it might even be comical. Marrket and Lacey had not seen Shay shin or the twins before. I saw no reason for their presence to be kept a secret from them, or anyone else really. I asked Shelly to explain her interpretation of Shay shin's presence in the conference room to Lacey and Marrket. The look on their faces was precious.

"Their ghosts?!" Lacey half whispered. And although Shay shin and the twins did not eat anything, still their conversations with Lacey and Shelly was more than interesting. Lacey was having a hard time believing her eyes. I tried not to get into shop talk, but Blake and Marrket asked about my meeting with McCane. The fact we were now responsible for the facilities in Pennsylvania, Florida, Colorado and California, brought some seriousness to the table. I suddenly felt more than inadequate of my position and title.

I felt my position was no more than a name or title, even though I now owned in total, one of the largest architectural corporations in the United States. The CEO's of these facilities would obviously know more about their local offices and responsibilities than I did, well, at least for the time being. Still there was the question of why Holdin hadn't made McCane the president? That was really starting to bother me. Everything was at his fingertips; the money, property, the control, all of it! With all that he was already responsible for, somehow to me that would have made more sense. And why didn't Foster make him the vice president? This guy had been with the corporation a lot longer than I had. Was I missing something? I mentioned my concerns to Blake and Marrket.

Although it seemed a curious situation, I saw no need for a background check. But there was one thing that kind of stood out just a bit; he was more job than people orientated, which made me a bit nervous. The girls seemed to be having a good time. Shelly was now brave enough to ask Shay shin some of the questions she thought were a bit pointed before. Lacey was curious about a lot of things that ghosts did and could do. To the dismay of Shelly and Lacey, Shay shin and the twins laid it all on the table. I should have been paying more attention, I might have learned something. Then Shay shin asked with her thoughts, if it would be okay with me, if Shelly, Blake, Lacey and Marrket spent the weekend with us? I had no objections, although I was wondering what Shay shin was up to? This could get more than a little spooky. I asked Blake and Marrket what they thought about the idea? They looked at their soon to be wives, who said they would love to. And they did! After Blake told them how majestic the house looked inside, they just had to see it for themselves. Let me tell you, five women in the kitchen is as scary as any apparition. Each one trying to make something they knew would be special for their mates, and at the same time, please the rest of the guests. After dinner was really special! Blake and Marrket made cocktails and we all went down into the sunken living room in front of the fireplace for about an hour. Then Shay shin asked that everyone (us humans) line up across the center of the living room. Then Shay shin and the twins stood about four feet in front of us and it began! When Shay shin had all our attention, she said;

"This is what we really look like!" So as not to scare the bee Jesuses out of anyone, Shay shin and the twins ever so slowly began changing into their normal apparitional form, right in front of us! Their human features slowly peeled away, as they became wispy skeletal floating apparitional forms, from their right to left, one at a time. A breeze seemed to be about them we couldn't feel, and the room noticeably became more than a bit cool.

"Holy shit," fell from Blake, even though he had seen Shay shin in this form once before.

"My god, they really 'are' ghosts!" Lacey whispered, now slightly hiding behind Marrket. Shelly and Marrket were mesmerized, and couldn't believe their eyes. Shay shin sent me her thoughts.

"Shay shin wants you to stand very still," I said, as the three girls moved right 'through' our human forms, then back to being in front of us again.

Then the twins absorbed into Blake and Marrket for a minute or so. Shay shin absorbed into Shelly first, then into Lacey. Then the three were again standing in front of us and changed back into their human or should I say, transmute forms.

"Oh my God! That was incredible," Blake stammered, with Shelly now tightly wrapped around his arm.

"Are you okay honey," Shelly cooed, still holding onto Blake's arm.

"That's how Shay shin can be with me all the time," I said quietly. Then the girls started their conversation on one side of the living room, while the guys traded BS in front of the fireplace. When Shay shin explained the ritual of my shower time to Lacey and Shelly, they both became more than a bit nervous, cause Shay shin didn't sugarcoat anything, and they both totally blushed. Shay shin explained about the difference of American and Oriental cultures and the way Asian women cared for their men and children. Then the responsibilities of her and the twins to me. Their conversations went on until almost one in the morning. Then the twins showed Blake and Shelly to the guest room downstairs. Then took Lacey and Marrket, to one of the rooms upstairs, across the open space between the walkways opposite from the twins rooms. Then it was time for my shower. But this time it was just Shay shin and me. Perfect!

The whole weekend went perfectly, a little strange at times, but perfect. The twins made several oriental dishes our guests just loved. To the dismay of Shelly and Lacey, the twins offered to give Blake and Marrket a special shower. Of course both guys had no problem with the offer, but Lacey and Shelly said "hell no!" Shay shin and I laughed so hard. From then on, the twins were totally off limits to Blake and Marrket.

"Shay shin, how can you allow those two young girls to be alone with Charlie in the shower? You don't know what they do with, or to him!" Shelly said assertively and more than a bit excited. Shay shin just smiled mischievously.

"I know exactly what they do with, and to him! They do whatever it takes to please his lustful animalistic desires. I also know Charlie is pleased with them, but that he loves only me, and that he shares that love with no one else, not even the twins.

He is their Lord and master, and if you watch carefully, you will see how they honor him. I will not interfere with their duties as maids and mistresses. There is a difference between sex and love. Charlie has sex with them, but loves only me. Is your love for Blake and Marrket not that strong?" Shay shin asked Shelly.

"Those two young girls could easily take our men from us, no matter how much we love them," Shelly said, now a bit aggressively.

"Not if the twins have no intention to, and your husbands truly love you," Shay shin said slyly. Shay shin could teach Shelly a lot about real love, but our society and culture is so different from theirs, and we think about love and sex differently than they do. It would take more trust than we allow ourselves or each other. Jealousy and love don't mix no matter how strong our love is. If the twins did in fact decide to love those two guys, they wouldn't need a shower to prove it! All they would have to do is stand in one spot, and their eyes and a very slight movement of their hips would cause a meltdown of someone's heart! Then I got to thinking about all of us being in that massive bathtub at one time. That would have been hilarious! It happened several times to me when I was doing my studies in Japan. It took some getting used to, but after awhile it seemed quite natural. Our little group broke up Sunday night to be ready for work Monday morning. The twins gave me my shower that night, then it was off to the love of my life. In her arms there was no question in my mind of who I really loved!

126

Marrket was now the CEO of the Wilton facility. I don't like to micro manage, but it was too soon to totally let go of the things that I had started. I had him get in touch with Mr. Spencer to see if we were having any issues with housing or the people adjusting to the area. I had two of the engineers go out to the tract and physically check the structural integrity of every single building. I also had Marrket look into acquiring the massive field on the west side of Hwy 87. Something had come to me out of the blue. I knew as soon as it came to me I was going to make it happen. In my mind things were moving so quickly I could already see it. Two housing tracts with their own support units, and the office building. We were in fact going to wind up with a whole new little town!

Blake was making plans and reservations with McCane for our upcoming visits to the other three facilities. This trip was mostly for my benefit, to learn and understand the differences of each facility. Their locations were also interesting. I spent a lot of time going over the thumb drives I got from Holdin's computer to learn what I could from them.

Then because of my new wealth, I naturally attracted a few politicians wanting to know where I stood in the political arena, but they were only interested in the money. Why would I take sides with people that can't see eye to eye to help our own country, and don't do what they were voted into office to do? I needed to keep Holdin's legacy in tact and that's exactly what I'm going to do.

The next six weeks were a bit hectic, bouncing from place to place in hotels and that little jet. We did some upgrading in some of the facilities and downgrading in other parts of them; but still maintained their locations. They were right where they needed to be. They were like three interlocked spiderwebs with connections all over the United States. Then it was time to take some of the pressure off McCane. Why that sneaky old man! That's when I thought I'd caught on to Foster's plan for the second wing! But in fact, the building I designed was Holdin's idea, not Foster! I moved four of McCane's drafters, two of his engineers, one of his accountants, three admin people and a secretary to the top floor of the South wing in the Wilton facility. They would handle inbound proposals and prints for new office buildings coming in from the other three facilities. The movement of any of McCane's operation would be into the south wing. Even though I was trying to move slowly, things were going to seem to be happening pretty fast in different places. I had McCane change the input addresses from the facilities in Florida and California, from his facility to the Wilton facility, and the ball kept rolling.

I had Blake get a hold of the general that did our Fosterville housing tract, to find out if he was willing to start another one just like it, even before the fire station was finished, or if he could do both at the same time. Then I asked Ricardo to pay me a visit. Then I asked Marrket to check on the progress of the Wilton fire house and asked him to double its size and equipment, and to have the fire chief start training people to man it. I didn't want to put any pressure on the mayor of Wilton, but I needed to be sure we had enough protection for Wilton, as well as the two housing tracts. Ricardo came in at about 10:30 the next morning.

"Whata I can do you for boss," he asked in his jolly manner.

"Rico, can you supervise another restaurant just like the one you have now; you know, two of them at the same time? You can put someone in charge of each of them, and you can be in charge over both of them," I said. He was very surprised at the question, and sat there thinking about it.

"I'm a pretty sure I can do that. Why, you a gotta another one hiding someplace?" he asked.

"Not yet, but I'm thinking real hard about it," I said.

"You should probably start training the two people to be in charge, because it's going to happen in about six months I'm thinking," I said.

"Okay boss; you let me know, I'll be ready," he said, stood up and he shook my hand, and left. My cell phone rang;

"Aldermon," I said.

"Mr. Aldermon, McCane here. Sir, do we have policy or proposal concerns regarding the San Andres?" he asked. Obviously the California facility was asking.

"The 'design' of a structure knowingly to be placed within ten miles of either side of that fault, or any other, would be a concern. The customer should notify our designers, engineers and drafters of the proximity of a fault or fracture. If a structure is to be placed within that proximity and it is not mentioned in the proposal, and the structure fails, the customer would be held liable for the failure and fatalities of that structure. So yes, we would have a concern," I said.

"Thank you sir, that's exactly what I needed to know," he said, and hung up. This got me to thinking. Mother nature has her own ideas of where things should be, and for how long she will allow them to remain there.

No matter how sturdy or strong or flexible a structure is, a tornado, tsunami or earthquake can quickly make all your efforts of design worthless, no matter how good an architect or engineer you are, or the precautions that are taken. Once in a science class, I was asked where on the continental US could you live and not have to be concerned about the wrath of nature? Of course the answer is 'nowhere!' Here, we design structures based on existing climatology and geological statistics for the areas requested.

We use the latest technology and the strongest flexible material known to man. But let's face it, if you put up a tent anywhere on this planet, your taking your chances! If it's not Her wrath, its her pets or some human asshole with an entitlement! My cell phone rang.

"Aldermon," I said. It was Blake.

"Charlie, they want a half a mil for that property the other side of 87; what do you think?" he asked.

"I have no problem with that. Be sure all the rights are included, then have Marrket and Lacey slowly start the drill we used on the Kingston move. I'd like that tract to be an exact replica of Fosterville, and I'm thinking it will be ready in a year and a half, but I don't want anyone moved until I give you the word. Something else may be in the works," I told him.

"You do realize your going to have a lot of wide open space to the west of that tract don't you?" he said with a bit of a chuckle.

"Not as much as you think Blake. Your about to become a very busy man my friend. Finalize that deal with the property and let me know when you have the title in the safe, then come to my office," I said. He said "okay," and hung up. My mind was in overdrive and I couldn't seem to slow it down. I needed to talk to the mayor of Wilton, this was going to have a hell of an impact on his town. Then I needed to pay the Department of Transportation a visit. I wanted an overpass between the two tracts over Highway 87, and I wanted that road to extend into that open space Blake was talking about. I was also thinking about the railroad company. I wanted a couple of railroad spurs out of Wilton for produce and products for a strip mall, and fuel for the aircraft and maybe the two gas stations. Then there was a water tower for the new town of Holdin Ind.! Maybe a hospital, a small airport with a short runway for business and medical flights. The pace of my mind was absolutely insane, and then it stopped, and my mind went blank!

I only knew of one way that could happen; Shay shin! Whisper soft, and as delicate as a feather came Shay shin's calming voice with an echo. That meant she was at the house, and that one of the twins was with me. If she wanted me there, it was important. *So* important *it would change my life forever!*

"Charlie…., come my dear," she said. I called Marrket and told him I was headed for the house if he needed me. It was more than unusual for Shay shin to do this, but I didn't hesitate. As I pulled into the driveway, the garage door rotated open; I hadn't touched the remote! Caution came to my senses, and I pulled my .32. The door opened just as I reached for the doorknob. "Shay shin," I thought. "In the living room my dear," came her reply. I put the .32 back in its holster.

She was in the oriental living room, in her apparitional form, but she wasn't alone! To her right was another apparition. It too had that wispy skeletal form, but it was all in white.

"Charlie, this is my friend I lin. She came to me this morning and gave me some insight to your endeavors. Her love too is named Charlie. I needed to slow your thoughts that you clearly hear my words and understand their meanings. You have asked yourself several times since I've known you, "how can this be happening to me?" The answer is within your heart and mind. Long ago when you were just an architect, you made a wish of three parts. To fall in love with an oriental girl, to be prospers and to advance in your profession. All of which you have accomplished. Do you remember that wish my love?" she asked softly.

"Yes, I remember," I said curiously.

"Yet of all your wish, only of the living was of your request. I believed I could be part of that wish, but it was not of my place or decision to make that choice," she said as I interrupted her as I caught an implication of what was going on.

"Shay shin, don't you dare tell me your going to leave me! Don't even think about it! I can't live without you Shay shin!" I said a bit more than assertively, and my anxiety level started climbing fast! I lin looked at Shay shin, took her hand and held it tightly.

"Charlie; your about to find me in another. I am the part of your wish that has truly not been fulfilled. I am the cause of that wish not being fulfilled. I beg of you, be patient with me as you have been thus far, and with what I must do to correct the situation to bring your wish to fruition," she said, and I came unwound!

"No! I won't let you do this Shay shin! To hell with the wish! I could never love anyone as much as I love you. I won't do it!

No! Leave things alone, leave things the way they are; change the wish, but I don't want to live without you!" I said aggressively. I lin took Shay shin's hand and held it with both her hands.

"Charlie, this is exactly how I lin's Charlie was lost to her love. He passed in her arms. Please, allow me to correct this mistake. I promise you will be happy and content with the outcome as I will be. Please Charlie, please do as I ask," she begged. Suddenly I hated me and everything I stood for. I'd give it all up, the corporation, our home, even my life to keep her!

"Charlie, please do as I ask, come to my grave, now! Please!" she said softly. With a heavy sigh and more than a bit pissed at the situation and myself, I stomped out to the garage and got in the car. This was ridiculous and insane! Still, I followed her instructions and drove to the cemetery where she was buried. In the cemetery, she guided me to her grave. Looking down at her picture on the headstone, I couldn't help it. My knees buckled and I collapsed. My emotions came apart. I started sobbing and cried out of control! Why? Why did she have to die? Why cant we just be the way we are? My God Shay shin I love you!! You can't leave me! Then I caught a whiff of Shay shin's sandalwood perfume, and heard her say;

"She was only twelve years old." I turned to look at Shay shin and got a hell of a shock! The girl standing just behind me was 'almost' an identical twin to Shay shin, but it wasn't her! This was a real woman, one that had the identical voice and features of Shay shin. Had Shay shin taken on another form? It became hard to breathe.

"My father told me to come here to see her, that joy comes of pain, and life comes of death. Did you know my sister?" she asked in a voice that was definitely Shay shin! I was still stunned and sobbing behind a wall of tears. I couldn't speak, and it was still hard to breathe! What was I supposed to say? I was staring at a living, breathing replica of Shay shin! This was no ghost!

"Ah, sorta, I guess you could say," I said through a wall of tears.

"Do you have a car?" I asked getting to my feet, wiping my face with a handkerchief.

"No, my friends brought me here," she said turning sideways so that I could see past her as she pointed. Next to a car at the curb were two girls standing side by side. My knees buckled again, and I fell to the ground!

Another set of second generation American Chinese identical twins, dressed in identical school uniforms, came running toward us. They took my arms and brought me to my feet. The shock was complete! I asked Shay shin's twin what her name was?

"My name is Mai Lin," she said softly, bowing her head a bit.

"Mai Lin, you and your friends need to follow me. I want to show you something your father did," I said, and headed for my car. Don't think Charlie, just keep moving! Don't think, just do! Things are confusing enough without you trying to explain something to yourself you know nothing about! They did as I asked, and followed me back to the house. They pulled into the driveway next to my car. When I got out of the car, my body was shaking as I stood next to Mai Lin, and took a deep breath.

"Mai Lin, this is the house your father built; this is where your sister died, and this is where I live, with the "ghosts" of your sister, and two of her friends, another set of twins! Do you understand what I just said?!" I asked. There, I said it. I wasn't even sure Shay shin and the twins would show themselves, but I had to tell her sister this just in case.

"Yes, I understand," she said, but it sounded like a question.

"There is nothing to be afraid of. Please, come in," I said and led them to the front door.

"My father has a picture of this house in an album. I was sixteen when they came to America. I stayed in China helping to care for my grandmother while my father built this house," Mai Lin said. That explained the size of the house; he was going to bring the rest of his family here. I took Mai Lin and the twins on a detailed tour of the house. Their remarks were the same as Blakes; "Wow!" in every room. Then I asked them to be seated down on the lower level of the sunken living room with the fireplace. Then with my thoughts, I asked Shay shin if she would become visible, but there was no reply, only a very light breeze that brought a trace of her sandalwood perfume and the coolness that always accompanied her apparition. She was there, but said nothing. Mai Lin looked at me questionably.

"Does your whole family live here?" Mai Lin asked, drawing my attention back to her.

"No, its just me and the ghosts for the time being. But because of the size of the house, I think your father planned on bringing your grandmother and a few more relatives here too," I said.

"It's a very big house for only one person. Do your maids live here too? Mai Lin asked. Where had I heard that before?

"Maids? No, I have no maids, its just me and the ghosts," I said. The three of them looked at each other questionably, like I had said something odd.

"Sir, the reason I asked the question is, there seems to be the distinct scent of a special kind of sandalwood perfume that comes only from China, throughout the house wherever we go. Have you recently had visitors from there?" she asked. Why did I suddenly have goosebumps all over me?

"No. That scent has been in the house since the day I moved in, and becomes stronger when the ghost of your sister Shay shin that I told you about is near. The air is also cooler when they are near," I replied.

"Would you excuse us for a minute," Mai Lin said, and the three of them moved a short distance away, and started a conversation in Chinese that went on for about twenty five minutes. Then Mai Lin turned and stepped to just in front of me. Why did I know exactly what she was about to say?

"Sir, I'm sorry, I don't know your name, but my friends and I were just discussing the situation of you not having someone to care for you and your home. That's not how things are done where we come from. If it pleases you, the three of us would like the opportunity to care for you and your home. Our cost will be up to you. We were also wondering if we could live here, using our payment of labor as rent money," Mai Lin said, then looked at the floor. Yup, that's what I thought she was going to say! I also knew Shay shin and the twins were still in the house, and somehow were having more than something to do with what was going on.

"Shay shin, what am I supposed to do with them honey? Say something or do something! I don't trust my own judgement here. What am I supposed to do about this?" my thoughts went to her. Her reply was strange, but logical. It was the three girls that felt the coolness and got a lot more than a trace of Shay shin's perfume. The three of them became calm and still as if Shay shin was speaking to them. Then Mai Lin spoke.

"Sir, I think my sisters essence is here with us!" Mai Lin said with just a tinge of fear in her voice, as the three of them huddled a bit closer to each other and began looking all around the room.

"My name is Charles Aldermon, and yes they are here. They are not regular ghosts, but trust me, if they didn't want you here, you would have known it by now.

I'm sure when the time is right, they will more than show themselves to you in one form or another, and they too speak your language," I said, trying to keep the conversation lighthearted. But the gnaw of Sha shin leaving me was still heavy on me. There was another quick conversation between the girls in Chinese with a bit of panic thrown in, and still they would look around the room, then back at me.

"Are you sure you still want the job?" I asked. They looked at each other and the twins said something to Mai Lin.

"Yes, we still want the job, if your ghosts approve of course," Mai Lin said, still with a bit of fear in her eyes and voice.

"Mai Lin, they are not my ghosts! The trace of sandalwood is from your sister Shay shin, the other two are a set of twins, Lenin Tao and Leunig Tao. By the way, may I ask your names?" I asked the twins.

"My name is Sue yin," the first one said and bowed. "And I am Lou chin," the second one said and bowed. That one had some strange eyes! That was simple enough; now I just had to figure out how to tell them apart?!

"May I call you Sue and Lou," I asked, and they said "yes," with a gorgeous smile that could melt your heart. Here we go again, I thought! Don't I have enough problems with females?

"Alright, Sue, you can have one of the two rooms over the master bedroom; Lou, the one next to Sue's room is yours. Mai Lin, you will be in charge of the house and your room will be the guest room downstairs. None of you will pay any 'rent'. Taking care of this house is a big enough job by itself. The sooner you move in, the sooner things will become normal, sorta. But there is something I have to show you first," I said assertively. I took Mai Lin and the twins into the kitchen, and to the backdoor. I explained about the bears and the electric fence. Then I showed them the gun, and explained it to them. I had each of them fire three shots in the back yard. Then I showed them how, then had them reload the gun. Then I took Mai Lin to the front door and showed her the office building where I work. I put my phone number on her phone and gave her a credit card for shopping.

I told her to get a car with that card as well. The look she gave me said it all.

"Yes, you can use this card for "anything" you or the girls need or want, including a car. Call me if you have any problems or questions about anything at all. I'm usually home about six o'clock or so, but right now I have to get back to work," I said. She looked so much like Shay shin, I found myself wanting to kiss her before I left; this is so unreal! But somehow I was going to have to make myself deal with it. Whatever Shay shin said, she meant, and that was the scary part!

I got in the car and headed back to the office. I could only imagine what was about to take place in that house, and it did! Boy did it ever! I had told Mai Lin how to tell if Shay shin and the twins were near by, so when they came it wasn't a complete surprise, and they came!

Shay shin came to them invisibly first, then verbally, and asked that the three girls sit in the oriental living room. Shay shin told the girls not to fear what they were about to see, as scary as it might seem. Then Shay shin and the twins slowly presented themselves. First in their apparitional form, then in their transmute human forms. Although Shay shin was the younger sister of Mai Lin, she spoke with authority. At first there was a bit of emotional joy between the two sisters, of the time they had not seen each other. Then came a formal discussion about the job. Most of it was about the house and its care. Then came who did what with who, (including each other) and where and how that would take place! This included Charlie's shower and bed. Shay shin had the new twins move into the old twins rooms. Everything in those two rooms now belonged to the new twins. Mai Lin was (for a short time) moved into the guest room upstairs, across from the twins rooms, and just above the master bedroom. Shay shin was contemplating future events, and had logical reasons and foresight for the moves. Not until the girls accepted the job, and the moves were complete, did Shay shin again sit the girls down and explain who Charlie was, what he did, and his worth. The three were more than a bit shocked! Of their way of thinking, Charlie was like a king. Shay shin brought on that "Master, Lord" stuff; the customs of their culture, respect and loyalty; their protocol and instructions of who did what with Charlie, in different places within the house, at the office, and restaurants. (*All that stuff made me nervous, because some of it was quite formal. Here I am trying to tell people I'm just a regular guy, and she makes me out like I'm some kind of royalty.*)

135

She explained Charlie's body guards; their reason and purpose, and why they seemed to always be there. Then she explained Blake, Shelly, Marrket and Lacey, and women that made it a point to become more than friendly with Charlie and why. She told them about Rico and his restaurant, the hotel restaurant and the waitresses there.

Then came the menus for the four humans, cooking, shopping, cleaning, and care of the house, and the timing of what happened when. *(It was going to be strange to see them eating.)* Then came the protocol of guests, other men, and especially 'if' Charlie brought home a female guest, alone! Then came Charlie's care! It was still according to their cultural customs, and that included Charlie's complete attire before going to work, his home clothes when he got off work, and his haircuts. Then came the methodical intricacies of Charlie's showers and baths, and their purpose of other than to get him clean! Then Shay shin assigned Mai Lin's taskings. If she and the twins accepted this job, without question or choice, Mai Lin was to become Charlie's mistress and of a time, his wife! (It would have been nice if I had been warned about this one). That she would be in charge of the caring of Charlie's emotions, passions and affection, and that the twins would care for Charlie's lustful sensual desires, but 'only' in the shower and bath. Mai Lin was to be the governess in charge of the house and its care. Basically, Mai Lin and the new twins were to take the place of Shay shin and the other set of twins in every detail. Then Shay shin asked them if they still wanted the job. The three looked at each other, but there was no hesitation, and they said "yes!" Shay shin then took the three girls into the attic, and they spent about three hours up there. Of course Shay shin didn't mention any of this to me. I was to find out all this stuff on my own over time.

That evening when I got home, as I went through the kitchen, things were very different from when I left. First there was the smell of real food, not a tv dinner, and it smelled delicious, and the timing was perfect. But the twins were waiting in my bedroom in the exact same sheer silk robes the other twins had wore for this occasion, along with the distinct scent of sandalwood. That meant Shay shin was there to make sure things happened somewhat in the way she wanted them to. But there was something different about these twins! Things in fact began happening exactly as they used to, almost! These twins undressed me, and their teasing started right there!

Their hands were all over me as they escorted me into the shower. But they didn't drop their robes onto the little bench as the other twins had done! These girls emphatically used those robes to entice and torment my mind out of control. It became obvious Lou chin was the controller of the two. Under the gentle spray of water, Lou chin, still in her robe, stepped barely in front of me and under the water! The sheer wet material of the robe took on a whole new design! Then Sue yin, still in her robe, stepped into the rain like water just behind and against Lou chin, her lips on Lou chin's neck, just below her ear, and her palms caressed Lou chin's shoulders. At this point I was almost out of control, and what happened next didn't help. Sue yin's palms slid ever so slowly down over Lou chin's sheer wet robe and cupped Lou chin's breasts, then parted Lou chin's robe. Holy shit; I lost it!

These girls were even more enticing than the first twins. Both of them guided my hands over their bodies making absolutely sure I saw, felt and touched, every mound, crevasse and curve on them. That my hands followed the liquid flowing movements of their bodies, that were absolutely perfect! Lou chin's arms wrapped around my waist, her palms and finger tips exploring every part of my body. These two didn't miss a thing, absolutely nothing! But there was something a little different about these twins; their eyes were green! Wickedly beautiful! But it was the way they looked at you that more than held your attention! It was like they could talk to each other using no more than their eyes. Tauntingly wicked and naughty, with more than a seductive begging come on, Lou chin drew me deep into those green eyes. In the shower she had no morals; none what so ever! She would wrap her legs around my waist and her arms around my neck, and kiss me, tormenting my thoughts and body like a wild bucking animal, offering more than I could give or take. She was more animalistic than Shay shin or Shelly had ever been. It seemed she was making a play to steal Mai Lin's thunder and passion. In the shower, they more than added to the seductive instructions of Shay shin, and she was letting them run with it. Their hands and bodies moved over my body like a team. How was I ever going to survive this?

When they finally got me into my home clothes and ready for dinner, I was a bit dizzy, weak and barely able to walk. Okay, what happened to my blue jeans, t-shirt and tenies? There had been an upgrade to my wardrobe. I looked like I was going out to play golf.

The twins had already prepared my clothes and shoes for the next morning. Then came dinner. You should have seen the look on Mai Lin's face when the twins escorted me into the dining room. I was starting to think she was as much mischief as the twins. How was I ever going to survive this night? This was all Shay shin's doing, I could tell! I was formally placed at one end of the table, and Mai Lin at the other end, with one of the twins on either side of the table in their place of honor. I'm never going to get used to this, and I hope I never take it for granted!

That night just after I went to bed, she came! She was a shadow standing in the doorway with the night lights behind her. It was Mai Lin in a very sheer white gown that was open down the middle. I was out of that bed in a heartbeat! She was now only about two feet in front of me when she looked up at me; something looked very....different! Even in the dim light I saw her eyes, just as the silky gown slid in slow motion from her shoulders to the floor. It was Shay shin! But not; I lost it!

"Shay shin said I should offer myself to you, if you think I am worthy. I'm yours if you want me Charlie," she said softly. Shay shin had said those exact words. Gently I picked Mai Lin up and laid her on the bed.

"This is where you will sleep from now on Mai Lin," I said. She was delicate, tender, and passionate; for the first thirty minutes or so; then something changed! She became assertive, then aggressive, then animalistic! Yup, this was definitely Shay shin! But how? We had made love just as before, and now we were going to have sex! This was part of what I had wished for a long time ago. But something was terribly wrong! What the hell was I doing? My lustful wants and gratification had been satisfied to an unimaginable extent by the twins, but something was missing! The tender loving arms of my loving Shay shin! I still loved Shay shin with my entire being! This affair with Mai Lin and the twins was not going to work! But how could I tell Mai Lin that without upsetting Shay shin? Although Mai Lin and I slept peacefully, still I longed for that special feeling only Shay shin could provide. Not to mention a heaviness that I'd been dragging around because I couldn't reach her. I know she wants me to get used to Mai Lin and fall in love with her, but it wasn't working! Mai Lin was the spitting image of Shay shin, with an innocence Shay shin had already gone through long ago. I knew Shay shin was still in the house somewhere, I was sure of it!

And somehow, I was also sure she was having more than something to do with having Mai Lin take her place. But this was a living human angel, a real woman I would have to teach the real world to. But first I had to teach myself to love Mai Lin, and I was pretty sure that wasn't going to happen, as good as Shay shin and Mai Lin's intentions were.

The next afternoon at work, I got a call from a Mercedes dealership in Corinth, about Mai Lin using my credit card. I told him it was all good, that I had told her to do so. He said Mai Lin wanted a car like mine, but he had no idea what I had. He said she just pointed at one of the cars and said that's the one she wanted. I told the guy the make, model and color of my car, and to make sure she got the top of the line, with all the bells, whistles, and cameras. And to be sure it had all the maintenance and mileage coverage they had to offer, and to put the title in her name. Also, to make sure she had the registration, and that the actual plates were on the vehicle before it left the lot. Then I gave him the insurance policy I wanted her under before she drove off the lot. I told him if there was any more questions at all about the transaction or the car, to call me back. He said "Yes sir." Then asked;

"Mr. Aldermon, what about bulletproof windows, driver and passenger doors and tires," and I said yes. I told him to give her a nice rental car until hers was ready, and to have the new car delivered to the house, then we hung up. About an hour later I got a call from Mai Lin, and she sounded like she was crying.

"Hello Mr. Aldermon; This is Mai Lin," she sobbed.

"I bought a car like you said. It's one just like yours, but they won't give it to me. They said they had to do something to it and gave me another car. The man said to drive that one until mine was ready. What am I suppose to do Mr. Aldermon?" she said brokenhearted and sad. I fell right into it! I wanted to call her honey or baby, and oh how I wanted to crawl through that phone and hold her in my arms, and tell her everything was going to be alright. I missed Shay shin's foresight; hell, I missed Shay shin period! And every time I looked at Mai Lin, I was seeing Shay shin!

"Mai Lin, you can call me Charlie. They're going to deliver your car to the house as soon as they have done what I asked them to do to it. Just be patient, it'll be all right; you'll have your new car pretty soon," I said. God she sounded pathetic.

It was three weeks before her new car showed up out in front of the house and they hauled off her rental car. Mai Lin was one very excited and happy young lady! Even if she didn't know how special that car was.

I remember the first time I told Blake about Shay shin. Wait till he sees Mai Lin, Lou chin and Sue yin," the twins! These were real live seductive looking, huggable females! But the way these girls gently moved their perfect bodies; and those eyes; oh my! And then there's the way they put their hands behind their backs, tilted their head forward just a bit and looked up at you. Their eyes drew you to them, as they toyed with your mind, heart and soul, not to mention your anatomy. Then there is their dainty like voice of an angel, that comes from lips that make it hard to breathe, because you want to kiss them forever, but you're too weak to move. Not to mention you suddenly can't think of anything else, because you're thinking you know the potential possibilities of what could be! Shelly and Lacey were going to have their hands full, big time! Wonder how Blake and Marrket are going to deal with these two?! But I too had a few surprises coming. Shay shin wasn't through with me, not yet; and neither was Holdin!

That week, Blake, McCane and I, got on that little jet and made an unscheduled visit to the facility in Florida. I was curious about how our structures were holding up to the hurricanes, their locations, and who was designing those structures? Then it was off to the California facility. There were several things that concerned me there. Locations specifically, because of eroding hillsides along the ocean front, mudslides, wildfires and of course earthquakes along the SAF corridor and Walkers Lane. Holdin had limited our structures in California to twelve stories, based on the substrata, and the substructures of our designs and their locations.

When we finally got back to the Wilton office, I did my rounds with Blake and Shelly, through both wings and the center section of the facility. Then we went outside. The progress across 87 looked like a battlefield. There were a line of drop decks crawling towards the cranes that were installing prefab walls for the homes and apartments. There could be an easy three or four hundred workers over the tract doing different jobs. The DOT too was making a special effort to put the overpass in place. Steel girders were already set in concrete over 87.

I could also see where the new restaurant was going to be; that too was a busy site. The weather was finally starting to cooperate as well, so things seemed to be moving along a little smoother. It was almost time for Marrket and Lacey to go to the PA facility to collect information from the staff and workers that would be moved to Wilton, so the move could begin on schedule.

But first there was something else I had to do. I asked Blake, Shelly, Marrket and Lacey to meet me in the conference room. They already knew about the three ghosts in my house, about Shay shin and the passing of the twins, so when we were in the conference room, I explained the strangeness of how my 'new' family had come about. I wanted them to meet Mai Lin, Sue yin and Lou chin, the new twins. I asked them to join us at the hotel restaurant that evening at six thirty. I called Mai Lin and told her not to make anything for dinner, that we were going to have dinner that evening at the hotel restaurant. When the three of them came down those stairs, I couldn't believe how absolutely seductively stunning they looked! They all wore the high collar traditional silk Chinese form fitting dresses. Short as they were, they were slit up the left side to where the panty line should have been. Mai Lin's dress was yellow, outlined in red and sparsely decorated in embroidered flowers, as was Sue yin's burgundy dress and Lou chin's dark red dress. The girls wore no makeup, and they sure didn't need any, and neither of the twins were wearing a bra.

There was now a car in front of mine and one behind it, my bodyguards! There were two other cars distant from us. I didn't like the idea of the limo, it seemed too flashy.

Still, billionaires have to take precautions. Two of the guards went in first, up to our private dining room where Blake and Shelly, Marrket and Lacey were already sitting in their assigned places at the table, opposite of each other, with Blake and Marrket closer to the head of the table. The table was now a bit wider as Mai Lin would be sitting next to me. I also insisted on a single chair at the other end of the table to be left open, as well as the two chairs closest to Mai Lin and I. So I'm a little old fashioned, or superstitious, or maybe something else. Blake and Marrket stood up as my little troupe was escorted to the table by the hotel manager. Even after Mai Lin and I were seated, my two cohorts, Blake and Marrket, were still standing there with their mouths open. Their wives too, seemed more than a bit in shock.

"Ladies and gentlemen, I would like to introduce you to my new family. This is Mai Lin, Shay shin's older sister, the lady of the house. And I hope I get this right; this is Sue yin, and Lou chin," I said gesturing to Mai Lin and the girls. These twins looked different from the other set of twins; more enticing, delicate and alluring, especially their eyes! But Mai Lin was 'almost' the spitting image of Shay shin, and that's what held everyone's attention for the moment. Blake and Marrket didn't say a word, it was safer that way, at least for the moment. All they could do was stare. First at Mai Lin, then at the twins. Come on guys, you have enough trouble sitting right next to you!

"Their all so beautiful," came Shelly's first comment. The twins eyes passed first across Shelly, and then Lacey, and you could tell something happened there. Their eyes alone could literally drain your soul. Shay shin had warned the twins about flirting with Blake and Marrket, and they did not look at them at first. Still, Lacey caught sight of Lou chin's simple glance at Marrket and was already fidgeting. Lacey laced her arm into Marrket's a bit tighter, who was sitting next to Sue yin, and facing Lou chin. Lou chin seemed to be conversing with Sue yin with her eyes; they were up to something! The twins were also wearing a mistic oriental perfume that acted like a tranquilizer to Blake's and Marrket's brains that were already unraveling. This was going to get complicated real quick! Where the hell was the brake pedal?

The head waiter was ready to take our orders. Our table in the secluded little nook upstairs had four other waiters as well, that had also become infatuated with the twins. To keep things simple, we ordered steak, lobster, scallops, and sides of shrimp, with wine for everyone. The wine came first. For some reason, Lacey now seemed terrified of Lou chin, who had again glanced up at Marrket for just a second, but that's all it took, and it didn't go unnoticed! There was a sudden strong trace of sandalwood perfume in the air, and for seemingly no reason, the twins switched with the empty chairs closer to Mai Lin and I. That seemed to ease the tension for Shelly and Lacey just a bit. Obviously, Shay shin was here, and in control. She had made the changes based on Lacey and Shelly's concerns and jealousy, and the guys submissive weakness. The twins were just that beautiful! All they had to do was look at you, and you were lost. But it was the 'way' they looked at you that made things really complex.

There were a few words said in Chinese by Mai Lin, and that look in the twins eyes changed drastically. I couldn't believe how gullible Blake and Marrket were, even with their wives sitting right next to them! I thought about it, but I didn't dare invite them over for a nightcap this time, for fear of what might happen. Guys will be guys, and right now their animalistic instincts were in plain sight! There was very little or no conversation between the girls as there had been with Shay shin and the other set of twins, and that made the situation delicate, even a bit scary.

"Is Shay shin and the other twins still at the house Charlie?" Shelly asked candidly.

"Most of the time," I said a bit dryly.

"But at the moment, the three of them are sitting at this table, and one is sitting right next to you, (Shay shin), the reason Sue yin and Lou chin have changed chairs. The other set of twins are now sitting next to Blake and Marrket. You might say the twins are still in training," I said quietly. Shelly blushed and Lacey hung tighter to Marrket's arm. They were still under the assumption these six girls were after their husbands, which was not the case at all. But it sure didn't look like it would take much to change that situation.

"Ah, guys, you need to focus on who's sitting next to you," I said quietly. Both their mouths closed and their attention was back where it was supposed to be. The rest of the evening was quiet, but the tension between the girls was more than a little obvious.

The next morning, Blake and Marrket were at my office door.

"How do you do it Charlie? How can you not be overwhelmed by those twins?" Blake asked.

"Do you guys love your wives? I mean really love them, or did that change after the honeymoon? Last night you were both acting like your hormones were on steroids and that you were on the make again. Your both executive officers. But at the moment, I'm thinking the waitresses at the hotel dining room could make you single again. Just do your job and love the woman you promised your love to, or your both going to loose someone precious," I said as genuinely as I could. Now they were both looking at the floor.

"Now, back to work you animals," I said with a chuckle, trying to stay on track myself.

Charlie, you talk a lot of shit, but at the moment you still want Shay shin and she knows it! I thought to myself. What was I supposed to do, just fall in love with Mai Lin and forget all about Shay shin?

"Yes," came a delicate voice right next to my left ear, and the scent of her sensuous perfume.

"Make your wish come true Charlie, and I will be happy," she said softly.

"Shay shin, this love thing is not a switch you can turn off and on," I thought, and she was gone! It was time for me to own up to my own words. Do your job and love the one your with! But how? I called Blake and asked for an update on the new housing tract, and the expanded fire station, and the new restaurant as soon as possible. Marrket and Lacey were off to McCane's facility with Steven the next morning, to gather info on who and what job titles we wanted to move to Wilton first, and so on. Blake and I went to Rico's for lunch and business.

"So, how are things going," I asked as we settled into our booth. Blake had called ahead and ordered our lunch; deep dish lasagna. Damn, did Rico ever outdo himself on this one!

"Well, first; the new fire station will be finished in about two weeks. Their updated and new equipment is another story. That won't be here until March 20th. That's still well ahead of the housing tract. They can use what they have until then. Second; The first six homes will be ready for tenants in a month and a half, along with three apartment complexes that will be ready at about the same time. The subs have delivered the carpets, brought in washers and dryers, central air, water heaters and that kind of stuff. Shelly has contacted the movers we used for the move out of Kingston. They said they will be ready when we are. Third; the general has a third crew working on the new restaurant, and he says it will be ready for inspection in one month. Fourth; they are laying asphalt on the overpass this week, but DOT said it will be another three weeks before its ready for traffic. The general says he's going to tunnel under 87 for a cross over into the existing drains and sewer lines that will hook up on this side of the highway to our lines. Then I talked to the town council about the inputs regarding schools, bus transportation, and putting in another post office. The gas, electric and water are ready to come on line as we make the hookups. This might be a good time to put in that water tower to maintain water pressure.

"Do it," I said.

"The council is concerned about the schools. Too many students per class room, lunches, and transportation," Blake said a bit concerned

"Have our general come to the office, and make an appointment for me with the mayor, town council and the board of education to meet as soon as possible. This is going to involve the expansion of the elementary, junior high and high schools, and require some new teachers. I don't want the town's tax base to go up to support the cost of this project," I said.

It was Friday and I was headed for the house. And even though Mai Lin, Sue yin and Lou chin were at home, I was still dragging around. God I missed Shay shin terribly. When I got to the house, there was the basic routine of shower, dinner and relaxation. Then Mai Lin was standing in front of me. God she had that 'mommy' look all over her!

"The ghost man said he wants to talk to you," she said softly and took my hand. I only knew one 'ghost man' and that was Holdin! She led me to the attic steps and we went upstairs. I didn't know if it was possible for Mai Lin to be able to make the pentagram function the way Shay shin had? Still, I sat where Shay shin had told me to sit and waited. In only a minute or so, Holdin's apparition was before me.

"Mr. Aldermon, it is a pleasure to speak with you again. By observance, your hectic pace and involvement in seemingly everything, seems to have increased somewhat lately, the reason I asked to speak with you. By now you should know what 'us' misty people are capable of, so don't even think about saying no to my request. There were several mistakes I made in my time, the results of which you saw at my funeral. The corporation was my life and death, but paid me no mind in my passing. Only in you, too late did I see there could be another side of life. But now even you have chosen a path that leads to an end of nothing but yourself. It's not too late for you Charlie; listen to Shay shin! She loved you so much, even her path became distorted with her want to please you, but she's attempting to correct that. Mai Lin is as you are, yet as a child in your world. Give her the chance you gave Shay shin. Show her the unbelievable and incredible world at your fingertips she has yet to dream of.

You have come to depend on Shay shin's presence, foresight and the comfort of her love so much, you have all but lost your way to use your own will and drive, that's put you where you are in reality this day. Treat Shay shin's love as a wonderful dream; that she was the path of your wish to Mai Lin.

With her humanistic faults and misgivings, give Mai Lin the opportunity to grow with the same love, compassion, and the guidance you afforded Shay shin, the corporation and its people. With your own eyes and mind, you have seen that power and wealth mean nothing in the end. Therefore Mr. Aldermon, it is my sincere request that you allow the fruition of this wish, by taking Mai Lin on a vacation that will come to you. Allow her into your world and your heart, as you did Shay shin. Use what Shay shin has shown and taught you to bring happiness, love, and compassion to Mai Lin, who is willing to do the same with, and for you. Don't look for her lacking of Shay shin's abilities, but search her soul and being for the light and joy of her innocence and love for you. She needs you as much as you need her. Together, you will find your dreams and that which you both wished for. I have taken much of your time. Heed that said, and have a good life," he said and was gone. For several minutes I just sat there thinking about what Holdin had said. I couldn't just turn Shay shin's memory off like a switch. Especially when every time I looked at Mai Lin, there she would be! There was a heavy feeling in my chest, and a tightening in my throat and jaws. I couldn't move. Then that glittering shimmer moved slowly over the pentagram. Was it asking me if I wanted to ask for something? So right then I asked; how could I let go of Shay shin's love? How could I love Mai Lin after loving Shay shin so deeply? Still I sat there with Mai Lin at my side, looking at me questionably. The pentagram became a dull red, went black, and again the glittering shimmer crossed over the pentagram.

"Did you hear what he said," I asked quietly.

"No Charlie; did he give you guidance to help you manage the corporation?" she asked.

"No Mai Lin, he gave me guidance to manage my life," I said as her hand reached for mine. Give it a try Charlie; let her into your heart. You came here to change your life, and here is an opportunity you need to acquire, before you lose what you asked for! (Accept or decline!). I looked into her eyes; this was Mai Lin, not Shay shin. Was I worthy enough, and was I really what she wanted and had wished for? Holdin had been right about several things.

I was again becoming a workaholic with no end in sight, and alone with no one to give a damn in the end. Could I do this? Come on Charlie, she's all but begging to be let into your heart.

Ever so gently I reached out and took Mai Lin's hand. Her eyes alone said, "please love me!" With what Holdin had just said, how could I not? Shay shin truly had been a wonderful dream, and the path to Mai Lin. I needed to accept that, and let go! I took Mai Lin's hand and squeezed it gently. Let go Charlie, let go!

Sitting at my desk the next morning, a name for the new housing tract came out of the blue; "Holdin Heights". Blake and Kaleb Hollister, the general contractor, met me in the conference room the next morning and we talked about school construction, and the distaste of temporary modules. I went over the stats and situation with Blake and told him what I wanted to happen, and he ran with it.

"Okay gentlemen, this is going to get a little complex, so I expect you to take notes," I said handing both of them a little notepad, and kept one for myself.

"Kaleb, your pretty stretched out with the housing tract and the fire station at the moment. How much more can I stack on top of that before you say enough?" I asked seriously.

"I can handle all you can afford Charlie, even if I have to bring in out of state guys that I really trust. What did you have in mind?" he asked in a somber tone.

"Explicit timing, speed, safety and material quality and construction that is going to have to be at the head of the list as usual. We all know that preparation is 9/10ths of the task. On this one, you're going to need all the materials on hand in front of you, and your people standing there waiting when I say go! That will be the evening of the last day of school on June fifteenth. Summer break for the elementary, junior and high school. We have coordinated with the mayor, school board and town council to make the last day of school the fifteenth of June. You'll have exactly three months to the day to totally complete the projects on all three jobs, not a minute more. Blake show him what you've got," I said. Blake rolled open the prints for all three schools on the big table and weighted them down. Kaleb went over them carefully, about thirty minutes for each one. Then he went over them again, this time taking notes for each set. Then he sat back in his chair and stared at me thinking.

"Do you think its even feasible Kaleb?" I asked. I had come to trust this mans word explicitly, but this was a lot to ask of him with everything else that was going on. Then Kaleb sat up and went through his notes. Blake and I waited! Then Kaleb sat back into his chair again and looked up at me.

"I can make it happen, but your looking at five mil per job site. That would include materials and manpower" he said quietly.

"Are you sure Kaleb? Because there's no extra time past that day! I'm going to hold you to your word, you know that. And you know what to expect if you don't come through," I said.

"Yes sir," he said without blinking.

"Make it happen Kaleb, please make it happen!" I stood up and shook his hand. He rolled up the prints, put his notepad in his pocket and left. Than I sat down and was looking right at Blake expectantly.

"What?" he asked.

"Well, now its your turn to prove your worth my friend. Can you hold all this massive corporation together without me for a couple of weeks? I want to take Mai Lin on a two week vacation," I said, and he jumped to a conclusion.

"Charlie, your going to get married!" he said a bit excited sitting up to the table.

"Woah, woah, woah! I said nothing of the sort. I don't even know if she'd want me to ask her. I don't know if she's wanting to go that far or not. She knows how I felt about Shay shin, but somehow I have to let that go," I said. I told him what Shay shin and Holdin told me, but I was still holding on to Shay shin. Somehow, some way, I had to let go! But how?

"Its only an idea," I said feeling a bit exalted.

"But without this corporation, I'm no different than any other guy. Would she want me if I was still just an architect and didn't have billions of dollars?" I asked.

"Charlie, are you not paying attention? Have you seen the way she looks at you, 'all the time'?! She don't care who, or what you are, or what you have, or don't have, she's in love with you Charlie! I know how much you loved Shay shin Charlie, but this is real, and as a friend once told me, I'm asking you to "pay attention to the one your with," does that sound familiar?" he asked.

Chapter 10

It was the words right out of my mouth over dinner when him and Marrket became infatuated with the twins. I just sat there thinking. Shay shin's and Holdin's words kept washing through my brain, and now Blake's. Would I be letting go of Shay shin for them, or for me, or Mai Lin? And could I really do that?

"Blake, I also need you to hold the fort down for a day or two. There's a couple of things I gotta do before I leave on this vacation, and I need to do it alone, and now!" I said, got up and left. I got in the car and went east to Hwy. 9, down to 29 and headed west to Gloversville. Its only about 35 or 40 miles, but I had to go there.

"Shay shin, I need you or I lin to guide me. You know where I'm going and why. A little bit of help if you don't mind," I said out loud. It was I lin who answered the call. She guided me straight to the graveyard where she was buried, and to her headstone; and Charlie's! Wow, what a rude awakening that was! This guy with my name, had gone through almost the same situations, feelings and emotions I had gone through with Shay shin. Sitting on the ground next to that statue of an angel, I lin told me the entire story. My God, it was scary and heartbreaking. Charlie had unequivocally loved I lin the same way I loved Shay shin, and look where that got him! Yes, I believed I still loved Shay shin; but there was only one way I could be with her, and that was not what she wanted me to do. Yeah, I'd be with her, but she would blame herself for how I got there. I sat there with I lin at her headstone for almost an hour and some. Shay shin was more than worth it, but that wouldn't be me. I looked down at Charlie's headstone and said;

"Okay, you did it your way my friend. I don't know if you found your dream or not. So, I'm going to try the other side of the coin and see how that turns out. The best to you and I lin," I said. I got back in the car and headed home, home to Mai Lin, and an uncertain future like most living human beings have. When I got to Wilton, I made another stop, then I called Blake and told him I was back, and that I'd see him in the morning. When I got to the house, Mai Lin and the twins were out shopping, but Shay shin was there.

"Charlie, I'm so happy for what you did, and the decision you made. This will be the last time I call on you, but you know how to call me if you need me. Love her as much as you loved me Charlie, and you will have a wonderful life together," she said and was gone; forever! Talk about feeling alone! But the cavalry came through the kitchen door right on time, loaded with packages of every description. With no reserve, Mai Lin ran up to me and kissed me with the loving passion only a wife can give. The twins played bashful, like two kids watching mommy and daddy smooching. This is what you chose Charlie, real honest to goodness life, and love! A real woman to hug you without reserve or guilt, to hold your hand and look into your eyes and make the world a better place. And what your thinking, hopefully will only make it better! Just remember what that old man once told you;

"First you laugh, then you cry; happiness is the beginning of a hurtful pain that will rip your emotions apart." Of this, I had already been a witness to, with Shay shin and the first set of twins, and then Holdin. As Shay shin said, death has no boundaries! Only the living shall parish, for that is the way of our existence. That's a harsh reality to think about when your trying to keep things together and make it from one day to the next. Still we keep trying, unto the end! And when your gone, to the world, its like you never existed. Who cares? I also remembered what Mai Lin's father had told her; "Life comes of death!" Mai Lin's eyes sparkled, standing on her toes with her arms around my neck, then came an echo as she said; *I will always love you Charlie!* It seems I've heard those exact words several times in the last few years. How could she love me so easily, when I found it so hard to fall in love with her?

"Mai Lin, how would you like to go on a vacation?" I asked quietly. The look in her eyes and on her face became confusing.

"Why do we need a vacation Charlie?" she asked, like I had said something wrong.

"Well, I'd like to spend some time with you, alone. I'd like to get to know you a little better, how you are with just you and me," I said, and Sue yin and Lou chin disappeared.

"I'd also like to get away from my work for awhile so I can devote all my attention on you. Right now, the time we have together is only in the bits and pieces I can spare from my work, and that's not fare to you or me. I'd like to be with only you to think about and nothing else," I said.

Your falling Charlie, but that's okay, because that's exactly how love comes about, and that's what Shay shin wants.

"Can't we vacation here in the house?" she asked quizzically.

"No, because you would still be cooking and cleaning and shopping and whatever. I want to take you away from that for awhile," I said. But she still looked confused.

"Is there anyplace that you'd like to go that you've always wanted to see? Some place that's quiet and remote, like Fiji or Samoa, someplace like that maybe?"

"Everyplace is too far, with too many people," she said softly. Then I had an idea! I made reservations at the best hotel they had on Santa Catalina Island, chartered a jet to Long Beach, and a car from there to the ferry out to Catalina. With everything confirmed, naturally, four of our body guards had to tag along. Two with us, and two that left the day before we did. With those guys underfoot, I still felt like I was at work. I called Blake and told him where we were going and staying, but try to keep from calling me unless it was necessary. Mai Lin and I left early the next morning and got to Long beach about eleven. We were at the hotel on Catalina by two pm. Mai Lin seemed totally awed at everything she saw. I had to keep reminding myself that China and Wilton were all she had seen. We spent an entire week doing absolutely nothing but goofing off and fooling around. Then it was time to get down to the real reason I brought her here. Without telling anyone, I had bought an engagement ring the day before we left. Here I didn't want to make a statement that would draw public attention, so I waited till we were back in the room sitting on the end of the bed.

"Mai Lin, I have two questions to ask you," I said.

"The first one is, if I was still just an architect, without that nice house and a lot of money, would you still care about me; I mean, do you think you could still love me?" I asked. It was like I lit a fire under that girl. She pushed me backwards onto the bed and put her hand in the middle of my chest.

"Charlie, if you had nothing, nothing at all, I would still be at your side. I love you! Not because you're an important business man, or you have a nice house and a lot of money. I just hope you could love me in curlers, when I have bad breath, and when I'm in my minstrel cycle.

And too, when I'm old and gray and falling apart, I hope you will at least care about me," she said looking down into her lap. I sat up on the edge of the bed and looked at her. Do I dare do this? Could we really grow old together? Holdin's words washed through my brain.

Look at her Charlie, look at Mai Lin! Do you not see her love for you? Do you not feel that she has given her heart and soul to you? Quit thinking about 'me' Charlie, think about 'us', I said to myself. I stood up in front of her, and she stood up too. Then I took the ring box out of my pocket and knelt down in front of her.

"Charlie, what are you doing?" she asked.

"The second question I have for you Mai Lin is; for better or for worse, through sickness and health, through riches or poverty, will you be my wife? Will you marry me Mai Lin?" I asked opening the ring box, and she fell back onto the bed and was sitting there in awe, covering her mouth with her hands, and she began crying.

"Charlie!" she gasped. I was hoping she was crying because she was happy.

"Charlie; Yes, oh yes Charlie, I will, I will marry you," she said through the sobbing and her excitement, and put her arms around my neck, kissed and hugged me tightly. When I finally got her calmed down, I put the ring on her finger and kissed it, then I kissed her tender soft lips. I let go! I was giving her all there was to give of me. The life of one person is precious and complex, and at times difficult to comprehend and keep together. To accept another person unto your existence, with their problems and issues, health problems, be they of the past or even with a devoted love on both sides, it might seem impossible, but it is less than the hell of a life alone!

I called my mom and dad and Blake and gave them the news. Through tears of joy and excitement, Mai Lin called her mom and dad, and Sue yin and Lou chin. By the time we got back to the house, her mom and dad, and my mom and dad were already booked into our hotel in Corinth, and preparations for the wedding had already begun. It was going to be held in a massive Chinese church in Corinth. Mai Lin, her mother, Sue yin and Lou chin and my mom had disappeared. Papa Xhong Jun said this was the way it was to be. That I would see Mai Lin on the day of the wedding and not before. Papa Jun and my dad were getting along great.

Papa Jun made no mention of Shay shin at all, but spent a lot of time looking out the back door! I could feel his pain and saw his tears. Me, I was starting to feel the same way about Mai Lin that I had felt about Shay shin. Yup, this is what real love felt like! I wanted her near me all the time; to hear her voice, hold her in my arms and smell her breath, her hair, and the scent of her body. To feel the gentleness and strength of her constant touch, and the funny little habit she had of looping her finger into my belt loop wherever we went. That was as far as we ever got from each other, unless we went to the bathroom or until I went to work. She was always there, trying to do something for me, or just showing me she cared, and I was always trying to do the same for her, and at the moment I was missing her terribly. Blake showed up to brief me on some things, and we all came together at the hotel, Blake and Marrket, both dads and me. I paced the floor like a caged animal, God I wanted to be with her! Blake said Shelly and Lacey had gone to wherever the rest of the women had gone. For three days I had to wait, and it was driving me absolutely crazy. I wanted to be with Mai Lin so much!

Friday finally came, and what a day that turned out to be! There had to have been over a thousand or more people at the wedding, including Ricardo and his people. It seemed the entire town of Wilton had showed up, including kids from the college. The corporation sent people from each of the facilities to attend. Almost every single person that worked at the Wilton facility was there. To me, it was all to glorify my wonderful Mai Lin; my love, my queen! Was I fulfilling Holdin's and Shay shin's intentions? I sure as hell was fulfilling mine and I hoped Mai Lin's!

At the front of the church, the tension of waiting was almost unbearable. Then finally the girls started down the isle toward us. Where was she? Where is Mai Lin? Sue yin, Lou chin and Lacey were the leading brides maids, with Shelly as maid of honor. The group was being proudly led by my mom and Mai Lin's mom, side by side. At the front of the church, was the priest, then Papa Jun and my dad waiting for their wives. Then there was Blake, my best man, and Marrket, and me.

Then she came! My lovely beautiful Mai Lin, one gracious step at a time. The joy in my heart was overflowing, and so came my tears. I really did love Mai Lin! I could feel it all over me. She had on a magnificent American wedding gown that trailed like a delicate cloud behind her. It was decorated with embroided silk flowers and lace.

153

Beneath her gown, she wore a formfitting white silk dress, slit up her left thigh and white high heels. God I wanted to hold her! *Patients Charlie.* Then finally she was standing next to me, and I couldn't look away from her. She looked magnificently beautiful! Then we went through the vows and the exchange of rings, then she turned towards me and I raised her veil.

Then something that wasn't supposed to happen, did! Shay shin paid us one last visit! Or so I thought! As I raised Mai Lin's veil, Mai Lin floated down to her knees right in front of me, and I caught more than a trace of Sandalwood perfume! When Mai Lin raised her chin, I saw it!! For some ten seconds, it was unmistakably Shay shin's eyes! Then Mai Lin smiled and said;

"I will always love you Charlie!" my knees buckled, and Blake caught me! When Mai Lin stood up, I kissed her, well, I was pretty sure it was her! We were one. I wanted to say she was mine, but that's so far from being the truth in any marriage. You don't belong to each other; you coexist and learn to take the good with the bumps. It should be called a compromise not a marriage.

Then it was time for the decorated limo, and to thank all the people that had come to help us celebrate this wonderful day. In the limo I asked her about her perfume. She said her mother had brought several bottles of it from China as a wedding gift. That night there was a massive street party in our honor, but we were home snuggling in each others arms. *Let go Charlie!* You truly love only once in your life, give it all you have, and don't look back at what was, or could have been. No maybe's or what if's. You're all each other have in this world, make it worthwhile. Love her with all of your heart and soul.

The next morning at the house, it was my mom and dad, Mai Lin's mom and dad, Sue yin and Lou chin. There was a conversation between Mai Lin and her parents, then she came straight to me.

"My mother and father have made a request of us. They ask if we could name our first daughter Shay shin. Do you approve?" she questionably asked softly, as if I would refuse.

"If that's what you want my dear, yes, I too think that would be appropriate," I said quietly. She went back and spoke to her parents. The three of them turned and bowed to me. That evening both our parents went back to the hotel and were on their way home the next day. Blake called the next morning.

"Okay boss man, its time for the honeymoon. I can handle things here for awhile. You guys need some time to yourselves. See ya in about three weeks, bye," he said and hung up. Sue yin and Lou chin got a room at the hotel that afternoon. I made sure their rooms and meals were paid for, and that they were well taken care of. I made sure they had enough money to do whatever they wanted to do, or go wherever they wanted to go; and of course they always had two escorts.

Now; it was just Mai Lin and I. Except for the toilet, we never got more than an arms length from each other for the entire three weeks. Truly this had been part of my wish! That was the most wonderful, but the shortest three weeks ever. Then it was time to start acting like a regular husband and wife. But it seemed we had no idea how that was suppose to happen. I'd go to work in the morning, but I couldn't wait to get home to Mai Lin. Mai Lin would always be waiting just inside the kitchen door with a reception that would make any other husband and wife jealous out of their mind! And still, Sue yin and Lou chin still did their ritual in the shower, that never seemed to phase Mai Lin. But outside the shower, my queen controlled all the goings on with the twins, at least I was thinking it was her. When Sue yin and Lou chin graduated from college, I sent them on a trip to China and Japan. Then to several places all over the world; Spain, Italy, Paris, Switzerland and Ireland, to broaden their knowledge of how things sort of went in other countries, and always they had two chaperons close by. The entirety of their trips lasted one whole year, but they were back just in time to meet the new arrival to the family, Shay shin! And Shay shin it was! Not only her eyes, but the movement of her hands and fingers and her little laugh. The guest room downstairs became the baby's room. There were many instances when I could have sworn little Shay shin had visitors during the night, and she did! Mai Lin and I were pretty sure who the visitors were, so we didn't interfere.

Sue yin and Lou chin make such a fuss over little Shay shin, you would think they are her mothers. Mai Lin took very good care of Shay shin, while Sue yin and Lou chin did the cooking and cleaning when they weren't pampering Shay shin. Packages started rolling in from both grandparents and friends. I didn't realize a baby could possibly need so much stuff. And even with the powder and perfume, how could a cute little bundle of joy smell so bad! Wow, I don't know how mothers can change those diapers and not puke their heads off! Hope I didn't smell that bad when I was little.

Still, little Shay shin was like a celebrity. Blake and Shelly became Shay shin's God parents, although Shelly still tried to keep Blake away from Sue yin and especially Lou chin. I wasn't sure weather she didn't trust the twins, or Blake?! One afternoon I asked Mai Lin if Sue yin and Lou chin didn't want to have a boyfriend and eventually get married too. Wrong question! The look I got was stern, and Mai Lin called to the twins. In English, Mai Lin asked the twins the question I had just asked her. Both of them dropped to the floor instantly.

"Are we not pleasing you my Lord," Lou chin asked in a trembling voice that sounded like a plea. Oh, oh, we were back to square one of Lord and Master!

"Mai Lin, this is America honey. Everyone has the right to live their own lives. I am completely happy with the twins, but don't they want to be as happy as we are?" I asked almost timidly, trying not to upset the twins again.

"Charlie, Sue yin and Lou chin have dedicated their lives to you, and will serve you until you, or they pass onto the next life, or you replace them. They have each other to console and have no need for a boyfriend or husband," she said assertively. Okay, it seems I'd missed something somewhere I just now caught on to, that Mai Lin had just brought to light. That brought some sense to what I was thinking about Shay shin and the other set of twins, and now this set of twins. There was another whole way of life in their culture this country boy had overlooked. I have no problem with it, I just needed to acknowledge it in my own mind. I really needed to pay more attention to what was going on around me.

"Okay, just checking," I said wrapping my arms around Mai Lin.

The next morning, it was back to the grind. The weddings(Blake and Shelly, and Marrket and Lacey) , the schools, the housing tract, the road, railroad spur, airport, and on it went. I was back into my hectic pace. It was the middle of May, and I felt like things were closing in on me. Maybe I had too many stokes in the fire this time, but still I was sure it was all feasible, I just needed to stay on top of things, and take them one at a time. I was going to lose Blake and Marrket shortly for their weddings and honeymoons, for about three weeks I was thinking. Even though I was the president of the corporation, it was time to get a little closer to my work.

First I checked in with Kaleb about the schools. He said they were standing on the doorstep of each school with all the materials, equipment and manpower that would be required. The overpass was complete, so I drove out to the housing tract. There were a hundred homes and two hundred apartments ready for occupancy. We already knew who was being moved and their jobs.

The moving trucks were also ready to start the move. My engineers said the new restaurant was ready for inspection and I called Ricardo. Ricardo brought over the new manager to the new restaurant. Then he selected certain people from his restaurant to move to the new one. He then hired more people to fully staff both restaurants. The new restaurant was in full operation in two weeks. The water tower was installed and ready to start pumping. I told Marrket and Lacey not to start the moves until the fifteenth of June. Their wedding, and Blake's and Shelly's, was going to be on the first of June so they would be back to work by then, and the move would start. Everything was coming together. I wanted to start several other projects, but decided to wait until the schools, housing tract and fire station was complete.

I shut down the facility on the day of the weddings. But the next day, I made a tour of the three schools. Then it was over to the fire station. They had got all their new equipment, and the station would be finished in two weeks. I was at the junior high school the afternoon of the fifteenth, when the last students left the building. Kaleb was true to his word; they were poised and ready for the last student to leave the school. There was a safety check to make sure no one was in the building, and the construction started. Three shifts, around the clock, none stop, and it was the same with the other two schools. The next day I visited the town council to see if they knew of any open prospects.

My precious little Shay shin was now five months old, but she still smelled bad at change time! I still don't know how Mai Lin deals with it. After she was changed, I'd sit her on my lap and the strangeness would start. She would sit there looking at me, like she wanted to say something. The look would become a deep stare, then she would raise both little arms to be held. She would put her cheek against my ear and whimper softly, with her little arms tight around my neck. She'd stay like that for an hour maybe, sometimes longer, sound asleep.

When she woke up, sometimes she would let go of my neck, lean back a little and again stare intently into my eyes, like she was trying to say something without speaking. There was no doubt in my mind that she had her aunty Shay shin's eyes! That baby has more company than I do. She has Mai Lin, Sue yin, Lou chin, and a twenty four hour line of sight guard, as did Mai Lin. Shelly and Blake, came to see her at least once, sometimes twice a week, and always brought her something, clothes or toys or something to add to her room.

And then of course there were her two strange cousins that were with her every night. And there was her name sake, Shay shin. I could go on forever about how cute she is, and the funny things she does. But when she's asleep on my chest in the rocking chair, I hush the world into silence, and nothing else in this world matters, except my baby and my loving Mai Lin. I hated to put her down or give her to Mai Lin, but I'd have to go to work.

It was the end of August, and Blake, the engineers and Kaleb monitored the school sites night and day. They were actually a bit ahead of schedule, but that made it easier for the landscapers to do their part. All three sights were going to be finished as planned. I asked the principals of each school to come in and tell me if I had missed anything in the furnishings of the class rooms. The janitors too came in to put the final touches on the floors and windows. The fire department and the health department came in for a thorough inspection. We went over the plumbing and ran the water through the whole system. On the fifth of September, all the equipment was removed from all three sights. By the tenth, you couldn't tell they had even been there. On the fifteenth of September, school started right on time. Then I had Kaleb bring every single man and woman that had worked on all three sites to the facility. In the west parking lot, I heartfully thanked them all for their accomplishments, and presented each and every one of them with a $2500.00 check. Each of the site bosses got an extra check for $250000. In the conference room, Kaleb was presented with a check for one million, five hundred thousand dollars, in appreciation for his work on the schools, the housing tract and the fire department. Holdin Heights was going to be the last project until next year. But already I had Marrket working on the hospital and airport. The town of Holdin was slowly coming into being.

As we moved people in from the Pennsylvania facility, two more choppers and pilots were added to our facility.

Then we brought in people who were okay with the move from California, Colorado and Florida, and two more choppers were added. This was keeping McCane and his bookkeepers busy for awhile. He was still in charge of the other three facilities. As much as I really didn't want to do it, I kept thinking if I moved McCane to the Wilton facility, that would in fact make our facility 'the' corporation headquarters! Then I had another idea.

What if I moved Marrket to the PA facility for one year and had McCane train him to do his job, then brought Marrket back to Wilton? McCane could stay where he was, Marrket would become the Chief CEO of the corporation and the Wilton facility would become the headquarters of the entire corporation.

It was time for a trip to the attic, and it knew I was coming! When I got home, Mai Lin met me in the kitchen with Shay shin. I hugged and kissed Mai Lin, and took Shay shin in my arms. I hugged my baby close to me and she hugged my neck. This was my world! Shay shin was now almost two. Mai Lin had taught her how to say "Papa". I was so proud and happy. I took my loving wife in one arm and looked into her eyes.

"I love you Mai Lin," I said softly and kissed her, and little Shay shin clapped her hands. Then I handed Shay shin back to Mai Lin and said;

"I got to take care of something honey," and headed for the office upstairs and the attic. I hadn't touched the button on the wall, yet the attic steps started coming down as soon as I stepped behind the bookcase. Shay shin! It had to be. She was still here. Just to either side of the ladder stood Lenin Tao and Leunig Tao in human form. I wanted to hug them, but something seemed different, kind of formal like. In the attic, I sat at the table where she told me to sit. Len and Leu sat just behind and to either side of me. Okay, Shay shin had to be here somewhere!? I don't know why but I closed my eyes. Okay, this is weird. My eyes are closed but I can still see everything in the room. There seems to be a deep humming vibration, a throbbing coming from someplace. And then I was tingling with that vibration all over me. Had I done something wrong? All the candles in the room lit at once without being touched! I was pretty sure I didn't do that! Then all of the candles left their containers and formed just above the circle around the star, and they were moving counter clockwise very slowly.

This hadn't happened before, even when Shay shin was with me. There was the smoke of sage and a trace of sandalwood incense. The smoke from the two slowly formed a blanket of a sort just above the star within the circle of candles. The color of the candles means something to some, but its flame is all that can be seen in the dark. And then in the center of it all came the spectral image of Holdin!

"Hello again, Mr. Aldermon. Thought I'd pay you a visit before you get too far ahead of yourself. It seems your pace is about to pass you. You need to slow it down some, that others may shine as you have, so you can see those unseen, and allow those seen, to rest in the glory you have given them. Your endeavors have accomplished much to help many. You can accomplish the same tasks slowly that you accomplish with your hectic pace. You might even see something you wouldn't have seen at the pace you are presently moving. You are the president of your corporation, a multibillionaire. Reach down into the earth and feel the truth of your origin. You are still just a man, and when death comes, neither of those titles will mean a thing! You have done well; you and your little family have brought happiness and joy to many. You have shown others by example, that a man with a dream and a wish can accomplish what is truly in his or her heart. Its time for you to sit back and enjoy the fruits of your labor, become the teacher and teach others that they can! Until next time my friend, as with Shay shin, I'll always be here to help you where I did not pay attention in the time of my own existence," he said and faded away. A shimmer crossed over the pentagram and the star turned a dull red.

"It now more than knows you Charlie," came Shay shin's delicate voice.

"Do you have a request of it," she asked. I had no requests, but my thoughts were many. Then one came to mind.

"Protect Mai Lin and little Shay shin for all time, I beg you," I asked humbly. The circle around the star became a bright red for almost a minute, then faded back to its matted black. All the candles returned to their holders and went out, and the smoke from the sage and incense disappeared. It was back to my baby and Mai Lin, waiting in the living room at the bottom of the staircase. I took little Shay shin in my arms and held her tightly. She too held tightly to my neck.

"I love you baby girl," I said, and she leaned back and looked into my eyes.

"I know papa," she said clear as day, and put her arms around my neck again.

That night there was a thunderous pounding against the back door! Then quickly came an explosion and a crash, then ten to fourteen gun shots rang out in quick succession. A bear had busted the entire door and frame right out of the wall, but it didn't get to take one step into the kitchen, he just fell backwards into the yard.

Obviously the electric fence hadn't slowed him down a bit. This was the biggest bear I had ever seen, even bigger than the one I had killed before. I called the sheriff, and him and his deputies came and got the bear. Our bodyguards had done what they were paid to do. Still, that night I moved the .444 into the bedroom. Again I had the door replaced, but with an addition, a trap cage with steel bars that would catch the bear before he got to the door!

Based on what Holdin had said, I didn't start anymore projects. It was time to let Blake and Marrket put their best foot forward. I'd just suggest things from time to time, and they usually ran with it. It was another eight years before the airport and hospital were complete and another project came to mind; a graveyard and a mortuary. I mentioned it to Blake and he took off with it. Lacey and Marrket moved out to Pittsburgh for a year so Marrket could learn McCane's job. McCane would still be in charge of the three other facilities, retain his pay grade, and not have to move from his home. Marrket would become Corporate Chief and eventually control all five facilities.

Once when Shay shin was five years old, I was holding her in my arms. She had her head on my shoulder and started humming an oriental lullaby near my ear. It was the same one her aunt Shay shin used to hum to me when she was content. That night I had to ask Mai Lin;

"Mai Lin, is it possible for little Shay shin to be possessed by your sister?" I asked quietly. Mai Lin was quiet for almost a full five minutes, but I waited.

"My sister says Shay shin is not possessed, but somehow has acquired more than a few traits of me and my sister. That Shay shin is a happy and healthy little girl, and that there is nothing to worry about," Mai Lin said softly.

"So, Shay shin is still in the house?" I asked a bit surprised.

"Only of her choice to babysit little Shay shin at night. My sister was the one who told the guards the bear was coming," she said softly.

"The other twins are here during the day to keep her out of mischief and safe while Sue yin and Lou chin are taking care of the house," she said. I was starting to think Shay shin was going to hold to her promise of not leaving me, ever, and just doing it in another way.

For me, things were starting to wind down a bit and I had less and less to do. So I started drawing again. Like Holdin had said, it was time to let Blake and Marrket shine. I also had more time to be with my little family. Blake was starting to catch on to the system and pace as well.

So I asked him into my office so we could have a little discussion about what we have done, what we were doing and where we thought things should go from here.

"Come on in Blake and have a seat. I'd kind of like to go over a few things to make sure I'm not leaving you or Marrket with a spaghetti ball, or to deal with something I started. Blake, I'd like to ask you; personally, from your heart, do you think and believe I have done the right thing here? I know we kind of got dropped into a couple of situations we no way could have contemplated to occur in our careers as drafters. Even in a life time, no matter how far up the ladder we were to go in our careers, under normal circumstances would they have happened. Have I or we, done all we should have to expound on those situations without being foolish? Have we done everything possible to improve the corporation, its people and the town of Wilton and the city of Corinth relative to the moves and changes I've made within the corporation? Do you think I've fumbled anything, anything at all that you can see or feel? Have I missed something you see that should have taken place, that still needs to be done related to the corporation? Do you think we have accomplished what Holdin would have wanted us to do? Not only for this facility, but the other four facilities as well? Do you think I've overstepped any boundaries or abused my authority anywhere?" I asked sincerely. Blake sat there for a minute or so thinking, and that's what I wanted him to do, was think!

"Charlie, I only know one way of putting this. You are the owner and president of this corporation. You have your own ideas of the corporations future and outcome; where you want it to go and how far. Weather its how many billions of dollars you want in the bank, or the quality and quantity of its progress. Or that you want Holdin Ind. to be looked to for what we've always done best; designing, drawing and engineering buildings that not only look good, but make people feel safe in.

I see not a single thing that you've missed or could have foreseen, that you did not do, relative to the people of this corporation, its management and leadership, and the accomplishments and events you made happen, to get it to where it is today. Truthfully, I think you've overdone a few things, but you've always had the people of this corporation, the town of Wilton and city of Corinth in mind to benefit from your accomplishments," he said sitting back in his chair.

"I believe you have surpassed anything the town of Wilton expected. You've become more than an icon for the people of Wilton and Corinth. By example, you showed them and me, that we and I, can accomplish our dreams and wishes no matter how far out they may seem. The quality of your work has given Marrket and I, a set goal in all we do. You have built an entire town from nothing, and brought people together from all over the US to accomplish the goals of this corporation. But most of all you've given those people hope for, and a future they didn't have. You gave them a pride in themselves that I believe Holdin, in his own twisted way, was trying to accomplish. But now, with all that you have accomplished, I think you and I need to get back to the basics of what we started out trying to be; just a couple of really good architects," he said quietly.

"You see Charlie; I too had a dream and made a wish, and you not only made those things possible, you made them happen, you made them come true, and I thank you!" he said.

"Now, I better get back to work before the boss shows up," he said with a chuckle, got up and went back to his office. I let out a big sigh and sat back in my chair to reminisce. What had I done? But at no time in my life was it ever just me, I had done nothing alone. When I was very young, a teacher reached out to me and drew a few lines on a piece of paper. That Christmas he brought me a drawing board. In my attempts to truly become of worth in my work, still there were others to clear and enhance the path of my future. Some were real, some were not; some were both. From the depths of my cold heart, Shay shin had taught me what real love was, and nurtured that path to Mai Lin. Foster and Holdin became my legacy and I theirs. Somewhere in the teachings of my life, someone had said; "Nothing of this world and life be of itself! My little family is the truth of that. And too, I was shown that belief and a prayer can bring a mountainous belief even for someone as empirical as me. Believe in yourself, believe you can! Just be careful what you wish for!

.